About the Author

Brooke Scarlett is a teenage writer living on the Central Coast of New South Wales with her parents, two sisters and a dog whose anxious attachment issues inspired some of the dragons in this book. She hasn't won any awards (yet) – unless you count school ones. Though, she doesn't. *Stealing Thunder* is Brooke's first novel of hopefully many more to come.

Stealing Thunder

Brooke Scarlett

Stealing Thunder

Olympia Publishers
London

www.olympiapublishers.com
OLYMPIA PAPERBACK EDITION

Copyright © Brooke Scarlett 2024

The right of Brooke Scarlett to be identified as author of
this work has been asserted in accordance with sections 77 and 78 of
the Copyright, Designs and Patents Act 1988.

All Rights Reserved

No reproduction, copy or transmission of this publication
may be made without written permission.
No paragraph of this publication may be reproduced,
copied or transmitted save with the written permission of the publisher,
or in accordance with the provisions
of the Copyright Act 1956 (as amended).

Any person who commits any unauthorised act in relation to
this publication may be liable to criminal
prosecution and civil claims for damage.

A CIP catalogue record for this title is
available from the British Library.

ISBN: 978-1-80439-576-9

This is a work of fiction.
Names, characters, places and incidents originate from the writer's
imagination. Any resemblance to actual persons, living or dead, is
purely coincidental.

First Published in 2024

Olympia Publishers
Tallis House
2 Tallis Street
London
EC4Y 0AB

Printed in Great Britain

Dedication

For Chloe, the most amazing reader, listener, friend, chauffeur and more. You are the literal best.

Acknowledgements

This book has been a whole trek of five a.m. writing sessions and crying at cringy dialogue and gossiping over my characters with my friends and cracking jokes and all in all, a lot of support from the people around me. Firstly, I want to thank God, without Him, none of this would be possible and there would simply be no words on the page. I am eternally grateful for Chloe who has been here since the very beginning. Like, the very beginning. She has read every draft I have sent her over iMessage and Instagram and various other platforms, staying up at ludicrous hours to do so. She has obsessed over these characters and this plot as much as I have and she will always be my #1 fan. Thank you. Massive thanks to my amazing mum and dad, who have been encouraging me to finish my stories since I picked up a pen. They have taught me so much and I could not have done this without them (both emotionally and financially lol). To my wonderful sisters, Edan and Tahlia, who, most likely, will never read this book. I love them so much and they have been there, supporting me for as long as I can remember. Thank you to Kani for being the best wingman a book could ask for. He has been hyping this book up since before he knew what it was about and has been essential in keeping me to my deadlines. To Raph for helping edit this book at its worst stage. To Chris for promising to write fanfiction when I'm famous. To Kyra for reading this book in class and sharing in all my excitement. To Sophie for always loving my silly stories and wanting to read them. To Kya for being an awesome writing friend. To Mrs Nicholls and Mr Hart for growing my love of writing and reading. I also want to say an enormous thank you to Danielle and Josh at Jopuka for helping foster my writing skills over the years. I am very, very grateful to all the wonderful editors, cover designers, production coordinators and everyone else at Olympia who has helped make this book a reality. None of this would be possible without you. And finally, anyone who picked this book up and read it. Thank you.

Part 1

Richmond Airport

Prologue

The clock struck twelve. And yet Jenkins remained the same, didn't lose his glass slipper and his mother's car didn't turn back into a pumpkin. Nothing. He looked down at the book in his hand, some stupid Cinderella retelling he had confiscated from a student that day at school. Scoffing, Jenkins tossed the useless book into the bin at the entrance of the desolate airport.

The airport hummed quietly, the lack of activity practically a sound in and of itself. No planes took off or landed, no, the airport was thoroughly abandoned. By most people, that is. Jenkins stuck his key in and twisted, the rust of the lock creaking in the stale night air. He once again locked the door behind him as he stepped into the frigid hallway of the abandoned airport, blank white tiles stretching ahead of him like some kind of haunted pathway. The whir of the coffee machine floated towards him and Jenkins grimaced, the closest to a smile you could get from him nowadays. He turned right and his eyes met with the barista barely visible behind the shiny machine.

The teenager's eyes were sagging in an effort to keep them open and they yawned before asking, "The usual?"

Jenkins merely nodded and waited as the pimply-faced boy pressed a button and out came that glorious caffeine. A familiar warmth spread through the older man's body as he took the cardboard cup handed to him, the coffee's glorious smell wafting up to him and immediately making him feel better. Jenkins continued down the hallway, a murmured thanks thrown over his shoulder to the barista. He took a long sip of the black coffee, savouring the burn on his tongue. Or, at least, pretending that he can drink hot drinks immediately after they were made and then realising, bitterly, that he can't and spitting the boiling coffee into the nearest bin. Jenkins scowled and cupped his hands around the coffee as he waited for it to cool down a bit.

Unfortunately, it didn't take Jenkins long to get to the Nesting Room. His face contorted, mouth pulling downwards as he shoved through the door. Rows upon rows of eggs stared back at him, varying in size and colour but, to Jenkins, they were all the same shade of boring.

"Hi, honey, I'm home," he scowled before nudging the door shut and taking a seat in the corner of the room, the dingy fold-out chair creaking beneath him.

Jenkins took another sip of his coffee, a smaller sip this time. Mercifully, it had managed to cool down a bit. His eyes scanned across the rows of eggs, wondering what could possibly be growing in them. Sure, they varied in size, but they were all pretty huge as far as eggs go. He supposed it would be fair to rule out the possibility of chickens. All Jenkins knew was that he was getting paid more to sit here and watch this room of eggs than he was getting for subbing a bunch of high school classes. That didn't make it any less boring, though.

Actually, Jenkins had first heard about the position from this woman at his regular Pilates class. He could still remember the day she first joined. He had been waiting outside the building, yoga mat in hand, trying to get some guy from the class to stop talking to him, when there she was. She had waltzed towards them, blonde hair tied loosely at the nape of her neck and the vague smell of rose petals surrounded her presence. It was safe to say, Jenkins was in love. Or at least, *he* thought so.

"Sorry," she had smiled at him, "do you know what time this building opens? There's supposed to be Pilates here but I'm beginning to worry that I've got the wrong place."

She laughed and Jenkins fought not to go mute.

"Yep!" he chuckled nervously, lifting up his yoga mat. "Someone'll come unlock the door soon for us."

"Perfect! Thank you so much."

"Jenkins. Uh, Stephen Jenkins," he'd said, hand sticking out abruptly.

But she merely smiled and shook his hand. "Melissa."

Eventually, the job had just come up in the super casual, super flirty conversations that they definitely had every day and Jenkins figured this was her way of saying she wanted to spend more time with him.

It was not.

Melissa didn't work here. Or, if she did, she never worked at the same time as Jenkins. In fact, apart from the guards and that teenage barista boy, Jenkins was beginning to suspect he might be the only one that actually worked at this abandoned airport. Perhaps this was all just an elaborate prank. Although, he couldn't quite think of anyone who might actually care enough to play a prank on him. The only person he really talked to was his sister and that was still only a few months ago at his mother's will reading. Oh! Actually, Jenkins had his cat. His stupid cat that needed stupid medication every three days. But at least he could talk to his cat. His cat wouldn't play a prank on him though, it was too sick. And a cat.

This job was turning Jenkins insane.

He huffed and rose from the chair, his foot catching on its leg and causing him to grimace as it clattered to the floor.

"I'll deal with that when I get back."

For now, Jenkins needed to piss.

*

The cool water rushed over Jenkins' fingertips, washing the soap down the drain. He shook his hands off and with a sigh, headed back to that blasted room. To make matters worse, the guards made sure you locked your phone in some metal box as soon as you arrived so you wouldn't share pictures or whatever. When Jenkins had first started working here, he thought he'd be fine, he'd just be able to play Candy Crush for a couple of hours and get paid for it. But no, no one cared that Stephen Jenkins was *bored.* He wasn't even sure why they hired him. Surely one of the guards could just do it? But for some reason, they wanted some shmuck off the street to come and watch a bunch of unhatched eggs and write down if something changed or the eggs hatched.

Jenkins wondered blankly whether if whatever hatched from the egg would eat him. That would certainly cure his boredom. In a way.

Frowning, Jenkins slowed his pace and crept cautiously towards the door. Muffled giggles and whispered shouts echoed towards him and his frown burrowed deeper. Who was in there? Why? The door burst open, almost smashing Jenkins' face in. He stumbled backwards and glanced up at what appeared to be a teenage boy, tousled light brown hair falling in front of his eyes. The boy blew the hair out of his face as he locked eyes with Jenkins and that was when Jenkins noticed what the boy was holding. An egg. *An egg!*

The giggles stopped abruptly and horrified, Jenkins' eyes dragged to behind the boy where a line of four other teenagers had stopped in a haphazard line behind the first, each holding an egg in their arms.

What the hell?

"Hey! What are you doing, put those back!" Jenkins commanded.

The boy at the front swallowed and without breaking Jenkins' gaze, yelled, "Run!"

Chapter 1

Marilyn-Jo

The air shifted as Marilyn-Jo pulled the window open with a grunt. The ear-bleeding creak of rust was worth it, though, as a rush of cool air hit her face and she sighed in relief.

"Marilyn-Jo, back in your seat, *now*," Mari's teacher's voice echoed dimly in her ears and she turned to face the front of the classroom.

"Sorry, miss," she replied, "but it was *so* hot in here, there was no way I could learn properly."

"Sit down."

Mari rolled her eyes and slumped back to her seat, albeit grumbling as she did so. She glanced around the room, already distracted and not paying attention to whatever formula her teacher was explaining on the board. Her leg bounced restlessly and her eyes were drawn to the clock at the front of the room. Seven minutes. She could survive seven minutes more, that was only one lot of five minutes plus two more minutes. See, she could do maths. Her eyes flicked back to the formula on the board but she'd not been paying attention all class, it didn't make sense to try and understand it now. Mari's eyes flicked back to the clock. Six minutes.

"All right class, I want you to complete this exercise for homework, but you can start on it now."

Mari groaned and slumped back in her seat as she fished her

maths book out of her bag. She flicked it open and made sure she took her precious time in turning to the next available page. Five minutes.

She fished her pen out of her bag and oh goodness, where did her ruler go? Mari searched her pencil case some more until she relented and pulled the ruler out. Four minutes.

Painstakingly slow, Marilyn-Jo dragged her pen down the page, ruling it. She wondered blankly whether they had any apples left at home.

Never mind, because the clock was ticking down and she would finally be out of here. For two weeks, that was, at least. Mari fought to retain her balance as she rocked back on the chair she had sat in every last period for nine weeks on a Friday afternoon.

Finally, the bell rang and Mari shot up out of her seat, hastily closing her book, zipping her pencil case, scooping it all into her bag and heading for the door. She, as well as everyone else in the class, ignored the protests of the teacher to stay and wait for the rest of the homework. Who did she think she was to try and stop the holidays?

Grinning, Marilyn-Jo made her way from the classroom and through the courtyard, towards the car park. She glanced around the rows of cars, hoping to spot the old Mitsubishi her brother had bought with his birthday money last year. She clicked open her phone, scrolling to message Reuben.

Mari 3:09 p.m.
Are you picking me up?

She waited a few moments for her brother to reply before sighing and going to message her mum. Before she could, Mari's phone pinged with a notification.

Gil 3:11 p.m.
Oi. Look up.

She glanced up only for her face to crack into a smile, spotting the hand sticking out of the pristine Audi three cars down. She heard Gillian's laughter as she came round to the passenger seat and climbed in.

"Thanks for picking me up,"

"Yeah, no worries," Gil replied, reversing out of his park. "Reuben messaged me earlier to see if I could."

Mari huffed. "Did he now?"

"Yep. Offered me a million dollars for it too."

"Right."

"Because it's *so* out of my way—"

"Oh, shut up, you're fine," Mari rolled her eyes. "I can give you petrol money though if you need it."

Gillian merely scoffed. "Nah, you're good. Besides, I doubt mowing the lawn for Mrs Patterson once a month could pay for even half a tank."

"Oh yeah because you're so righteous in the way of having a job," Mari mocked.

Gillian pointed a finger at her. "Hey, don't judge. I literally have an interview tomorrow."

Mari hummed thoughtfully. "You're going to be one of those uni students who just eats two-minute noodles every night, you know."

"Hardy-ha-ha."

She glanced over at her friend. Gillian was only a year older than her but was two years ahead in school. She had always found it unfair that he got to graduate earlier just because he was born in January. And be in her brother's year at school. That was heinous. Gillian had been their neighbour for as long as she could remember, perhaps he had been there forever, perhaps not. Not that Mari remembered much of what happened before her mum had brought her over from Japan when she was two.

"Your hair is too long, you know," Mari said jokingly.

His hair had started to curl at the ends, insanely dark, so much so that it looked black unless Gil was standing in the sunlight.

He made a sound of disgust. "You sound like my dad."

"Ew! Don't say that!"

They laughed and the car rumbled along peacefully, their street approaching just around the corner. Gil turned the car and soon enough, he pulled into his driveway.

Mari hopped out with a wave, thanking her friend for the ride once again.

"Don't forget to study!" Mari yelled just as Gil was about to disappear through his front door.

Gillian merely groaned and rolled his eyes, Mari chuckling as she closed her door behind her. At least that was one advantage, she didn't have to do her finals for another two years. Mari dropped her bag at the kitchen bench and opened the fridge door mindlessly, eyes scanning the shelves for something to eat. The sound of her mum's car pulling into the driveway echoed through the house and Mari closed the fridge door.

"Hey, Mum," she called.

"Hey, honey," came her mum's reply, accompanied by the sound of the door locking, "how was school?"

"Yeah, you know."

Her mum leant against the kitchen counter, her brow just

creased.

"Sorry I couldn't come get you, honey, I only just got off work."

"It's all good," Mari replied. "I'm gonna go check on Reuben, though. Make sure he's not died off in that shed."

Her Mum chuckled and waved her off, giving her a quick kiss on the forehead before Mari wandered away.

*

The shed was located in the back corner of the Breneger's backyard, though it hadn't always been used as Reuben's little hideout. According to their mum, the shed came with the house but the previous owner had failed to mention that it also came with a family of possums living in its roof. Mari's mum had spent the better part of a year trying to get rid of them and finally when she couldn't, Mari and Reuben convinced her to hire a professional. Fast forward ten years and teenage Reuben's room was cluttered with his various "experiments" and "research". Mari had lost countless nights' sleep listening to her mum yell at Reuben to clean his room.

She had told him that if he wanted to "cook up schemes", as her mum put it, he was not allowed to do it in his room. Mari didn't know if she had ever seen her brother so focused. He had cleaned out the dingy old shed in a week. Another week later and he'd begun filling it up with whatever project he was working on. In hindsight, Mari realised she could have used the space for herself but she doubted she would have had the motivation to actually clean the thing.

Marilyn-Jo nudged the shed door open with her foot. Reuben was hunched over at the workbench, muttering something incomprehensible as he drew lines across what appeared to be a printout of Google Maps. She stood there for a moment later before speaking.

"Hey."

Reuben jumped in his seat and he turned around, scowling. Mari merely smirked.

"Got you."

"Yeah shut up. I'm in the middle of something."

"Shouldn't you be studying?"

Reuben frowned and turned to her fully, "For what?"

"Oh my gosh."

"Oh right. The finals. No, no. This is more important," Reuben muttered before swivelling back to whatever he was working on.

Reuben had to have been the only year twelve student in the entire nation not stressing out about exams. Which was weird because he was also the most anxious person she knew. Mari huffed and shuffled her brother over on the bench he had stolen from the family piano and she sat down. She peered at the documents spread across the desk, mouth downturned as she tried to interpret them.

Reuben moved them away from her. "Can you please go away?"

Mari ignored him. "What are you working on?"

"None of your business."

"Plenty my business. What is it?"

"You'd laugh."

"I wouldn't."

Reuben narrowed his eyes, assessing her. Mari made a gesture over where her heart was.

"Cross my heart and hope to die. There? Now will you tell

me?"

Reuben paused and looked back at the papers.

"I don't want to," he said slowly.

"Reuben."

"Ugh fine," he glared at her, "but you have to take what I say seriously."

"As if."

He shook his head and let go of the documents, sliding them back over the desk to rest in front of Mari. She assessed them once again. There was the Google Maps printout she had glimpsed earlier, though she wasn't able to figure out where it was or what all the lines and arrows Reuben had drawn meant. Then there was a PDF about some old coffee place that shut down years ago. And then a list of websites.

"What are the websites?" she asked him.

Reuben looked over at the piece of paper. "You know those rumours of experiments going around? The ones about like the government-endorsed team that was tampering with animal DNA and stuff?"

Mari nodded. Of course she knew. Jurassic Park nerds turned conspiracy theorists had taken to every social media platform trying to convince the general public that the government were evil scientists that were trying to bring back dinosaurs. Absolute nonsense, obviously, but Mari had got fully invested in the TikTok drama that had arisen from it. She was surprised Reuben was actually mentioning it now, given he had huffed and rolled his eyes every time she showed him a video about it.

"So," her brother continued, "though the rumours of dinosaur resurrection were probably not true, I have reason to believe that some type of creature actually is being created."

Reuben paused, waiting for Mari to speak but she didn't,

merely waving for him to continue.

"Australia is often quoted for its many dangerous animals, right? What if we harnessed that, what if the *military* harnessed that?"

"What are you saying?"

"I'm saying," Reuben rolled his shoulders and sat back, looking Mari in the eye for just a second, "I think they're making dragons."

A small, choked giggle escaped Mari's throat and she threw a hand up to cover her mouth. Reuben's face fell and he snatched the papers back.

"See, I knew you'd laugh."

"No!" Mari threw up her hands, swallowing her laughter. "No, I'm not laughing. It's just, well, it is a little far-fetched."

Reuben scowled.

"Well, you went from rumours to dragons. Which don't exist—"

"*Probably* don't exist."

Mari sighed. "I just, I don't know. When did you become a conspiracy theorist?"

Reuben stood abruptly from the bench and Mari frowned, watching as he hastily grabbed his research and moved to leave. Damn it. Mari was constantly trying to get Reuben to talk to her and now here she was, shutting him down right as he was about to do that.

"Wait."

Reuben stopped but didn't turn around, waiting for her to say something.

"I'm sorry I laughed. Will you tell me your plan?"

Reuben smiled.

Chapter 2

Reuben

Reuben watched through the minuscule window of his little shed as the first rays of sunlight peeked through the glass. Pretty. He glanced away just as quick, however, focusing his attention back on the scattered papers on the desk in front of him. He knew it was far-fetched; he would be idiotic to think it wasn't, but he still wanted to go through with it. Why? Well, why not? He had nothing better to do with his time. Except maybe study for the finals exams coming up, but that could wait. This was infinitely more pressing and it was also far more interesting. He shuffled the papers into one neat pile, moving pens and stationery around until the desk was neat again. He couldn't afford a bad impression when the others got here. He had spent a long time thinking about who he wanted to come to help prove his theory. He would need someone just as smart as himself but someone with a science and biology mind would help, given the subject matter. It wouldn't hurt to have some bulk on the team as well, or at least that was what Reuben had learnt from movies. He figured there wasn't much more to it and the number of people that Reuben knew amounted to about that much too. Maybe if he spent as much time getting to know people as he did in his shed, he would have more friends. That's what his mum told him anyway. She didn't understand, though. Reuben was happy, despite his current lack of social presence.

He would be able to pick up Nora and, since Mari seemed pretty eager to help him, she could fetch Kish for him. He and Kish had gone to school together and had been friends briefly in primary school. He wasn't sure Kish would actually want to come over, but it was worth a try. He would constitute the brawn. Then Nora. Nora, who smiled at Reuben on the first day of year seven when he didn't know anyone and was so scared he thought he would faint. Nora, who had smiled the exact same the day of graduation when Reuben had to deliver a speech to a crowd of peers he had barely talked to. Her smile wasn't the point though. Nora was smart, scary smart. She had come out on top in almost all her classes and Reuben was fairly sure she'd be receiving dux once their ATAR's came out. Plus, she was a huge science fanatic and that was exactly what Reuben needed for his theory. It had nothing to do with her smile.

Reuben yawned as he stretched and forced himself off the work bench and out of his shed, routinely shutting the shed door with the hefty padlock he had bought from Amazon. He made his way through the house, up the stairs and down the hallway to Mari's room. Her door was littered with stickers and a small whiteboard that said "Mari's Room" with little hearts and stars around it. Plus, a not at all menacing message of "keep out!" written in cursive. He knocked. Reuben waited for just a moment before knocking once again. When she didn't answer, he opened the door.

"Wake up."
She didn't, unfortunately.
"Mari, wake up. Come one."
He leant beside her bed and shook her shoulder.
"Go away," she mumbled.
"No. Come on, get up."

Marilyn-Jo groaned and swatted at her brother's face. "Why?"

"You said you wanted to help me. Now, come on." Reuben stood.

Mari's eyes shot open and she pushed herself up somewhat on her bed. "With the dragons?"

"Yes, with the dragons."

"Ugh, okay, fine. Just, don't do anything without me. Wait till I get up."

Reuben huffed and left the room, shutting the door behind him.

"All right, fine," he said, "but hurry up, we're running on a tight schedule today."

*

Reuben fought not to yell at the car he had spent the majority of his savings on as the engine sputtered and refused to catch. He rolled his eyes and slammed the car door behind him, walking sulkily over to the garage and grabbing the bike he hadn't ridden in a year and a half. His legs were far too long for it but he simply did not have any other options. His piece of crap car wasn't starting and his mum had taken the family van to work. So, cycling it was. How was he going to bring Nora back to the house? Would she have to drive? Would she think he was strange for riding a bike to her house? They didn't live *that* far away from one another. It would only take about an hour to ride there. Not that Reuben was in particularly good shape, despite his lean frame. Well, it seemed he would just have to push down any embarrassment, he had no choice.

Thus, Reuben set off down his street, beginning the long and arduous journey that was the road to Nora Fairweather's house. The road was littered with potholes and Reuben swerved to avoid them, his neck sore from constantly checking behind him to see if a car was approaching. What was he supposed to say when he got there? He *really* should have thought about this more, should have planned out what he would say, how the conversation would go.

Hey, Nora, want to go break into a government facility because, as my sister said, I've turned into a conspiracy theorist and I believe the military is creating dragon-like creatures for the purposes of warfare?

Yeah, because that sounded so logical. This was dumb, why was he doing this, again? Sure, he and Nora hung out at school. But that was only because they were in the same classes and somehow Reuben had ended up sitting with her group of friends at lunchtimes. But, to do this? To ask her of this? That was pure insanity. And yet, Reuben kept on riding. And sending his sister to get Kish? That was perhaps even more idiotic. Marilyn-Jo had never even met Kish and the last time Reuben had had a proper conversation with the guy had been five years ago. Not to mention that Kish ran in completely different circles. He was on the basketball team, he hung with the rugby jocks, with the crowd that Reuben continuously avoided at school. It was too late now, he was too far gone. He was almost at Nora's street and he had already sent Mari off. He was doing this; *they* were doing this.

Her pristine, white concrete, two-storey house approached rapidly and Reuben pulled his bike to a stop, scraping his worn-down Vans on the bitumen below. A gulp ran its way down his throat as he eyed the bright red door of her house. All he had to do was knock, that was it. Just a knock, a simple, little, knock. That wasn't too hard. And yet Reuben seemed frozen in place, sweaty hands gripping the handlebars of his bicycle as he stared that red door down.

He muttered incoherently to himself before nodding decisively and carefully placing his bike against the kerb. Reuben wiped his hands across his pant legs and made his way cautiously towards Nora's house. Breathing deep, he knocked. Reuben waited for a moment, then a moment more, staring at the grooves in the crimson paint.

The door swung open and Reuben was met with the sight of *her*. Her dark hair sprung back from her face in ringlets, held back by a Nike sweatband. Her brown skin shone in the early morning light and Reuben thought he might just fall over from the way his nerves were racing. She gave him a tentative smile.

"Reuben?"

He grinned back awkwardly. "Hey, Nora."

Chapter 3

Gillian

Gillian turned over in his bed, ignoring the shouts coming from outside and the banging on his window. He grumbled something, hoping they would go away as he burrowed further beneath his duvet.

"Let me in!"

Gillian groaned and shouted something back but the pounding on his window was incessant. He scowled and pulled his lanky frame out of the bed, pulling his blinds open with an aggressive tug. On the other side of the window was Em, grinning stupidly as she waved. Though known as Marilyn-Jo by everyone else, Gillian's younger self had insisted that she needed a shorter name and, thus, she became Em. He had tried calling her MJ once but that had not gone down well, apparently Spider-Man wasn't her thing.

Gil's tired eyes glared at her through the window.

"You woke me up," he scowled.

She merely lifted a hand to her ear and mouthed, "What?"

He huffed a sigh and yanked the window upward.

"I said," he grumbled, "you woke me up."

Em merely shrugged as she climbed through his window and made herself at home on his swivelling desk chair. He groaned and climbed back into bed, pulling the covers up over his head.

"Hey, what are you doing?" Mari asked, shaking him.

"Going back to sleep."

"You're not even going to ask me why I came over?" Mari shook him again.

"I don't really care."

She gave a short grunt of frustration before jumping on the bed and jostling everything.

"Gillian," she drew his name out, "I need your help."

"Gillian's not here. Go get someone else."

"Gillian!"

"Ugh fine. This better be worth it or I'm making you buy me KFC."

He pushed the covers back and sat up in his bed, pulling his pillow up to rest behind his head. He yawned before taking in his best friend, kneeling on the other end of the bed, grinning like a maniac. The sunlight had streamed in through his now open window and had turned her eyes from black to a warm brown, her ebony hair pulled haphazardly back from her face. She really was beautiful, though Gil tried not to notice it nowadays. He was happy with their friendship, he really was. And he had worked hard to be, too. Plus, he respected the fact that Mari didn't want to be with *anyone*, probably ever. He just had slip-ups sometimes when the feelings came back, not that he would ever put that on her. She didn't need to know.

He raised his eyebrows expectantly and Em's grin turned sheepish.

"I need you to drive me to Kish Lancaster's house," she said, her eyes imploring his hopefully.

"No."

"Please!"

"Why?"

Kish Lancaster was in the same year as Gil at school and had hung with that sporty type crowd that had taken a particular interest in making Gillian's life hell. Not that all sporty types were mean, no, just this particular batch it seemed. Gillian had thought that when he moved school, he wouldn't have to see that damned jock or any of his friends ever again. How did Mari even know Kish?

Em sighed. "Reuben wants him for a project or something, I don't know."

Gil shifted uncomfortably. "What sort of project?"

Historically, Reuben's endeavours hadn't always proved safe and before Gil had started hanging out with Em more, he had consistently been a victim of these "projects".

"Oh well," Em started, "nothing hugely dangerous or anything. Reuben's just got it in his head that the Aussie military is creating dragons."

Gil laughed and rose from his bed. He looked back at Em, her face serious, and laughed again. Mari merely threw her hands up and followed Gil out his bedroom door and into the hallway.

"Ugh, I know. But it might be fun to go along with it. And plus, what if talking to Kish actually gives you closure?"

Gillian scoffed. "I don't need closure."

"Yeah sure, whatever you say."

"Plus," he continued, "it's not as if it was actually Kish who bullied me, it was his mates. I just also happen to not like his personality or really, anything about him."

Em laughed. "Bit harsh."

Gillian stopped walking a moment and sighed. "Just give me two seconds then I'll drive you over. Not talking to Lancaster though."

Em merely clapped.

*

The car putted along the street, engine grumbling. Gillian pulled alongside the kerb and put his car in park, glancing expectantly at Em. She shot him a thumbs up before climbing out of her seat and out of the car, making her way a few houses down the street. Gil watched as she bounded up the stone steps up to a front door. He leant up over the steering wheel, trying to get a better glimpse. The door swung open and Em stepped back, smiling easily as she offered a greeting. And there he was.

Kish freaking Lancaster.

He leant casually against the doorframe, looking down at Mari as she explained, what Gil presumed, was a brief, persuasive summary of what Reuben wanted him for. Gillian's mouth turned downward in disgust, Kish thought he was *so* cool, he just thought he could waltz through life shooting hoops or whatever the hell he did during his downtime. Gillian didn't care. Stupid Kish. He saw Em finish off her explanation and Kish nodded, shrugging as he yelled something back into his house. Gil sighed and leant back in the driver's seat as he waited the few precious moments before they made it back to the car, moments that unfortunately did not last very long.

The door slammed shut behind the others as they climbed through into Gillian's car. Gil's eyes flicked to the rear-view mirror to see Kish nod a greeting.

"'Sup," the other boy said.

Gil smiled politely, though it could have been mistaken as a grimace. "Hey."

Em smiled widely, clicking her seatbelt in place. "Well, now, this is fun. Off we go, Gillian, start the engine!"

He did just as Em had said, and started the car, steering them back towards Reuben's house.

Gil's mood was thoroughly sour by the time he pulled into the Brenegers' driveway. Kish and Em had chatted the entire way, Gillian not being able to offer one word, not that he particularly wanted to anyway but that was beside the point. He turned off the engine and didn't wait for the others before he got out of the car. Which just made him look like an idiot as he waited for Mari to unlock the door. When was this going to be over?

Em led the way through her house, passing Mrs Breneger in the kitchen.

"Afternoon," Kish smiled at Em's mum.

She smiled back warmly and Gil blankly wondered what it would have been like to grow up with a mum like Mrs Breneger.

"Kish, my goodness, haven't you grown up?"

He chuckled and Gil simply stood there, unsure what to do with his hands. Kish and Mrs Breneger chatted for only a couple more moments before Em grabbed both Kish and Gil by the wrists and dragged them through to the backyard and to Reuben's shed. They entered and were met with the sight of Reuben hunched over some kind of workbench, sneaking glances at the girl next to him. She glanced up, pushing her glasses up the bridge of her nose and smiled when she saw them come in.

"Gillian?"

Oh my gosh.

"Nora?" he grinned.

She jumped up and gave him a quick hug.

"How have you been? How did the new school go?" she smiled wide.

"Yeah, yeah, it was fine. Their chess club was nowhere near as good, though."

She rolled her eyes good naturedly. "Well, duh. We were

always the best."

Gil's eyes were diverted away from his old friend as Reuben stood up and raised his eyebrows at his sister.

"Okay thanks Mari and…" His eyes flicked quickly over at Gillian. "Gil? Anyway, you guys can go now."

"Excuse me?" Em's voice was stricken.

Reuben merely replied with a puzzled look.

She shook her head. "Whatever you're planning, I want in."

"Absolutely not," Reuben laughed.

"I'll tell Mum."

"Sure."

"I will."

"She won't care."

"*You* won't care."

"What?"

Mari stared her brother down and Gillian went to take her away, grabbing her lightly by the arm. She just shrugged him off. After an eternity of Gil standing awkwardly by Em's side, Reuben groaned and relented.

"Fine! You're so annoying. I wish we never adopted you."

Em smiled sweetly. "You love me really."

Reuben rolled his eyes. "Yeah, yeah. Now sit down so I can explain this thing."

Chapter 4

Kish

Kish flicked the speedometer in his minivan before grunting in satisfaction and backing out of his driveway. A flicker of doubt crossed Kish's mind as he began the drive to Reuben's house. He tried to push it away, he didn't get doubts. He didn't second guess. He made decisions and he moved on with his life. Yet he couldn't help but wonder how long they were supposed to be away for? He had thought it would only be for the night but what if it was longer than that? Reuben didn't exactly explain much. Would Kish need his toothbrush? Kish scoffed at himself, worrying like some mother hen. Who was this? Certainly not the Kish Lancaster he'd thought himself to be.

Nah, he'd be fine. Kish glanced at the clock, he bet Nora and Gillian's parents would have just a few questions about where they were headed at this hour. Not Kish's though. No, his mum was probably too busy with what she thought was her "secret boyfriend" to be worried about his own night-time activities. And his dad, well he didn't want to think about his dad. Though, Kish was worried about his sisters. His teeth played with his lower lip as he tried to tell himself they'd be fine. Jill was fifteen, she could take care of the twins just fine. But if anything happened…

No, they'd be fine. Jill had his number and his dad was at work. If there was a perfect night for Kish to be away from the house, it was this one. And to think that he was spending it with a bunch of conspiracy theory nerds. Speaking of which, Reuben's house emerged out of the shadows as Kish slowly drove into the driveway. The urge to honk the horn entered Kish's mind but he pushed it away with a shake of his head. With a yawn, he climbed out of the minivan and started towards the steps.

A shadow in the corner of his eye shifted and Kish whirled around, defensive stance immediately locking into place as the figure jumped the fence over into the front yard.

"Who goes there?" Kish called, feet locked and fists raised.

The shadowy figure continued approaching and raised its arms as if in sarcastic supplication.

"Woah calm down, Balboa. It's just me."

Gillian stepped onto the porch, eyeing Kish warily. Kish hastily relaxed his frame; attempting to appear friendlier.

"Oh. Hey, Gillian. Sorry about that."

Gillian grimaced. "Don't even worry about it."

What could Kish have possibly done already to cause such a reaction? He sighed and raised his arm to knock on the front door. Gillian's own hand shot out and closed around his wrist, sending little sparks of electricity down his arm. Kish forced himself to turn and look Gillian in the eye and raise an eyebrow.

"Their mum's probably asleep, dummy."

Kish raised both eyebrows now. "Dummy?"

Gillian rolled his eyes but let go of Kish. He rubbed his now cold, sparkless wrist as he looked back up at Gillian.

"So, what now?" he asked. "Do we text them or…?"

Gillian seemed to hesitate, teeth lightly biting his bottom lip reluctantly in thought before turning and muttering, "Follow me."

The night seemed to wrap around them as Kish followed Gillian's lanky figure through Reuben's front yard and along the fence dividing the houses. The fence continued on even as Gillian came to a halt, Kish very nearly bumping into his back.

Kish turned his eyes to the side of the house, the large window's curtains pulled back to reveal Marilyn-Jo sitting in the shadows on a lush double bed. She hopped gracefully off the duvet and strode over to the window, hoisting it up in one movement.

"Took you long enough," she said to Gillian before turning piercing brown eyes over Kish's way. "Hey, Kish."

"Hey."

Gillian pushed past him and climbed somewhat clumsily through the window into Marilyn-Jo's room. Kish pulled his own muscular frame easily through the too-small window gap, smirking at Gillian as he did so. He was met with a scowl.

"All right, we better get going, Reuben's going to lose his mind if we don't find him soon," Marilyn-Jo said, striding towards the door of her still dark room.

"Hey, uh, Marily—"

"You can call me Mari, you know,"

"Oh. Well, *Mari,* how come we're in the dark? Can't you turn on the light?" he asked.

"No," she said slowly as if explaining the incredibly obvious, "my mum thinks I'm asleep, dummy."

Dummy? *What?* Kish looked between the two people standing before him and shook his head with a small chuckle.

"What?" Mari asked, eyebrows knitting together.

"Nothing. Just… has anyone ever told you guys you're incredibly similar?"

"Never," Gillian said, sarcasm dripping from his words like icicles.

Mari rolled her eyes at Gil and he looked down at her with a smile so warm it would have thawed even the coldest winter's day. What Kish wouldn't do to have someone to share that look with. He didn't need to worry about that, though, did he? He could get *any* girl he wanted. *If* he wanted them, that was. Although, he had to be honest with himself, he didn't, and that just seemed to make them flock around him even more.

"Isn't Reuben expecting us?" Kish interrupted with a forced cough.

"Right, yes. Come on," Mari said quickly, turning and leading them out of the door.

She strode softly through the halls ahead of them and he and Gillian followed her through the hallways of her house and eventually towards the backyard and Reuben's project shed. A shot of déjà vu hit Kish as the image of Reuben sitting next to Nora on the workbench hit his eyes. Nora seemed to be reading something on her phone while Reuben was sitting, tense, beside her. The old mate had a crush. And he was not going well. Reuben shot up, chestnut brown hair falling in front of his eyes as he jumped towards them.

"Everyone ready?" he said eagerly.

This guy really needed to calm down. Nevertheless, they all nodded and Kish shouldered his backpack more securely.

"No, no, no," Reuben took it off him. "You don't need to take anything with you."

"My phone—" Mari interrupted.

"No phones." Rueben's voice was matter-of-fact and brooked no argument.

The twins. Jill. What if Kish's dad came home from work early? What if Jill needed him? What if?

"Mate, I need my phone," he insisted.

Reuben looked at him, hazel eyes firm. "No phones. I can't

risk any of you posting this."

Scowling, Kish let Reuben take his backpack from him. One night. They would be fine for one night. Jill would take care of the twins and herself. They would be fine. Just for one night.

*

Kish's hands gripped the wheel of the minivan, sweating. He just hoped none of them would look at the steering wheel when he let go.

"Reuben, what exactly are we doing?" Nora asked from the backseat.

Mari was between her and Gillian, Reuben next to Kish himself in the front passenger seat.

Kish watched from his peripheral as Reuben pulled a printed screenshot of a map from his pocket and turned to the others in the backseat.

He pointed to somewhere on the left of the map. "It's an abandoned airport, so it's pretty big. I'll get us in at the South West gate but it's still important that we enter in absolute silence. Did you hear that, Mari? *Silence.*"

"What? Oh right, geez okay. I got it."

"Good. From there, Nora and I will scout ahead to make sure there's no one in the way and once we check that, we will lead you all here," he slid his finger across the page, "to where, according to my knowledge, there will be uniforms. The probability points to this room being locked so if that's the case, we'll need you to lockpick it, Gillian."

Gillian started. "What? Why me? I-I can't use a lockpick."

Reuben snorted. "Oh please, the amount of times you've forgotten your house key is alarming."

"Reuben please stop spying on us," Mari frowned.

"I'm not spying, you guys are just incredibly loud when returning home at one A.M."

Marilyn-Jo scowled but let Reuben continue speaking.

"Try not to touch too many things," Reuben stated, "and we only need access to the file cabinets. Nothing else. Got it?"

Murmurs of 'sure' and 'yep' rebounded through the van and Kish readjusted his grip on the steering wheel. Through his rear-view, Kish could see Nora shift in her seat.

"What do we do once we have access to the files? We're gathering information but what for? What happens after that?" Nora pressed.

Reuben didn't meet her gaze, didn't meet any of their eyes as he turned back to look through the front window. His silence bore a heavy presence in the vehicle and Kish swallowed a dry breath. What exactly had he got himself into? Kish supposed that he should have been discomfited by Reuben's blasé, almost unprepared, attitude to what they were about to do but he still felt just as enthusiastic. Apart from having to leave his sisters at home, Kish had actually been looking forward to the night. He didn't quite know why.

Chapter 5

Nora

Nora's eyes stayed determinedly fixed on the landscape outside. The rolling hills were coated in the night's darkness as Kish parked the van behind a hedge surrounding the perimeter of the abandoned airport. She had this gross feeling left over from lying to her parents earlier. She'd told them she was going to a sleepover at Olivia's house. Not that she really hung out with Olivia much any more since Liv had started dating her latest boyfriend and left Nora in the dust. But they didn't know that. Plus, this was a once-in-a-lifetime opportunity. What if Reuben was right? Then they would be exposed to the most groundbreaking experiment in the last few decades. Perhaps ever. No, that's not true, Nora chuckled inwardly at the thought. A true scientist shouldn't talk in such superlatives.

She followed the others as they hopped out of the minivan and felt the soft, dewy grass underneath her battered Converse. The airport loomed above them from behind the hedge, a great big block of red concrete, its curved roof overshadowing the glass exterior. The desolate runway sat next to the building, cages stacked on one side and the surface littered with potholes. Nora's breath caught but she continued to follow Reuben all the same.

She did so as he cautiously went around the hedge, each of them following suit and she did so again as he led them through to the waiting point. Reuben pointed to behind the cages on the runway and gestured for them to wait there. She and the others scattered behind the cages as Reuben approached the airport door and raised his fist to knock.

What was he doing? Nora sucked in a breath, eyes fixed on the stocky, broad-shouldered guard who swung the door open, his face expressing quite clearly that he was already fed up with Reuben. Reuben's face took on a bored slackness, a scary contrast to the animated anticipation she had seen in him earlier. Nora frowned as she watched the two of them side by side and she realised that Reuben was wearing clothes almost identical to the ones the guard was dressed in. Not the actual uniform but close enough that in the dark, a sleep-deprived guard would probably mistake it for one. He began talking to the guard slowly and Nora wasn't game to let go of her breath lest the guard should hear and figure out their ruse. The guard replied and disappeared inside the building for a moment. He returned shortly with a small bag under one arm and exited the building, clapping Reuben on his back as he did so.

Nora stared, bewildered, not bothering to hold her breath any longer. She waited till the guard disappeared before she gestured to the others that they could come out. They jogged up to Reuben who appeared at attention in the doorway of the building.

"What the hell?" Gillian spluttered.

"No time, follow me," Reuben said quickly.

Nora furrowed her brow. If something went wrong and they lost Reuben somehow, they would be screwed and not even able to finish the mission because he had seriously neglected to tell them anything. She kept her mouth shut, however. She didn't really know these people all that well, or at least hadn't spoken to them in years, and she didn't want to give a bad impression. Reuben shut the door near silently behind them once they had all filtered through and began leading through the hallway. He turned his head towards Nora and the others and raised a finger to his lips. Nora nodded back sagely and the ghost of a smile flickered at the corner of Reuben's mouth. When they reached the end of the hallway, Nora came to halt a few paces back from where Reuben had done just the same.

He glanced around the corner before grabbing Nora's hand, not looking back and pulling the both of them round the bend.

"I don't know why we need two people to check the coast is clear," Nora whispered.

Reuben looked at her and raised his finger to his lips once again, eyebrow arched.

Nora scoffed; her own eyebrows raised in retaliation. Nora's hand became empty again as Reuben let go of it to wave her over to a plain grey door. She crept over just as Reuben tried the handle. It swung open eliciting an eye-roll from Reuben, making Nora laugh quietly. Just as Reuben had said, the room was filled with uniforms of those that worked there. Nora and Reuben silently began to peruse the racks, looking for the right sizes for everyone. Although, the question was really were these all-in men's sizes? As Nora continued to examine the uniforms and check the tags, it seemed the answer would be yes. Ridiculous. She grabbed two coveralls off the racks, hoping they would fit, basing her entire judgement off of sight. She followed Reuben out of the uniform room and back to the others who, miraculously, were still deadly silent. Nora handed the smaller uniform to Mari who turned to Reuben with a look of disgust.

"Are we supposed to just strip here?" she demanded.

Reuben sighed, shaking his head. "Just put it over your clothes, Mari."

Mari made a little *hmph* sound but changed, nonetheless.

Once they were all in uniform, Nora watched as Reuben beckoned them to come in close, huddled.

"All right, Mari, you take Kish and Gil to the left. See if there's anything useful down there. Nora and I'll take the right," Reuben whispered.

They all nodded back and just like that, they were dispersing. Nora and Reuben veered off from the group to the right, heading down a dimly lit hallway. The prelude to a horror movie if there ever was one.

They continued the rest of the way in silence, which was what Nora expected but she felt tense from the heaviness of the unspoken, nonetheless. The room they came upon was unlocked and Nora wrapped her hand in her sleeve as she turned the door handle. The less of themselves they leave here, the less chance people will know they committed a felony. The room stretched away into rows upon rows of filing cabinets, the lighting overhead flickering ominously, casting the dark grey cabinets in sickening hues of green and yellow.

"How are we supposed to get into the files?" Nora asked, mouth dry.

Reuben remained silent. Out of the corner of her eye, she could see him set into motion, suddenly rushing around the room. His almond-brown hair washed in the hues of the lights as it fell over his eyes. Finally, Reuben looked up, spark suddenly ablaze in his eyes and held up a key, grinning. They would probably have to take that key now, but she couldn't bring herself to shut down the joy on Reuben's face. He unlocked a cabinet and immediately set to rifling through the files. He handed the key to Nora, not bothering to meet her gaze as he continued through the manila folders.

Nora went to another filing cabinet and set to looking

through her own files. She looked up, however, when a chorus of giggles and muffled shouts echoed through the hallway and into the file room. Nora glanced at Reuben, his spark gone, replaced by a stoic expression that sent shivers down her spine. She grabbed a couple of the folders and rushed out of the room, Reuben replicating the movements beside her. Her steps seemed too loud, too fast, as she rushed to see what was going on. She and Reuben emerged from the hallway and Nora's jaw clenched.

No. No. This wasn't the plan. They weren't following the plan. Anything could go wrong now. She watched in horror as the figures of Marilyn-Jo, Kish and Gillian crept into a room that was definitely not planned for them to go into. Reuben immediately went after them, face fuming. Oh, Nora could cry. This wasn't the plan. She forced herself to take deep breaths, in and out, and told herself it was fine, over and over. With one more breath, she followed the others into the room, it wouldn't be good to get caught out there alone in the middle of empty hallways. The room she entered beheld a stark difference from the ones they were supposed to be exploring and, well, it most definitely confirmed Reuben's theory.

Tens, dozens, of abnormally sized eggs lay in artificial nests all over the floor and walls of the room. The egg's sizes were increasingly varied and they were covered in a myriad of patterns and colours. Nora spun slowly, jaw slack with shock. Reuben was right. And this was more proof than any file could contain. Then she remembered how they got here. Nora marched across the room to the other three, stepping over the eggs as she did.

"What were you thinking?" she whispered. "This room was not where you were supposed to go. There could have been people in here, we could have got caught! You—"

"Nora. It's all right," Reuben's voice filtered across from the far side of the room.

Nora backed down. She still was fired up from the straying from the plan but... Reuben took the lead on this, she supposed.

Instead, after muttering a quiet apology, she began to go around the room and inspect the eggs. They really were quite beautiful. As Nora did, she could categorise them into three groups. The first group was a number of eggs that had a shiny or metallic exterior, she noted that these were predominantly the larger eggs. The smallest eggs, however, were drenched in pastel hues and were speckled, much like that of a sparrow's but perhaps thirty times larger. Then, there were the plain eggs. In a full range of sizes, these eggs, Nora examined, were merely white. Or perhaps... it may just be like a polar bear's fur and there were so many layers of the clear exterior that it appeared white.

Bouts of giggling once again drew Nora out of her research and turned, with a sigh, to face the others once again.

Nora's eyes widened as she and Reuben took a collective gasp.

"Kish..." Reuben said slowly, approaching Kish in the same manner, "I need you to put that down."

"Why?" Kish said flippantly, holding the egg nonchalantly in the crook of his elbow.

Its metallic red hue glinted in the synthetic lighting of the room. What was he doing?

Kish continued on. "You could take one, Reuben. Research it more. Plus, you'd be like, sticking it to the man or whatever."

Reuben paused. No. He couldn't be serious. He couldn't possibly be considering that?

"Reuben—" Nora started.

She fought to let out a noise of frustration as Reuben bent

down to pick up a plain egg. Nora once again breathed deeply. Research. This could be good for research, perhaps Kish was right. Mari approached Nora slowly, thin brows furrowed together.

"Nora, you all right?" Mari said softly.

Nora nodded and unclenched her eyelids, indulging Marilyn-Jo in a small smile. After all, this wasn't her mission. It was Reuben's. She was merely here to help. Maybe... Well, maybe she could have some fun after all, she wasn't the one who had to be in control. She didn't have to be the one keeping it together, she could let go of the reins.

Nora once again began to peruse the eggs scattered around the room, with a far different purpose this time. A strange warmth seemed to draw her to the back wall. It pulsed seemingly in tendrils, thin from the source and thickening when coming closer to her as to envelop her in its comfort. Nora obeyed its beckoning and drew closer, closer, closer. The warmth unfurled from her body and began to pulse just around one egg. It was one of the plain white eggs and was about the size of a small throw pillow.

Awestruck, Nora extended her hands to wrap around the egg and the joy that emanated from it at the touch was unmistakable, shooting through the egg's exterior and into Nora's veins. Nora lifted the egg off its nest and the joy doubled. She cradled it softly in her arms, a small smile creeping out from behind her defences.

When she, at last, turned back to the others, she noticed they too all had an egg in their hands.

"We should probably leave now. You've still got the files, Nora?" Reuben said, face still glowing despite his seemingly flat expression.

Nora nodded and Reuben signalled for them all to file out the door. Nora wished the others would be a little quieter with their laughs, at least wait till they weren't in danger of death or imprisonment. Nevertheless, they fell into line behind Reuben as he twisted the knob of the door to leave. Nora clung to her egg as she abruptly ran into Reuben, now standing stock still. Why'd he stop walking? Nora peered around his frame and almost vomited with panic.

Mr Jenkins, the substitute teacher Reuben had told them worked here, was standing right outside the doorway, face slack with shock.

Reuben gulped. "Run!"

Chapter 6

Marilyn-Jo

Marilyn-Jo didn't need any further encouragement. She took off, legs burning as she ran and ran and ran, the pale, speckled egg cradled in the nook of her elbow. She distantly heard the slapping footsteps of her peers as they, too, ran as if hell itself were on their tails. Mari couldn't help but let go of the bubbling laugh that escaped her throat as she skipped a little in her run. This was too much fun. Of course, the threat of jail time and a criminal record put a sour filter over the whole occasion but—

Mari pushed that from her head and instead focused on the hallways in front of her. She could hear Mr Jenkins' flustered shouts as he lumbered after them. Another laugh fought its way out of Mari and she pushed more of that energy into her legs as she continued running. They skidded round a corner and Mari cried out as she fought to stop in her tracks. A burly figure dressed in navy stood smirking in the middle of the hallway. *Seriously?* Mari thought. Jenkins finally came around the corner, albeit panting. He laughed and said something that none of them seemed to understand, pointing with a look of superiority on his face. The guard took a step towards them.

"You kids are coming with me," he said, voice rough.

Reuben's hands seemed to be shaking. Not just from nerves, Mari knew. No, Reuben was thinking. And thinking hard. If he could just think a little *quicker*, that would be nice. The guard came to Gillian first, reaching to restrain him. Yet as Mari watched, Gillian's fist swung up, connecting with the guard's jaw with a shocking crunch. Marilyn-Jo let out something between a gasp and a giggle. The guard leant over, rubbing his jaw and groaning. Gillian looked at them all, eyes wide.

"Run! Oh my gos—"

They took off once again, Mari's mind reeling. Gillian punched a guy! Gillian *punched* a guy! The adrenalin from before was nothing compared to this. Mari grinned at Gillian as they ran harder down the halls of the not-so-abandoned airport. He threw a shaky grin back at her and soon enough they were hurtling through the door they had come through. Mari barely registered Reuben's shouts to run faster, nor the opposing protests of Mr Jenkins. All she knew was the hard gravel flying beneath her feet, the wind snapping at her bangs. The energy coursed through her as she gave in to the wild thrill of danger. And the egg. Oh, shoot, the egg. Mari glanced down at her arms quickly and fought the urge to sigh in relief. No time. In front of her, Kish practically threw himself into the van, fingers fumbling with the keys. Then Gillian's lanky figure fell in. Mari kept running and running, finally vaulting herself in. She cradled the egg, landing on her back on the floor of the van, crushing Gil's ribs beneath her.

"Sorry," she said quickly as she scrambled to make room for Nora, sprinting towards the van.

Before Reuben had even closed the door, Kish was slamming on the pedal, accelerating out of the military institution like a madman, dragon egg held between his thighs as he drove. Mari glanced back at the disappearing figure of her old substitute teacher. Of course, she couldn't go back to school after this, could she? Thank the heavens. She slunk into the seat, breaths coming heavy.

"What a night, eh?" she grinned at them all.

Reuben groaned.

"What? We broke into a government facility, stole some *dragon* eggs and escaped!"

"That's what worries me," Nora murmured, promptly appearing to fight back the urge to vomit.

"Gillian punched a guy! An armed, buff guy!" Mari protested, hands waving.

Gillian chuckled nervously. "Yeah, I did do that."

Kish glanced back at them in the rear-view mirror, his smirk wide enough to swallow the moon.

"Between that and your lockpicking skills, you'd best try not to land yourself in jail," Kish warned.

Nora retched again. "I don't think you guys get it. We *will* go to jail for this. We got caught."

"She's right," Reuben added, his voice quiet. "We're not even on the freeway yet and you guys are already cracking jokes."

The car shifted and they fell silent. Mari frowned. Sure, jail was a very possible outcome but, well, they could also all have pet dragons now so that was pretty cool. But yes, Reuben and Nora were right. They were probably going to jail. Though she had been fairly excited at the sight of her best friend punching the security guard, there was a reason he had stayed doubled over for longer than necessary. Gil wasn't *that* strong. They knew that they could just arrest the kids in the morning.

It was fun while it lasted, Mari thought, though it didn't exactly last very long.

Reuben spoke again. "We need to come up with a—"

"No more plans for now," Marilyn whispered, "only sleep."

The others didn't respond and Mari didn't wait to see if they would. She merely let her eyes drift close and settled as comfortably as she could in the middle seat of the car. Sleep came easy, erasing for just a moment what had just happened.

*

The jerks of the car rounding a corner roused Mari from her slumber. The moon was still high and she could just make out the outline of a simple, two-storey building in the darkness. Kish rolled the van to a stop and Mari pushed herself further upright in her seat. She rubbed her eyes, her hand fisted and yawned. She felt Nora leave the seat beside her. Gosh, she was tired. Mari's still half-unconscious brain jerked with panic. The egg. Damn it, she really had to pay more attention to that. Thankfully, it seemed she had held onto it pretty effectively while sleeping.

It was a very aesthetic egg, she had to give it that. A beautiful cream colour, with pastel pink splotches scattered across the surface. She had just had… a feeling about it. There was no other way to describe it. As soon as Mari had seen it, she knew. She felt as if the egg had known too. They were destined to find each other. Not that Mari particularly believed in fate or destiny or anything like that but there had been a few circumstances in her life that had felt… right. Like they were meant to happen.

Like when Reuben and her mum had found her when she was a baby, when she had first met Gillian and now when she found this egg. Mari adjusted her grip on the egg, only about the size of a football and settled back into the seat. She leant her head down on Gil's shoulder beside her and closed her eyes once more. She felt a breath escape him just as his own head came to rest on hers. She kept her eyes shut but could not bring herself to sleep, despite the overwhelming exhaustion clawing at her conscience. Afterall, she couldn't risk the egg.

Chapter 7

Nora

The moon was way too bright for Nora's liking. She took yet another deep breath and willed her disobedient feet to move from the front porch.

Just go inside. It's easy, come on Nora, you can do this.

She was suddenly glad her mums hadn't given into her protesting for a porch light. That would have been really bad. All she had to do was put the key in the lock and step inside. Nora flicked her eyes to the glint of her golden watch. Damn it all, it was only quarter to eleven. Her mums were probably still up, watching one of their true crime shows. Oh, heavens above, *Nora* was a criminal now. None of this was in her life plan. She had laid it all out meticulously. Graduate high school, then do the same with university. Then she would get a respectable job that paid well, grow that career. Somewhere in her thirties she would probably get married and have a couple of kids. Grow old. Keep working. And working. And working. It was her ideal lifestyle, she had thought. Now all that was probably going out the window because she couldn't resist that stupid crooked smile Reuben had thrown her way yesterday morning.

Nora eyed the balcony above her. Maybe she could climb up and break into her room from there. Climb up. With what was basically an exaggerated chicken egg. Even in her head, it sounded ridiculous. Ugh, she really thought they'd be getting back later than this, it'd be a hell of a lot easier to sneak back in a few hours. Maybe she could go out and just come back later? Go to... what was open at this time of the night? McDonald's?

The creaking of the front hall's floorboards startled Nora and she quickly shoved the egg into her mum's lavender bushes. She ignored the shrill cry she thought she heard and returned to a standing position quickly. The door swung open and Nora gulped as she took in her mother's dark brown skin wrinkled with what Nora couldn't decide was worry or rage. She hoped it was the former even as she swore she saw steam coming from her mum's nostrils. Her other mum hovered behind; blonde hair streaked with grey strung up into a knot on the top of her head.

"Nora Jean Fairweather, where the hell have you been?"

"Um, honey," Nora's mum wrapped her pale cardigan around herself, "maybe start by asking why she's out here."

"I think it's pretty clear, Emily. She snuck out."

"Well, not necess—"

"It's okay, Mum," Nora said quietly. "Look, I was just taking a break from studying, getting some fresh air on my balcony when I... I tripped."

Her mother's near-black eyes narrowed. "Tripped?"

Nora nodded, hoping sheer confidence would distract them from her incredibly shoddy logic. Her mum hurried out from the doorway, wrapping her arms around Nora's shoulders, grey cardigan scratching.

"Debbie, honey, Nora has clearly had quite the fall, all right? I think she just needs to get back on up to her room and get to sleep, yes?" Her mum's tone was warm and Nora saw her mother's eyes soften.

Nora wasn't looking at her mum, but it was clear she was shooting her mother a look that told her to *drop it and we'll discuss it in the morning.*

As Nora passed, her mother pecked a quick kiss on her forehead. "I love you."

"I love you too, Mum," Nora whispered.

Nora was silent as her mum walked her up the carpeted stairs and through the short hallway to her room. She sat down quietly on her bed as her mum closed the door behind her. Her pale blue eyes were sparkling with mischief but her age showed in the delicate crow's feet at the corners of her eyes and the way she kept wrapping that long cardigan around herself.

"Nora—"

"Mum. I tripped."

Nora's mum laughed, the sound scratchy with age. "Nora you are wearing a janitor's coveralls that stink of wet animals. I got you out of there so I could hear the story without your mother yelling over the top of it so if you won't be honest with me, I can just as easily bring her up here."

Nora gulped. She had a point. Also, the uniform did smell really bad. She couldn't believe she was *still* wearing it.

"Okay, okay. I'll tell you, then," she sighed.

Her mum grinned and hopped down on the bed beside her.

"All right! Where'd you go? Ooh! *Who with*?" she wiggled her eyebrows at Nora.

Nora slipped her headband out of her hair, the curls springing up around her face.

She told her mum about how they went for a drive out to the abandoned airport. She didn't tell her about Reuben's conspiracy. She didn't tell her about them getting caught. Nor the dragon eggs. Nor anything that could make her mum think her daughter was a criminal.

"So, this was that Reuben boy's idea?" her mum asked.

Nora nodded.

"Ah well, your mother and I went on a few late-night drives of our own in our day. You didn't need to lie about that," her mum said with a wink as she rose from the bed.

Nora recalled her mother's face at the doorstep, her black hair pulled tightly back from her face, only accentuating the fear-instilling rage.

"Didn't I?"

Her mum swallowed. "Actually yes, you probably did."

Nora laughed, a light sound and her mum's own raspy laugh joined her.

"All right, honey, time to get some sleep, I love you."

"Love you too."

*

Nora did not get some sleep. She waited until she was positively certain her parents had gone to sleep, all the lights in the house winked out for the night. The chatter of their late-night talks had dissipated at least an hour before Nora was game to walk past their bedroom and down the stairs. She slipped out the front door with almost silently. She was close to sick of trying to be quiet, she'd done it that much tonight. A small voice seemed to be whining and Nora wished the kids across the road would shut up. She stooped down to the lavender bushes and scrambled to find the egg. Her hands finally closed around it and scooped it out of the cluttered bush. The whining stopped abruptly. Weird.

Eyes narrowed, Nora slowly bent back down and placed the egg on the ground. Silence still. Must be her imagination. She had to be sure, though. Multiple tests and all that, of course. Nora stepped back a few paces. Nothing. She went back inside the house, reaching to pull the door closed. There. The whining resumed, high-pitched and squealing. Was it coming from the egg? It was so loud! How had no one come out to see what was happening? Was society so damaged that these people just didn't care about anything any more? Nora rushed over to the egg and scooped it up. Just because no one was coming out of their houses, didn't mean that her parents wouldn't be able to hear it and be woken up.

The whining cut off abruptly once again. She was *almos*t a hundred per cent sure it was coming from the egg. Nora frowned but rested the egg between her arms. She made her way back through the house quietly. She returned to her room and with a weary sigh, placed the egg on her desk. Nora groaned as yet again the egg whined excruciatingly loudly. She grabbed the egg again. Silence.

"What? What do you want? I can't hold you all the time," she whispered to the pale egg.

A small voice seemed to float up from around the egg, wrapped in the same feeling as when Nora had first felt called to it.

Mother?

Nora thrust the egg away at arm's length, eyes narrowing suspiciously. After a few moments of deliberation and coming to the conclusion that if this was her madness finally coming, then that was that.

"No. I'm not your mother," she said slowly.

The egg was silent and Nora placed it carefully on the bed next to her. When the voice came again, it was tentative and questioning.

Mother?

Nora raised an eyebrow at the plain, white shape of the egg

next to her. "You probably don't have a mother, honestly."

The wailing was louder this time. How had her parents not heard this?

"Okay, okay, calm down—"

Nora had never been good with kids. She didn't know how to talk to them or what they wanted and she was quite sure they didn't know either. This was just like a small child, in all the worst ways. Except it was literally an unborn dragon. Talking to her. Heaven help her, she was going insane. And damn it all, said unborn dragon was still wailing.

"Um, hi there. Dragon? Look, you probably don't have a mother but—"

The wailing increased.

"Ah! Okay, what I'm trying to say is that I can look after you. Yes?"

The wailing died down and Nora could have sworn she heard what sounded like a sniffle.

Mother?

"No, not mother. No, don't scream! Okay, I can't be your mother but I can look after you. Like a mother would, kind of. I think," Nora cringed.

At least it wasn't wailing any more. In its silence, Nora took the time to marvel at what was before her. Somehow this unborn organism, probably still growing inside that egg, was able to communicate with her. It was amazing, really. A scientific miracle. What she wouldn't have given to be a part of the team that brought this about. Although, the government's science team weren't exactly renowned for their kindness.

Nora twisted her lamp to shine over the egg. The colour was hard to describe, reminiscent of milk almost. But with darker, creamier, strands that appeared, when under light, much like veins. Under the harsh glow of Nora's lamp, a blurry figure could just be glimpsed within the egg.

"I'm Nora, by the way," she whispered with a smile.

The egg made a sound and if Nora could have seen the dragon, she thought it would have cocked its head.

"You need a name, don't you?" Nora mused

The egg did not reply and Nora took that as confirmation. Nora glanced around the room, wracking her brain for an appropriate name. Her eyes snagged on the copy of the periodic table resting on her desk, printed out from her chemistry textbook. Magnesium? No, that was stupid. Copper? That sounded like a good name, right?

"I'll name you Copper," she announced to the egg.

The egg calmed and Nora chuckled. She might like this little egg after all. Not that it was that little. The egg was about the size of a human head, after all.

"Can you say much yet?" Nora queried.

The egg made that same inquisitive sound again.

Nora hummed. "Interesting."

She swiped a notebook from the top of her desk and flipped it to the next available page. Nora hastily clicked a pen and began scribbling her notes on what she'd learnt about this egg so far. About how no one else heard it. About how it knew minimal words such as 'mother' and how it communicated with Nora. About its size and colour. Tapping her pen absent-mindedly against her chin, Nora's mind wandered to exactly how they had managed to create a creature sentient enough to communicate with human minds. The first theory she came up with was that chips had been inserted into the creature's mind while they were being made. But Nora didn't have a corresponding chip in her own brain. Never mind, she would keep thinking about that later.

After she got some sleep, perhaps. Nora finished up on her notes and, grinning, grabbed her phone. Grin still strong, she opened up Instagram and scrolled through her DMs. There. Reuben. The last message was a happy birthday from two years ago. Her grin slipped a little but she continued. He would want to know this. Right?

Nora – 12:09 a.m.
Reuben! You will not believe what just happened!

Nora hesitated over the send button. She deleted the message and went back to the home screen. Reuben was probably asleep; she didn't want to wake him. Plus, it's not like they usually messaged each other. It would be weird. She'll just tell him later. Nora put her phone down and went to lie down on her duvet, eyes trained on the egg sitting peacefully on her desk.

Chapter 8

Reuben

What in the actual flaming hell had he done? They'd got caught. They had got caught. Sure, they weren't in jail *right now* but it was only a matter of time. Reuben lay star-fished across his bed, hazelnut hair mussed with stress. He'd doomed all of their futures. *He* had done that. Crap, all he'd wanted was confirmation of his theory. And now he had a freaking dragon egg sitting underneath his bed. He had gone too far, yet again. People always told him to just think about it, not everything required action. He had scoffed. If only he could go back and actually listen to their advice.

The sun pushed stubbornly through his bedroom blinds but Reuben shut his eyes with fervour against it. He did not want to wake up. Maybe if he went to sleep it would all go away. Reuben knew he was acting like a child but, to be perfectly honest, he didn't particularly care.

If it was just him, it would have been fine. Well, he wouldn't be *that* comfortable with prison but it wasn't like he had made many plans for his future anyway. He bet the others had, though. And he'd just gone and shot it all away. Of course, they did make the decision to come with him. He was very confident in their success, though. He couldn't blame this on them, he'd as good as brainwashed them. Was he evil now?

Reuben shook his head and sat up, blood rushing back down

through his body. He needed to get up; get on with his day. Stop obsessing over something that may or may not even happen. Reuben rubbed his eyes with a yawn. He pulled himself out of bed, chucking on the hoodie that had fallen on the floor. He lumbered out of his room and down the hall to the kitchen. Mari was already dressed in biking shorts and an oversized T-shirt. She had her hair pulled back into one of those claw clips she had said were the trend nowadays, the same thing she had said when she had cut her own curtain bangs.

"Morning," she called, voice more chipper than usual.

"Mhmm," Reuben mumbled, pushing past her to get to the toaster, "do you really have to make a smoothie this early in the morning?"

"I've been up for four hours, Reuben."

Reuben furrowed his brow. "What time is it?"

"Eleven thirty."

He groaned and went past the cupboard, not bothering with the toaster. He merely grabbed the slice of crust out of the bread box and started chewing. Mari glanced at him with a look of rancid disgust, eliciting an eye-roll from Reuben.

"Hey, Mari," he asked, swallowing.

She made a sort of humming noise of affirmation.

"What do you think will happen now?"

Mari paused, leaving the berries half crushed inside the smoothie bottle.

"I think—"

Reuben doubled over, clutching his head. His fingers knotted in his hair and he squeezed his eyes shut. An unbearable, high-pitched... What was it, screaming? A high-pitched sort of screaming filled Reuben's read with murderous, unceasing continuity.

"Reuben? Reuben! Did you even hear what I said?" Mari came over and shook his shoulder.

Reuben fell to his knees. How could he make it stop? Could Mari not hear this? He let out a short scream of frustration.

"Reuben! Oh my gosh, what's going on?"

Mari's voice was distressed but all Reuben's mind could focus on was that blasted noise. He forced himself onto shaky feet and stumbled down the hallway, Mari's concerned footsteps right behind. He burst back into the bedroom and hoisted the dragon egg onto his bed, fingers shaking along with the rest of his body. The sound stopped and Reuben collapsed. What was that?

Reuben.

Reuben's eyes widened and he leapt from the floor in a tangle of limbs and messy hair.

"Who was that?"

He turned around his room, searching. He relaxed his frame, however, as he saw Marilyn-Jo standing in the doorway.

"Oh," he sighed, "it was just you."

Mari's brows lowered and she peered at him. "I didn't say anything and I didn't hear anything either. Reuben, are you okay?"

Reuben looked at his sister. "Yes. No. I don't know, it's probably just the stress."

"Okay," she didn't look convinced but Mari walked away nonetheless. Reuben sat back down on the bed.

Reuben.

Reuben yelped. He rubbed his forehead and peered at the egg. Maybe the unborn dragon knew how to communicate. Although, that was quite a stretch if he was being honest with himself. Not that it was really a time for rational conclusions, given his current mental state. And the existence of dragons. A hum of affirmation came from the egg. Interesting. Reuben eyed the egg warily. Hold on, did it just read his thoughts? Yep, that was pretty weird. Another hum.

"So that was you who was screaming before?" Reuben mused accusatorily.

That same hum of affirmation came from the egg.

Reuben frowned. "You're literally a foetus, how do you already have attachment issues?"

A soft whining sound emanated, much like that of a wounded puppy.

"Oh okay, I'm sorry. Geez. But seriously, a bit of a warning would have been nice."

The egg, well the growing dragon foetus, didn't respond.

"Okay, I'm going to leave now," Reuben warned as he began to back out of the room slowly.

The screaming pierced his conscience yet again and he clutched his head, the pain from the sound coursing through his skull.

"Ah! Okay, okay! I'm staying!"

The egg seemed to quieten at that. What was his life? Seriously, what had happened? He was speaking to an almost inanimate object, for all Reuben knew, he needed to be shipped off to the nearest psychiatric ward immediately. With a resigned sigh, Reuben returned to his bed and flicked on the small box television sitting on his chest of drawers. Bland images from programmes he didn't care about flashed across the screen and he huffed, falling back onto his wrinkled duvet. The buzz and crackle of the television speaker registered dimly in Reuben's ears drowning out any sound from outside of his room. Or, at least, he had thought it would. Through the on-screen voices,

Reuben could just make out the sound of the phone ringing. The phone being answered. His mother yelling in outrage. Something about the other person being wrong, Reuben couldn't hear the exact wording. Then the fated, heavy, steps of his mother prowling through the hallway to his room. This couldn't be good. His door slammed open and Reuben flinched before pulling himself into a sitting position.

"Reuben Maxwell Breneger," his mum said quietly, "what exactly have you done?"

Crap.

Chapter 9

Kish

The cereal was way too dry. Although, Kish supposed that was to be expected given he was eating it straight out of the box. Clad in just a singlet and basketball shorts, Kish wandered down the halls to his room, crunching on handfuls of cereal as he went. He swung into his desk chair and flipped on his LED lights. That was better. Kish set down the box of cereal and opened his laptop. What was he doing? He couldn't remember. Needless to say, Kish opened Google Chrome only to begin playing the Dino game. He wondered whether the thing in the egg he'd stolen would come out looking like that. Probably not.

His bedroom door swung open to reveal Jill, leaning against his doorframe, unsaid words betrayed by the gnawing on her lip.

"You all right?" Kish swung round on his chair to face his sister.

She was only fifteen but already growing out of people's empty remarks about how similar they looked. Sure, they both had hair the colour of coffee beans and a pale brown complexion but that was about where the similarities stopped. Their dad had moved over from London when he was twenty for university and ended up meeting, to quote his father, "the most beautiful girl he'd ever laid his sorry eyes upon" at the university and dropped out. Kish's mother had, at that time, come into a scholarship that had given her cause to move from Palestine to Australia. Kish had always loved listening to his parents recount the story of their elopement, his dad's eyes alit with love, passion and simple adoration as he gazed at Kish's mum. Fast forward ten years and Kish barely saw them in the same room anymore.

"Yeah," Jill conceded. "Why? *You* all right?"

Kish nodded, letting the dinosaur on the screen crash into a cactus. "Everything okay last night?"

Jill rolled her eyes. "Kish, you weren't even gone for two hours. We were fine."

Not even two hours? Kish blew out a breath, it had sure seemed longer. He didn't think he had driven that fast in his life.

"Anyway, what do you want?" Kish asked.

Jill shrugged and merely dragged herself out of the room. Seriously? Well, at least everything was okay while he was gone. He never thought he'd say this but everything had been fairly boring after school finished. He had nothing to do. His work had recently run out of business which was a bummer, Kish supposed, but he was starting a paid apprenticeship soon so it was fine. He might look at another job anyway just for that extra bit of cash.

Kish looked over at his half-full washing basket where he'd stashed the egg. It was a chunk of an egg too, at least a third of the size of the washing basket it was in. It had a rippling pattern on its metallic red surface, resembling what could be scales. Yet as he shifted in his seat, that rippling pattern also shifted. Maybe it was a trick of the light. He wondered if there was some cosmic connection or something that had compelled him to grab it. He'd felt called to this egg more than others but that was probably just the gut feeling he'd learnt to trust over the years. It's not like the dragon had talked to him or anything like in all those fantasy stories. No, this was just some rip-off created by money-hungry government scientists and officials. It probably wouldn't even hatch.

A sharp ringing sound snapped Kish's gaze away from the egg. He swung his chair over to his bed and lifted his phone off the duvet. Unknown number. Weird. Kish tapped the answer button and held the phone up to his ear.

"Hello? Kish here."

The voice that answered was flustered and out of breath with notes of high-pitch panic.

"Kish! Thank goodness, um, it's Reuben. You gotta come over here right now! Please, just, I gotta—"

"Woah, dude, slow down. What are you talking about?"

Kish heard Reuben take a deep breath and when he spoke next, Kish could have sworn this voice was one devoid of hope. One with a desperation that just knew not much could help it. Somehow, this was way more alarming than the panic.

"Kish," another deep breath, "Kish, the police are coming."

"The police?" Kish asked confused.

"Yes. They're coming to my house. And maybe yours, I don't know. But we need a plan- maybe we give the eggs back, mayb—"

"Hold on. Calm down a bit, mate, I'll be right over."

Kish's mind began to reel despite the façade he had put on for Reuben's sake. The police? No, no, no, no, no. He couldn't go to jail; it would ruin his sisters. He'd never be able to find a good enough job after that. Stuff the apprenticeship, he could kiss that goodbye too. Damn it, why did he have to agree to go out last night? Although, he couldn't blame it entirely on that. He was the one who'd wanted to take the eggs. He was the one who had led them all into that room. He was the one who had sped away in a sketchy van.

This was so bad. It was so, so, so bad.

"Okay," Reuben's voice jolted Kish back to the present.

The beeping of Reuben hanging up echoed in Kish's ears and he slumped down onto the ground, eyes finding that blasted red egg across the room. That was what this was about. He had stolen government property. Kish shook his head; he shouldn't have gone this far. He'd always had a bit of fun during school with the occasional prank or practical joke. But he'd never outright broken the important rules. And now he'd gone and shot all his morals down the drain just for a stupid egg that a guy he barely knew thought contained a dragon.

Stuff it. Kish stood and grabbed the egg, pushing it into a reusable Woolworths bag as he left his room.

"I'm going out for a bit," he called through the house as he snagged a jacket from off his bed and patted his pocket, making sure the pouch with his Epipen was secure.

Various mumbles of affirmation rumbled back through the hallways to him. He was in this mess now and he may as well roll with it because the other option was moping in his room and waiting for the cops to come and get him. And that was *not* a Kish Lancaster move.

*

Kish pulled into Reuben's driveway and hopped out, Woolworth's bag swinging softly. He really had to be more careful. Over the fence, he could see Gillian rushing out of his house and hopping over the fence, a suspicious lump underneath his shirt.

"Who knocked you up?" Kish called.

Gillian merely rolled his eyes as he hurried over to the front step.

"Gee, okay, it was a genuine question, dude."

Gillian gave Kish a sour look and slipped the egg out from underneath his shirt. Their eggs were identical save for the hue. Where Kish's was a flaming red, Gillian's egg had a dark, writhing blue that felt as if Kish was looking into the depths of the night sky.

"Reuben call you, too?" Gillian asked.

Kish nodded sombrely, jokes aside for that moment.

"You have big plans?" Kish asked.

Gillian cast Kish a questioning look as he rang the doorbell. "For what?"

"I don't know. Life? Higher education? Not jail?"

"Oh yeah, I guess those things aren't much of an option now, are they?"

A sharp hissing sound drew their eyes from the still-closed door. Mari was standing round the corner, fire written across her face as she waved them over.

"Gillian! What were you thinking? You are holding the egg in plain sight and you ring the doorbell! Why didn't you just come to the window?" Mari demanded as soon as they'd jogged over to her.

Gillian shook his head. "I don't know. Sorry. I... uh, I was distracted."

A rush of déjà vu hit Kish as he climbed through Marilyn-Jo's bedroom after her and Gillian once again. Although, everything was a lot clearer in the daylight. As soon as Kish cleared the windowsill, Mari rushed over and slammed the window down, closing the blinds with undeniable aggression. Kish wouldn't admit it but it kind of scared him.

"Um, Marily- I mean, Mari. Are you okay?" Kish ventured.

Mari whipped her head to him, eyes wide, muscles tense. She shook her head and visibly relaxed. She sighed, eyes closed, before opening them again and looking back at Kish.

"Yes. It's just Reuben... Well, he's not going so well. And by not well, I mean really, really weird. So be careful."

Kish raised an eyebrow. Be careful of Reuben? Oh please. That guy wouldn't be able to hurt a fly if he tried, no offence though. Kish's regretted such thinking as soon as he followed Mari into that ramshackle little shed in their backyard. Reuben was pacing the length of the shed, hair knotted and spiked, dark bags under his eyes. His hazel irises had a dark shadow and were widened as he muttered to himself. Mari was right. He was being really, really weird.

"Reuben?"

Reuben snapped his head towards them and stopped his pacing, sinking to the floor.

"Oh good, good," he muttered, "you're all here. Wait, where's Nora?"

"She's not here yet," Mari said gently, approaching Reuben slowly. "Reuben, I say this with love but you're acting crazy. Like scary-old-man crazy."

Reuben closed his eyes and shook his head. Reuben whispered something to Mari and she nodded. Kish leant over to where Gillian was standing beside him.

"What do you think got into him?" Kish murmured.

Gillian replied in the same manner, albeit a lot drier. "Probably the fact that he's going to be in a prison cell sometime in the next twenty-four hours."

Kish's mood flattened. "Yeah, probably."

A loud crashing sound drew Kish's attention away from the other boy and towards the doorway of the shed. Grass stains on her knees, Nora was pulling herself from the ground and rushing towards them.

"I'm here! I'm here!"

Reuben's head snapped out of its daze and Kish could immediately see the difference. Where once was dazed distress was now only intelligent clarity.

"Nora, it… it talks."

Chapter 10

Gillian

It talks? What talks? Gillian's thoughts were flying all over the place and he couldn't concentrate with Kish breathing so damn heavily next to him. Seriously, what was he doing before this? A marathon?

Reuben took a deep breath. "The egg. It spoke to me."

Gillian took a step back and forced himself to take a seat on the workbench.

Nora nodded emphatically, large brown curls bouncing. "Yes! Mine too! What did yours say?"

Kish stepped between them after setting his red egg down next to Gillian. "Hold on, your eggs talked? Mine didn't!"

Reuben and Nora shrugged in sync. Gillian's egg hadn't made even a sound since he'd brought it home last night. He peered at it now quizzically. He knew this was the egg he wanted as soon as he'd seen it. It was as if those swirls of deep metallic blue had just spoken to him. Well, not spoken to him, not like Nora and Reuben were proposing. Gil stood up, leaving his and Kish's egg leaning against each other.

"Kish has a point here. How come your eggs talked to you but ours didn't? Em, did yours?"

Em shook her head, eyes wary of the situation. Before she could elaborate with her words, a figure came rushing through the backyard and into the shed. Gillian turned his head to see Em and Reuben's mum in the doorway, blue eyes filled with worry, hair frazzled.

"Reuben! Oh, honey. They're coming."

"Who? Who's coming?" Gillian asked.

"Oh Gillian, bless you. The officials. They aren't even police; I don't know what they are but... They're coming and you guys need to leave. Right now," her voice was frantic.

"Are you sure?" ventured Em.

"Yes! Now go!"

Gillian stared wide-eyed at the others. Would the logical explanation not be to just return the eggs and get whatever reduced charges they could scrounge up? Before Gil could protest, the others hurried out of the shed, Reuben and Mari stopping to hug their mother goodbye. Gillian waited until Em was finished before rushing out with the others. This was crazy. Kish was ushering them all back into the van and Gillian climbed in just as Em vaulted herself over the backseat.

"Em! Get out of the boot, man."

She snorted. "There're seats back here, calm down."

Gil shook his head but clicked his seatbelt into place right in time for Kish to slam on the pedal and zoom out of the driveway. This could not be happening. Not to him. Gillian was just the boring neighbour, that kid in the background of high school that no one paid attention to. Em was giggling in the back, warming her face with the sun streaming in through the window, utterly unperturbed by the situation at hand. It was ridiculously beautiful. Gil wished he could merely freeze time at that moment but no, they were, unfortunately, trying to escape the government not in some fantasy fairy tale. If Gil's thoughts had been more organised, perhaps he would have conjured enough conscience to object to their choice of action at that moment. And yet he had somehow been struck dumb.

Kish swerved the van onto the M4 with frightening carelessness. A shot of panic rushed to Gillian's head. The egg. The mother freaking egg. He really had to stop forgetting about it. A sigh of relief filtered out of his lungs as he spotted the egg on the floor of the car. He should probably be more careful with it.

"Oh," Kish murmured from the front.

"What?" Gillian asked.

"I, uh, I think I forgot it."

"You forgot *what*?" Gillian asked slower, warningly.

Kish gulped, taking his time replying. "The egg."

Various choruses of "Kish" and "Oh my gosh" and "You idiot!" were thrown at the driver's seat as Kish cringed. As soon as the next exit came, Kish swung around into a U-turn and began driving at breakneck speed back to Reuben's house. More reprimands followed.

"What?" Kish protested. "We're already speeding!"

Everyone settled back into their seats. This was going to be a long day.

Before long they were traversing the M4 again, this time with all five eggs in the car. It didn't take long, with Kish going far past the speed limit, for the group to then exit the M4, pass Glenmore Park and ease into a more relaxed, though still tinged with panic, cruise down the road.

Gil leant forwards in his seat. "Where are we going?"

"I thought we'd stop at the dam." Kish shrugged.

Seemed smart enough. Plus, Gillian really needed to stretch his muscles, he was not used to car trips. He supposed living your whole life in one place didn't lend itself to long amounts of time in the car, especially when he could just walk everywhere. Except, of course, when visiting his family's holiday cabin. Although, those visits were infrequent and hadn't happened in years. The time went by quickly and before Gillian knew it, Kish was pulling into a car park on the side of Warragamba Dam.

"What are you doing? We're not nearly far enough away?" Reuben asked fervently.

"Yeah, I know. I just thought it'd be good to stop here for a couple of minutes. Also, I really need to pee," Kish said.

"Too much information!" Em yelled from the back. Gillian chucked his jacket over his egg and climbed out of the car, the others following similarly. Kish immediately rushed off to the public bathrooms nearby. Presumably. Gillian couldn't actually see any restrooms but Kish would figure something out. Hopefully. Gillian leant onto the railing, gazing out at the rushing water below. There was something soothing and yet truly terrifying about it. The water could swallow you whole and yet it was also capable of bringing life. Drowning or quenching your thirst. It all depended if you knew how to swim, he supposed.

"So, what now?" Reuben murmured.

They all paused for a while, staring at the never-ending rushing of the water.

"We go somewhere," Mari shrugged.

"We don't have a somewhere," Nora replied despondently.

Gillian chewed his lip. It was risky to suggest what he was thinking of, he knew that. But, like Nora said, they didn't have a somewhere yet. Maybe what he was thinking of could be their somewhere. For the time being, at least.

"I might have a place," Gillian ventured quietly.

Three heads turned his way.

Gil took a deep breath. "My family owns a holiday cabin in

the Southern Highlands over at Bowral. We haven't been there in a couple of years so it should be okay to hide out there for a little while."

Three near-identical smiles cracked the faces opposite him and Gillian offered them a small grin in return.

"That's brilliant, Gillian!" Reuben congratulated, heading back to the van.

Nora passed him too, giving him a little pat on the shoulder. "Thanks, Gillian."

"Gil," Em bounded over to him, "you sure?"

Of course, she knew exactly what he was thinking. Somehow, she always did.

"Yeah, no, I'm sure. I promise."

Mari eyed him warily but ended up smiling and giving him a light punch. "Okay, if you say so. I'm going back to the van, you good to wait for Kish?"

Gillian nodded and watched as she skipped her way to the boot of the car and crawled in, giving him a little wave as she did so. Gillian wasn't sure if he had just told the truth or not. It should be fine, both his brothers were currently deployed somewhere with Australia's military so there was no way they'd be there. And it'd be fine for a little while until Gil's parents figured it out. But they could stay at the cabin for a couple of days at least. Gillian just hoped he was right and wasn't about to doom them all.

Part 2

The Reptile Park

Chapter 11

Jenkins

Jenkins gulped. He was absolutely, terribly, undeniably done for. He bounced his knee as he fought to keep himself seated on the extremely uncomfortable sofa cushions in the lobby of Parliament House. He'd had no idea those kids had come into the facility. Where had Hank been anyway? He was the one in charge of entrance and exit security. Jenkins had to go find Frank who was in charge of some other part of security to help him with the hooligans. Frank! That wasn't Frank's job! Or maybe it was? Jenkins always got them mixed up, all the guards' names rhymed anyway. They were pretty much all the same person, if Jenkins was being completely honest.

"Mr Jenkins?" the receptionist called, causing him to stand up perhaps just a tad too eagerly. "He'll be out soon."

Oh. Jenkins lowered himself back onto the uncomfortable chair. He'd never met the head of Australia's military. He'd never had cause to, he was a substitute teacher for Pete's sake. What would they say to him? At best, he'd just be fired. At worst... well, he didn't even want to think about it. He hardly thought this was a matter worthy of such an audience, but he wasn't about to try and argue with his superiors. Clipped footsteps echoed through the lobby straight to Jenkins' ears. He peered up, gulping at the sight before him. A towering six-foot-something man stood there, dressed completely in military garb, head shaved, hand out in what appeared to be an invitation for a handshake. Jenkins stood shakily and with just as much nerves, he gripped the commander's hand.

"Robert Gregorian, pleased to meet you, son," the man said, voice deep and raspy.

Jenkins choked. "Uh, yes, hi. Um, I'm Stephen Jenkins. I heard you wanted to see me?"

The man turned, abruptly letting go of Jenkins' now very sore hand. He started a brisk trot through the reception and Jenkins figured he had no choice but to follow. The walk was silent and Jenkins suddenly found himself in a small office which, if he was being brutally honest, looked as if it used to be a supply cupboard. Mr Gregorian shut the door behind Jenkins and moved around him to sit behind the small desk. Jenkins was acutely aware of each movement. Gregorian gestured for Jenkins to take a seat on the opposite side of the desk. As he obliged, Jenkins' eyes snagged on a small photo frame in the corner of the military commander's desk. There was something so familiar about the woman in the photo. The blonde waves. The chunky glasses. Who was she?

Gregorian chuckled. "Beautiful, isn't she?"

Jenkins nodded emphatically. "Yes, she is, most certainly, sir. If you don't mind me asking, who is she?"

"My wife, Melissa. I love her very much."

Melissa. That's where he knew her. Melissa from Pilates. He guessed this kind of damned all his chances of asking her out. Melissa. Geez. Just his luck, he supposed.

"Now," the general said, "I heard an unfortunate... incident occurred at our Richmond Nest a few days ago?"

"Yes. An unfortunate incident did occur, sir," Jenkins gulped.

The man shook his head with a rueful smile and Jenkins leapt forwards with his words.

"General Gregorian—"

"Please," he held up a hand, "call me Robert."

"Robert. I can explain what happened."

The man chuckled cruelly. "I've already been briefed on the events of the night but if you have something to add, go ahead."

Jenkins shifted uncomfortably. "Well, actually, no, I don't. But, I can help you. I know these kids. I've taught them before as a substitute teacher." Gregorian rolled his eyes and Jenkins had never felt more inadequate in his life, yet he kept talking. "And I was there when they broke in. I can help you find them. I can…"

Jenkins trailed off as he caught sight of Robert's expression. His bushy eyebrows were lifted and he was clearly waiting for Jenkins to finish his crazed ramble. With a condescending collecting of breath, Robert steepled his fingers and levelled his gaze at Jenkins.

"What makes you think you would be more successful at tracking a bunch of worthless teenagers better than my squad of military-trained professionals?"

Jenkins opened his mouth but no words came out. He willed himself to shut it but nothing happened. This was entirely humiliating.

"All right, son. I'll make this a bit easier. Give me one reason I shouldn't fire your sorry arse right now."

Just one reason, Stephen, it's not that hard. You know you need this money, your cat is dying, it needs medicine, just think of something!

Jenkins racked his brain for something when it hit him. He had spent a year at these kids' school as a permanent teacher. It had been hell. He'd done a parent-teacher interview with that Gillian kid's family. They wouldn't stop boasting about their other sons and how they were going away for a family retreat that long weekend. Stupid rich parents. But where? Where had those arrogant bastards been going?

"I know where they are!" Jenkins burst.

Just maybe Jenkins may get to keep his job today after all.

Chapter 12

Kish

The early afternoon light shone through the windscreen into Kish's eyes. One of the others *could* have offered to drive at some point but Kish didn't mind so much, he felt useful. It seemed he had been unofficially anointed the group's personal chauffeur.

"Hey, guys," Mari called from the back of the van.

Various hums echoed from the rest of the group.

"Wouldn't they be able to track us super easily because they know the licence number or whatever of the van?"

Silence ensued. She had a point. Kish eyed the exit into a small town out of the corner of his eye. It looked fairly quiet. Well, it was this idea or nothing. He swerved into the town and cruised down a few streets before he spotted a viable option. Kish pulled alongside the kerb, ignoring the stares and pointed questions of those around him.

"Trust me guys, we have to do this."

"Does he need to pee again?" he heard one of them murmur as he left the van.

Kish circled around to the boot of the car and pulled out his toolbox. Mari eyed him suspiciously but he merely pulled out one of his screwdrivers. That one should be right. If only Jill could see him now. *You're so weird*, she'd said, *what eighteen-year-old needs screwdrivers in their van?* Kish smirked, this eighteen-year-old did.

He slammed the boot fairly conspicuously and crossed the street. He crouched down as he approached the car across the road from them. Silently, Kish raised his screwdriver to the licence plate and began unscrewing it. Before long, he had removed it from the vehicle. As he moved to the front of the car, he glanced back over at the others. Four pairs of widened eyes stared back at him. Nora was shaking her head slowly, the others just stared in shock. He ignored them. Kish once again crouched down and began unscrewing the licence plate at the front of the car. He glanced across at the van, swearing he could hear muffled shouting. Oh well, probably just paranoid imagination. He flashed them a thumbs up and set back to work. Gosh, the shouting was getting louder now. Kish looked back at the van. His friends were banging on the windows and pointing behind him with terrified looks of alarm plastered across their faces. Confused, Kish turned slowly around. A navy-clad police officer was fuming towards him, mouth open in a shout, fists clenched. Kish just tried not to laugh at the police officer's comical position.

"Kish, get back here, you idiot!" Reuben yelled out the window of the van.

Right! Kish yanked the licence plate the rest of the way off the car and sprinted towards the van. The shouting of the cop behind him was starting to grate on his nerves. He needed to be able to think to drive and the police officer's irritating voice wasn't letting him do that. Kish slammed the van door behind him and chucked the licence plates into the back seat, eliciting a yelp from Nora. Kish slammed on the accelerator, going back out onto the road from before. He laughed as the ever-shrinking figure of the policeman disappeared in his rear-view mirror.

"What was *that*, Kish?" Nora demanded.

"Think about it," Kish said, easing on the pedal a little, "if the government wants to track us, all they have to do is look up my number plate in the records, which Mr Jenkins saw, remember? So, we get a different one."

"*Steal*, you mean."

"Same thing."

"It's done now," Reuben sighed.

Nora leant back into her seat. "If you're going to do something illegal, you should do it properly at least. And not laugh when you're being chased by a cop."

"What," Kish scoffed, "do you happen to make a habit out of *stealing* licence plates?"

"No," Nora replied slowly, "but you should have taken ours off first so that you could put them on that other car and—"

"Yeah, because I definitely had time to do that."

Nora huffed and shook her head, giving up albeit her stubborn frown persisting. Kish kept his eyes focused on the road; he'd done what he had to do. She'd thank him later. Soon enough, most of Kish's passengers had nodded off, save Gillian who had to occasionally lean forwards and whisper the next turn or direction to get to the holiday home. He still couldn't quite believe Gillian's family had a holiday house.

"Just the next left, then it's an easy road up the path," Gillian said quietly, not wanting to wake the others.

His voice was husky when quiet and maybe it was just that combined with the near silence of the car but Kish suddenly couldn't think straight. He gritted his teeth and forced the thoughts of Gillian out of his head. No point entertaining that crowd.

Kish followed Gil's directions and took the next left. The path he followed was bumpy, a dirt trail, really, combed on either side by towering gumtrees. The early evening light filtered through their leaves, casting splatters of shadow across the dirt road in sparkling patterns. It was like something out of a holiday calendar, much like the one his aunt had bought Kish's family the year before his mum had met Derek. He shouldn't be thinking about any of that, though. Geez, today was not a good day in Kish's mind. He just couldn't seem to keep his thoughts in order.

Happy thoughts, Kish, he willed himself.

"All right, you should be seeing it soon." Gillian's voice echoed from the back.

He pushed the van the last little way up into the cabin's driveway. It was a quaint little log cabin, a chimney sticking up out of the roof. Kish looked at it in awe as he put the car into park. It was honestly beautiful. The perfect getaway. He just wished the circumstances for his being there could have been different. No time for could have, should haves, though. Kish hopped out of the van and slapped the roof to wake the others up.

"Come on, sleeping beauties, we're here!" he called to them.

Groggily, Mari lumbered out of the boot. "Did you just call us beautiful?"

"No, I called you sleeping beauty. You know that hobo that lived in the woods?"

"Weird take on a classic fairy tale, but okay," Gil muttered as he too joined them on the driveway.

Kish ignored Gillian and moved to the boot to rescue his egg, still clad in the armour of the Woolworth's plastic bag. He peeked inside to make sure it was still okay, not cracked or anything. Kish breathed a sigh when he saw none. It'll be all right. He jogged to catch up with the others, locking the van on his way. Couldn't be too careful, even out in the middle of nowhere. As soon as they'd all entered the cabin, the others dispersed immediately. Presumably in search of a warm bed or at least somewhere to sit. Kish couldn't blame them.

Yet he couldn't tear himself away from joining Gillian in the cosy sitting room. If you could call three stout armchairs and a two-seat sofa huddled haphazardly around a small fireplace a sitting room. Barely three steps over was the kitchen. Ornately tiled, with pine cabinets. The whole cabin seemed as if it should be lived in and yet it felt so... abandoned. Neglected. The whoosh of dust drew Kish's attention back around to see Gillian crouched at the fireplace, fingertips coated in old dust.

Gil chuckled nervously. "Haven't been here in a while, I guess."

He trailed off, eyes averted. Kish nodded awkwardly and sat himself down in one of the armchairs.

"Uh, that's—" Gillian cleared his throat, "that's my seat."

Kish jumped up and moved over to another armchair quickly.

"Oops, sorry," he chuckled.

Gillian nodded and murmured something about it being no big deal. Kish rested the bag on his lap, not willing to let the egg out of his sight after he'd forgotten it the last time. Gillian slid himself over to the side, hauling a log of firewood into the fireplace, bundling it up with kindling immediately after.

"How'd you learn to build a fire?" Kish asked.

Gillian paused. "I watched my dad do it a billion times. Then my brothers after that."

"Huh. How many brothers do you have?"

"Two. Garrett and Griffin, they're both in the military now. You have sisters, right?"

Gillian's tone was warm, friendly even. Such a stark contrast to the coldness he'd shown Kish thus far. Kish didn't know the reason for the sudden niceties but he certainly wasn't about to object.

"Yeah. Jill's three years younger than me and the twins just started kindy earlier this year," Kish replied.

Gillian stood to grab the matches off the top of the fireplace. He levelled his blazingly green eyes at Kish. Kish was stuck in his gaze and for the life of him, could not break it.

"What are their names?" Gil asked.

Kish watched as Gillian once again turned away from him, striking the match and placing it carefully beneath the small tepee of kindling and wood he'd built within the fireplace.

"Sasha and Lydia."

The flames tickled at the edges of the kindling, climbing higher and higher until *whumph*. The kindling was utterly engulfed in the flame, its burning blaze gnawing away at the sides of the log. The kindling was gone in less than a minute. The flames kept eating away at the log anyway. For some reason, it irked Kish. Even though the log withstood the fire for longer, it held out against the onslaught of flame far better than the kindling did, it didn't matter. It didn't matter whether it was burnt within a second or two years, it all became ash in the end. One and the same. Gillian closed the fireplace door and Kish shook himself out of his daze. Weird. Gillian fell into the armchair beside Kish with a sigh of contentment.

"I can't tell you how good it is to be back here," Gillian breathed.

"Did you come here much as a kid?"

"Yeah, now and then. Less when Garrett graduated and even less so when Griffin left."

"Two years now, hey?" Kish ventured.

Gil nodded, eyes downcast in thought.

"What are you thinking?" Kish asked.

Gillian shook his head, chuckling.

"Come on," Kish pushed with a grin. "Look, I'll tell you what I'm thinking in return."

Gillian's lips pressed together and he made a sort of huffing sound. "No, no. You're just as bad as Em, always trying to pick apart my psyche" he laughed, "no. You can't make me talk like that, man."

Kish shrugged. "Have it your way. Become a grumpy old man."

Moments passed as they sat in silence, gazing at the crackling fire. Kish could have sworn there was a metaphor in there somewhere but he couldn't honestly be bothered to go and find it. Metaphors weren't his thing anyway.

"Do you ever wonder what your life would be like if you'd done one thing differently?" Gillian said softly, not looking over.

Kish huffed a laugh. "Was that your thought?"

Gillian began to protest but Kish rumbled a low chuckle and held up a hand. "Relax, I get it. And yes, I do wonder that sometimes."

Gillian seemed to accept that answer and leant back into his chair. The room had started to warm comfortably.

"Why didn't you ever stop them?"

Gillian's voice had gone quiet again, as it had in the car.

"Who?"

"Your friends. They weren't exactly very nice to me back in school and I know you never explicitly did anything to me, so kudos I guess, but surely you knew what your mates were like? You don't seem anything like them, so why did you hang out with them?"

"I—"

Kish was at a loss for words. He'd had no idea. He'd only passed Gillian in the halls a couple of times, barely even, before they'd properly met for Reuben's mission.

"I'm sorry. I didn't know. I mean, I knew they could be jerks sometimes but… but I didn't know they like, targeted you or anything."

Kish mentally punched himself. *Stupid, so stupid.* Of course, his friends had picked on Gillian, that's what they did and Kish had kept being friends with them. Like a total idiot. That completely explained why Gil had been so cold to him.

"Yeah, well…" Gillian trailed off once again and they both merely sat back, soaking in the warmth of the fire.

Maybe Kish could right this. *Hopefully* he could right this.

Chapter 13

Marilyn-Jo

Mari gazed at the ceiling. This was the worst idea ever. She groaned and scooted up to a sitting position on the bed she'd claimed upon first arriving. Who was she to think she'd be able to nap? She'd *never* been able to nap, why would she have been able to start now? It had taken her all of seven minutes and twenty-three seconds of keeping her eyes closed to know that there was no way she was doing this for an extended amount of time. There was zero chance that she would have been able to fall asleep with the sun still out and blazing and it was absolutely far too boring to just lie *there*. She could be doing something way more fun or productive with her day. Never mind the fact that she couldn't go anywhere besides this cabin.

Mari looked at her egg, trying to perceive what the foetus inside might be feeling or thinking. It totally wasn't fair that Reuben and Nora's eggs *talked* to them when Mari's egg had never said a word, nor communicated in any way, shape or form. The closest she'd come was when she'd first seen and she'd known that was the egg she wanted. If you could even call that communication.

"I'm hungry," she said to no one.

With a decisive hop off the bed, Mari strode out of the room, picking the egg up as she went. Might as well have some company, even if the company didn't talk to her. Marilyn-Jo strolled down the hallway, eventually coming to knock upon the door of the room she'd seen Reuben disappear into.

"Come in," her brother called.

Mari pushed the door open softly to see her brother lying on the bed, eyes wide open. Had she interrupted a nap? Oh well, he could deal.

"Do we have any food?" she asked.

Reuben merely shrugged.

Great leadership skills, clearly, Mari thought with a scowl. He took them all on this crazy mission and couldn't even be bothered to organise any food. Mari groaned loudly with exaggeration and dragged herself out of the doorway. She supposed she could check the kitchen. That would obviously be the logical place to go. With a new purpose, Mari took herself through the short hallway and out into the small sitting room, passing by Gil and Kish as she did.

"Hey, Gil," she called, "do you mind if I have a look for some food around here?"

"Knock yourself out," he called back.

Great. Mari grinned in thanks and headed over to the kitchen. It was a small thing but as long as it contained some kind of pleasant-tasting nutrients, she didn't really care what it looked like. As she rummaged around in the cupboards, she could hear Gil and Kish chatting behind her. She was glad they were finally getting along. Mari spotted a pack of spaghetti in the back and pulled it from behind the pots and pans with forced dexterity. She pulled out a saucepan as well and set it on the stove. She cracked the spaghetti only to hear shouts come from the sitting room.

"Em!"

"What, what?"

Gillian rushed over to the kitchen and snatched the split

spaghetti from Mari's hands.

"That is not how you cook spaghetti. Honestly, Em, what would Gordon say?"

Mari shrugged, looking down sheepishly. Gillian went to the cupboard and pulled another pack of spaghetti miraculously out of the cupboard.

Kish stood from his armchair. "I'm just going to put that snapped spaghetti in a Ziploc bag, we might need it later."

Gillian filled the pot with water and set it onto the stove top before coming round behind Mari and placing the spaghetti in her hands, fingers an inch from hers as if to make sure she didn't snap it again. Once the water had boiled, he guided her hand to place the spaghetti gently in the water. Quickly, he let go of her hand and stepped back.

"Do not snap the spaghetti," Gillian said determinedly.

He took another step away, hands pushing back his unbuttoned flannel to rest in his pockets. Mari looked up at him, black locks falling around his face like the leaves around a tree.

Gil threw her a lopsided grin. "What?"

Mari peered at him quizzically.

"Nothing," she assured.

"Okay," Gil shrugged and walked casually back over to where he'd been sitting.

Marilyn shook her head.

Weird, she mouthed to her egg. Letting go of the moment, Mari went in search of something to season the pasta. She couldn't serve her friends plain spaghetti. It really was a shame they didn't have cheese, cheese made everything better.

*

Marilyn-Jo sashayed over to the dining table, her tiny hands engulfed in oven mitts as she cradled the huge dish containing the mass of spaghetti. She could sense the salivating eagerness of the others as she set the dish down.

"Spaghetti á la salt. Bon appétit!" Mari grinned.

The others took no hesitation in digging in, heaping piles of salted spaghetti onto their plates. Mari, too, took a seat at the rustic dining table and loaded her plate. She was *starving*. Despite her companions' grimaces, they ate and ate.

"Look," Mari sighed as she saw Reuben flinch from the pasta for about the tenth time, "I did what I could, okay? Be grateful there was even spaghetti in the cupboard."

Her friends merely nodded through more grimacing and chewing. Despite the dish's tastelessness, the group seemed to go through the mound of spaghetti with speed.

"So," Mari said as soon as she gulped down her last bite, "what now?"

"I feel like we ask that every five seconds," muttered Reuben.

"You're the one that's been pushing us to make plans, remember?" Mari shot back.

"I stand by that but it just gets a bit repetitive."

Mari scoffed.

"Okay…" Kish said slowly, "if we can just put down the sibling rivalry and actually figure out what we're going to do, I think that would be good, yes?"

They all mumbled a yes in response to Kish.

He cleared his throat. "Okay, good."

The table fell silent.

"I think," Nora's voice was small, tentative, "it might be a good idea to put the eggs in a room together, like how they were at the airport?"

Mari shifted uncomfortably in her seat; she didn't like the idea of parting with her egg. Even though it hadn't done anything like speak to her like Nora and Reuben's had, she still felt... *connected*. Must be like a maternal instinct or something. Not that she'd ever felt that motherly but oh well.

"Can't do," Reuben said confidently. Probably the most even his voice had ever been when talking to Nora, "my egg *screams* every time I leave it alone."

Reuben gestured his fork over his shoulder where the pale white egg rested on one of the armchairs near the fire. "See? Even now I have to be in the same room."

Nora's dark brows furrowed a little and her eyes glossed over as if she had retreated back into her thoughts, trying to figure something out.

"Did anyone else hear the scream?" she queried.

"Nope," Mari answered for her brother, "he looked like a total weirdo."

Reuben levelled a glare at her. "I was in a lot of pain, Mari."

Mari shrugged. "Okay. You still looked weird."

Reuben let out a withering sigh that was much too reminiscent of their mother for Mari's own liking.

Nora, across the table, hummed thoughtfully, fingers absentmindedly drumming the table.

"Interesting," she murmured.

They all watched her carefully. It took a few more moments before Nora drew her gaze back up and was startled when she noticed they were all staring at her. Mari watched as Nora regained her perfect posture, drawing her shoulders back and lifting her head up straight.

She cleared her throat and levelled her gaze at the group.

"My hypothe—I mean, I believe that Reuben's egg and my egg, due to similar occurrences happening to both of us and the eggs' resemblance to each other, well, I believe these eggs specifically may have some sort of telepathic abilities."

Mari rested her elbows on the table as she mulled the thought over, all her mother's lessons on etiquette flying out the window.

"It'd make sense, I guess," Mari said casually.

After all, her egg hadn't deigned to make any sort of communication with her. The little bugger. Reuben nodded as well, his eyes racing with his tell-tale signs of a new fixation. Honestly, sometimes Mari's brother scared her. Gillian and Kish merely leant back in their chairs, almost identical in posture. Save for the fact that Gillian had his arms crossed and his default 'the world sucks and everything in it' look, whereas a slight smirk was at ease on Kish's face.

"I," Nora began tentatively as Marilyn-Jo forced herself to rake her eyes away from analysing the similarities of the boys sitting next to each other. "I took a quick look at the files we took from Richmond. It seems to imply that they created approximately three breeds of dragon and potentially are in the process of making even more."

Reuben was practically out of his seat he was leaning that far forwards. When Nora glanced across at him, however, Mari noticed he abruptly collected himself and sat somewhat leisurely back into his chair, an embarrassed blush creeping over his neck.

He cleared his throat. "Um, well, if you will excuse us, everyone. I think Nora and I need to investigate this further."

Nora and Reuben pushed away from the table and, eyes fixated on the floor, began to head out of the dining room. Kish stood to follow but Gillian's hand shot out and pushed him back into his chair. Kish glanced at Gil and then at Mari, confusion seeping across his features.

Mari patted his hand reassuringly. "Don't worry, it's not that they're *excluding* you, per se. It's just..."

Mari couldn't quite put the phenomenon into words. Thankfully, Gil could.

"Those two have been denying their feelings for each other since year eight, so trust me when I say you would not be welcome in their little science party. Here are some rules about it, okay?"

Gillian didn't seem to bother waiting for affirmation. He merely began listing, counting off on his fingers as he did.

"Don't comment on their situation in front of either or both of them, don't try and understand their language. You'd probably have to memorise the periodic table or something," he paused, "and read into social cues that don't apply to anyone else, for that matter. And do not, under any circumstance, ever, you hear me? *Ever* get involved."

Gillian took a deep breath, his eyes locked with Kish's. Mari fidgeted awkwardly wondering if it maybe would have been better to have followed the nerds. Kish gulped audibly and nodded. Mari somewhat wished that the rest of them could have been included in the research, but she and Gil had come up with those rules for a reason. Gillian shook his head tiredly and with a quick goodnight to Mari, he abruptly reported it was time he head to bed. At seven thirty. Mari peered after him, her eyes flicking between the points of the room as she ran through Gillian's actions. Strange, really. Maybe it was time she headed to bed as well.

Chapter 14

Reuben

The doorway of the small sitting room was surprisingly high for the small woodsy cottage. Reuben wasn't particularly fond of how it seemed to loom over him, watching, waiting for him to do something incredibly stupid.

"So," he began hesitantly, "what were you saying about the types of eggs?"

He moved over to the large, oak desk in the corner of the room where Nora had situated herself. Reuben only just then allowed himself to notice the three manila folders spread over the surface of the desk. Nora's slender fingers skimmed them carefully, almost reverently. "I started reading these after the egg spoke to me," she said, eyes trained on the folders.

"It doesn't exactly say anything explicitly but I'm hoping maybe the information in the folders will help us figure out how to care for the dragons later on when they hatch."

What she said made sense. Reuben estimated they didn't have much time before the dragons did hatch and they would be far better off if they started learning everything they could before then. He opened the first of the folders and extracted a sheet of paper from within. A dozen diagrams of DNA were scattered across the page, uneven lines connecting the drawings with scrawled notes in the margins.

"I studied this for hours, Reuben, but I can't figure out where they got their DNA samples from. I tried Google image searching it but… nothing."

"A dragon isn't exactly like every other animal," Reuben replied.

Nora huffed in frustration. "No. But they can't make something out of nothing. That's scientifically impossible. Unless they're God."

"I highly doubt that," Reuben said, frowning.

Nora's brow was furrowed, her lips pressed together tightly. She raised a finger to push her glasses back up the bridge of her nose and brushed her dark hair over one shoulder.

"I don't get it." Nora whispered the words as if she were at a confessional. Reuben knew the feeling. That nagging at the back of your head, the shame that maybe you weren't *smart enough* to figure it out, that maybe you wouldn't ever figure it out. And maybe a lesser person would have given up at that point but that wasn't Nora. Nor was it Reuben.

"Hey," he said softly, flicking his hazel eyes up, "you'll get it eventually. In the meantime, I'll help you. I'm sure we'll get an answer soon enough."

Reuben knew his words didn't carry much weight but Nora indulged him with a small smile anyway.

"Is it the same with the others?" he asked.

Nora opened the files and lifted them up. "There's some that are recognisable. I matched them with DNA examples I found online and in my bio textbooks. Different species of birds, alligators even but… there's still the unknown DNA. I just wish—"

Nora cut off mid-sentence, a gasp bursting forth. She pushed her glasses up again and stood abruptly away from the table. She began bouncing on the balls of her feet and Reuben suppressed the smile that threatened to come out.

"I got it!"

Reuben raised his eyebrows, finally giving in and letting the corner of his mouth rise. He couldn't help it, her excitement was unreasonably contagious.

"You figured out where the DNA is from?"

She waved her hand at him dismissively. "No, not that. But I have an uncle who works at the Reptile Park. He got some obscure degree in animals or reptiles or I don't know, my mum doesn't really like him."

Nora continued. "Anyway, I'm sure he could help us! He'd probably recognise the strands and maybe he'd have a good idea of how we can care for them!"

Reuben could admit it was a fairly decent idea. An expert would be greatly appreciated right now, especially one that wasn't working for the people trying to hunt them down. He was worried about one thing, though. The Reptile Park was an insane tourist attraction. It was bound to be filled with kids and families and large crowds. Not to mention guards and probably a bunch of people that could report them at a moment's notice. He voiced this concern to Nora and she bit her lip thoughtfully but he could tell the excitement of an idea that could work was still coursing through her. She walked carefully over to where he was still sitting and placed her hands on his shoulders lightly. The moon shone through the window, highlighting the glint on her glasses and the soft reassurance in her gaze.

"Hey, we'll figure something out, okay?"

He nodded, not trusting himself to not say something stupid. She smiled brightly and with a borderline awkward step back, left the room.

Reuben let out his breath and slumped in his chair.

*

The grass had been slightly damp when Reuben had lowered himself down onto it. He didn't venture far from the cabin, there were too many horror stories of teenagers wandering off alone in the woods at night. Though the idea of camping had never appealed to him, he could admit that it was oddly peaceful away from the bustle of society. It was as if a weight had been lifted, a weight he had barely acknowledged before, a weight he only realised the heaviness of once it was gone. He'd never minded the pressure, really. It was the one thing that kept up with his mind. He had thought it had pushed him, helped him to do better, produce higher marks. That's what his mum had said, what his teachers had said, what he'd said. It was as if he had been seeing his purpose, his life through a one-sided mirror and suddenly he had just crashed through it to the other side and could finally see clearly. It wasn't as if the pressure wasn't still there, it just wasn't so apparent.

Reuben?

Reuben chuckled mirthlessly. "Oh so, you're into speech now? Done with the incessant screaming?"

The egg remained silent and Reuben looked away from it. Somehow, even in all the panic Reuben had forced himself through, he didn't think he had actually yet processed the reality of what he had done. To himself. To his friends. To the world, honestly. He wasn't even quite sure whether he was ready to process such a thing, nor whether he was capable. Maybe it would have been better if he had just sat and waited for the authorities to take him. He could have taken all the blame, said that he had stolen Kish's van and returned the eggs.

Reuben glanced at the milky white egg next to him and felt a flow of disapproval from it. Perhaps not. Regardless, he had not been thinking earlier in the day and now they were all reaping the consequences. That was the problem, though, wasn't it? *Thinking.* Reuben was sure he was either thinking too much or not at all and he was tired. He felt as if at any moment he might just fall to the floor from the weight of his thoughts. Out here, though, in the cooling night air, just on the edge of civilisation… it was quieter. His thoughts now had space, had time, if only for a few moments. If only. He breathed in and the sigh flowed out of him as a river did from a cave mouth as Reuben slid himself to a lying position on the grass. If only this moment could stretch out and he wouldn't have to think of a solution to the absolute crap bag of a situation he was in. Alas, Reuben eventually made his way back inside, egg in his arms, to return to his shuddering reality.

Chapter 15

Gillian

Who was here last? Oh, that's right. Me.

Gillian shook his head as he murmured to himself, head plunged within the cabin's kitchen cupboards. He had tasked himself with acquiring sufficient provisions for their next leg of the journey. Reuben had woken them all bright and early that morning to announce the news about Nora's uncle. Then he had just walked off. For all his methodical planning bravado, Reuben really didn't seem to think things through. Thus, Gillian, seemingly the only right-minded one, was stuck with making sure they all didn't starve, which as it turned out, was an increasingly difficult task. Em really wasn't kidding when she said there was only spaghetti in the cupboard. Gillian had last been here a year ago and that was only to dust everything off and make sure everything was locked up and safe. His parents hadn't been since at least the year before. He hadn't stayed long enough on his last trip to need any meals so hadn't bothered to check if the cupboards were stocked up. How old was the spaghetti they'd eaten, anyway? Could uncooked spaghetti go off?

Well, it is what it is, Gil supposed.

If Mari had unwittingly subjected them all to food poisoning, it would honestly be the least of their problems.

"You find anything in there?" Em called from her perch on the kitchen bench.

Gillian pulled himself from the cupboard, coughing up the dust and rolling his shoulders. "Nope."

She groaned. "I'm so hungry, man."

Gillian rolled his eyes. "Me too. Hey, actually, I think I might know somewhere we can get some cash to buy something once we leave."

Em raised her eyebrows and hopped off the bench to follow Gil as he strode out of the cramped kitchen space, the cupboard door swung softly behind him. He paced confidently down the hallway and through the elaborately carved doorway of his parent's bedroom. They had always loved extravagance, to the point that it sometimes sickened Gillian. He jumped up onto their pristine, yet dust-coated, white duvet and swung out the fake Van Gogh painting above the bed. When the shining, silver safe was revealed, Gillian could practically hear Em's eyes widen.

"Are we in a movie?"

Gil laughed at Mari's awestruck face before turning back around and punching in the code. His parents hadn't changed it since he was little and it hadn't taken him long to figure the passcode out. Griffin had told him. Twelve. Zero. Eight. Garrett's birthday. Some parents tried to hide the fact that they had a favourite child, but not so much in the Andrews household. He was surprised his parents hadn't called or texted him. Sure, he spent most of his time locked away in his room or at Em's house but seriously, they weren't even a little worried that he hadn't been home? He shook the thought out of his mind and pulled open the door of the safe. The bed creaked slowly as Mari stepped up onto the duvet next to him.

"What in the mafia boss is this?" she breathed.

Inside the safe lay several stacks of hundred-dollar bills, held together by strips of paper. It was certainly a sight to behold.

"This should get us at least a couple of hotdogs, right?" Gil chuckled.

Em burst into laughter and doubled over, her hands on her knees. Her ebony hair fell around her face as she jumped up, whooping. She came over and leant up on her tiptoes, only just reaching Gillian's shoulders with her hands.

"This could get us *anything*, Gil, anything!"

Her laughs and whoops of joy echoed throughout the cabin as Gil slowly retrieved the stacks of money from the safe. Even as he did it a small, a very small, part of him felt sorry. Yet, then he remembered his parents had neglected this building and had good as forsaken it for years. As with the money it held and, he supposed, Gillian himself.

*

The music blasted Gillian's eardrums, cementing his belief that the front passenger seat was indeed cursed.

"It's not cursed!" Kish yelled at him over the music, fingers tapping relentlessly on the steering wheel, out of time, notably.

Gillian had tried to explain to him that time he was in year two and it was his first time in the front passenger seat. His mother had pulled over to help a man on the side of the road. His face had been haggard, gaunt scraps of bead trying to cling to his face, bags stretching down from beneath his eyes. Gillian's mother, who was at the time convinced of her own goodwill, had rolled down Gillian's window so that she could ask the man if he needed help. Gillian's protests had gone unheard, of course. He was a child. Neither seen nor heard. Of course, it was Gillian, trapped in the front seat as a helpless eight-year-old who had to suffer through a strange man vomiting on him through the window of a brand-new Subaru. Then, *then*, that same man who had just heaved his lunch onto Gillian, was *invited* to take Gillian's seat! His jaw clenched just at the memory.

Gillian's face stretched into a snarl as he forced himself to not think about smacking Kish just to stop him from tapping. The tapping and the music. Gosh, he was annoying. Kish must have seen his face because the music went down a notch. A notch. Which did absolutely freaking nothing. Gillian reached over and, maybe a tad bit too aggressively, turned down the music.

"GILLIAN!"

"Woah, Em, calm down, I'm literally like a metre away."

"I've been yelling at you for the last hour, Gil!"

"Blame it on Kish's stupid music."

Kish gasped. "How dare you call Olivia Rodrigo stupid."

Gil rolled his eyes and turned to face his best friend in the back.

"You know what, I can't even remember what I was trying to tell you," Em huffed.

Gil shrugged and went back to staring, bored, out the front window. Once again, Kish's tapping resumed. Gillian clenched his fists and took a deep breath.

"Wanna play a game?" Kish said.

"No."

Kish glanced over at him, eyebrows raised. "Geez, someone's in a crappy mood today."

Gil raised an eyebrow right back at him.

"I spy—"

Gillian glared at Kish and he stopped abruptly. Mari, however, decided it was the perfect time to pipe up.

"Don't worry Kish, it's nothing personal, Gil is just a grumpy old fart sometimes."

"I am not a grumpy old fart," Gil grumbled in a very similar manner to that of the old man from *Up*.

He wasn't *grumpy*, exactly. He was just... tired. And he didn't have what one would call a bubbly personality. He seemed to attract those upbeat types of people anyway, they had enough positivity that he really didn't need to bother. His mother used to say it was refreshing since he didn't spend time with anyone other than Em growing up. He'd tried making friends with the boy who lived next to him on the other side but the third time he had gone over to Patrick's house he had ended up with his head doused in toilet water. It was not a pleasant experience. Not to mention that had been a mere two weeks after the vomiting hitchhiker incident. Second grade hadn't exactly been the best year. After that, Gil had learnt to stay in his lane. He quickly figured out who he was, well more specifically, who he was comfortable being. The last, and sometimes forgotten, brother, Marilyn-Jo's friend, your average student. And he was okay with that. Most of the time.

"Hey," Gil leant over and tapped Kish's shoulder, "stop here, I'm going to go get us some hotdogs."

Kish nodded and pulled into the petrol station by the side of the road with ease.

He smirked at Gil. "Watch this, I'm about to go undercover."

He then proceeded to pull a battered, red baseball cap from the centre console and stuff his unbrushed hair underneath it.

"Voila, disguise," Kish said smoothly.

He chucked Gil a wink and hopped out of the car to fill the van up with petrol. Gil, however, merely shook his head and grabbed thirty bucks from the massive bag of cash they had stolen from his parents. No. Not stolen, *liberated*. From hands that no longer had need of it. In a very Robin Hood-esque way, if he did say so himself. Gillian climbed out of the van and made his way over to the servo's little store inside. It turned out that they didn't have any hotdogs at the petrol station. Which he honestly should have expected but hey, the body craves what it craves. Instead, Gil grabbed four travel meat pies and some sort of spinach pastry for Em. He shuffled towards the counter, not bothering to have grabbed a basket. Gillian dumped the pastries unceremoniously onto the counter and waited for the cashier to count them up. His eyes wandered around the store, settling on the small television just above the counter. A news reporter spoke in a deep voice and Gil could do nothing but watch in abject horror as five different school photos flashed across the screen, accompanied by the sound of a police report. Gil's year twelve portrait stared back at him with a daunting warning. This was very, very bad. Two deep voices drifted from across the small store to Gillian and despite knowing better, he strained to listen, eager for a distraction away from his doomed future.

"... see them?"

"Yeah! They came so fast I couldn't even be sure what they were."

"Military vehicles, right?"

"Probably, I think they were headed for the holiday houses up in the hills."

"Yeah, I think so. There's probably another fugitive or something..."

Frick. Frick, frick, frick, frick, frick. Damn it. They had to move and quick, at that. This day could not get any worse.

"Sir? *Sir!*"

Gil snapped his consciousness back to his situation.

"Sorry," he said to the cashier, a flush creeping up his neck, "what was that?"

"I said, it's fifteen dollars fifty," the cashier said, a sigh definitely forming.

Gillian gave a twenty to the lady quickly.

"Hey, um, do I know you?" the cashier asked slowly.

Gillian lowered his head and shook his curls over his face, painfully aware of the news report still blaring above the conversation.

"Probably not, never been here before," Gillian huffed out as the cashier handed him his change.

She made a sort of humming noise and Gil hurried out of the little store, almost bumping into Kish on his way out.

"Kish! Kish, stop!" Gillian grabbed Kish by the shoulders forcefully. "You can't go in there."

Kish seemed to freeze beneath Gil's grip before he eventually forced his eyes up to Gil's and cleared his throat. "Sorry, uh, why?"

"The cashier almost recognised me and some locals were talking about military vehicles passing here and heading towards the holiday houses."

Kish blanched. "Military vehicles?"

Gillian grunted and shoved Kish back towards the van. They rushed into the vehicle and Gil chucked the pies at the others as Kish frantically tried to start the engine.

"Is everything all right?" Nora asked.

Kish finally got the engine going and they roared out of the petrol station, not bothering to check if anyone was following.

"Care to explain what just happened?" Reuben asked, his voice's calm composure doing nothing to convince Gil that that was how he was really feeling.

He gave a brief explanation to the others. He was met with silence. Although, in Em's case, he was pretty sure it was just because she had already started eating her pastry. They all thanked Gil for the pies and the vehicle settled somewhat, everyone disturbingly quiet about the matter at hand.

"Hey, Gillian," Kish began, "you wouldn't have perhaps checked the ingredients on the pie, would you?"

"No, I just grabbed them," Gillian replied.

Kish merely nodded and readjusted his grip on the steering wheel. Was he going to offer an explanation or was he going to force Gillian to have to keep the conversation going? Gosh, he hated this.

Finally. "Why do you ask?"

"Dude, I have anaphylaxis."

"You have what?"

"If I eat dairy or shellfish, I die. Have you seriously never heard of it before? And I have a gluten intolerance."

"Geez, you could have told me that earlier, how bad are your genes, anyway?"

Kish raised an eyebrow and smirked at Gillian. "Well, they can't be too bad if I look like this."

Gil turned to fully face Kish and took his time, taking in the sight sitting before him.

Finally, he just turned back towards the window with his pie and said, "Eh."

He didn't hear a gasp of outrage or an overly dramatic reaction as Em probably would have, not that he'd say anything like that to her. All Gil could discern was a slightly awkward shift in the other boy's position. Not that he should have been comparing the two, anyway. Why would he do that?

Chapter 16

Nora

The noon sunlight filtered through the old van's windows, reflecting off of Nora's gold-rimmed glasses. It had been a narrow escape from the petrol station, by her standards anyway. The others had already relaxed, the kind of thoughts racing through Nora's head probably far from their own minds. Except for perhaps Reuben. He was trying desperately to hide his panic, unsuccessfully, though. She needed to distract herself. Nora reached under her seat where she had stashed the files she'd stolen from Richmond Airport at the beginning of all this mess. Heavens, that felt like an eternity ago. She stared once again at the clusters of DNA. Whoever had been working on these files had labelled the pages with some obscure words. The first page, the one where she had correlated strands' of lorikeets, kookaburras, parrots and more birds' DNA with images from her Google searches was simply labelled *Tanin*. Not to mention, there was something that looked vaguely reptilian. She supposed it would make sense when the dragons hatched. She grabbed up the other file and flicked through until… *there*. She knew she'd seen those words somewhere else. The *Tanin*, the government's second attempt at creating a dragon life form. A small polaroid picture rested in the corner of the page, held on just barely by a rusted paper clip. In it was depicted an egg, pastel pink overshadowed by tendrils of darker pink, somewhat resembling pink tie-dye. It almost looked like…

"Hey, Mari," Nora called over her shoulder.

"Hmm?" she merely answered from behind.

Nora lifted the file up awkwardly to show Mari in the far backseat. Mari peered at the page as Nora pointed to the photo in the corner.

"Don't you think that looks like your egg?"

Mari lifted up her egg, considerably smaller than the others, pastel pink and most definitely resembling the egg from the photograph.

"Yeah, it actually does. What does that mean?" Mari asked.

"Well," Nora said, not actually quite believing it, "your egg may have been one of, if not *the*, first of that species of dragon they created. Or perhaps the best surviving prototype thus far."

Marilyn-Jo's eyes widened and traced her finger over the DNA diagrams on the page.

"What are these from?"

"Birds, a lot of birds, and some reptile, I think."

Mari's face contorted. "Dude, what kind of person makes a dragon out of birds and reptiles?"

Kish's scoff echoed down through the van from where he was driving. "Is a dragon not just a croc with wings?"

"I always pictured them more lizard-y?" Reuben mused.

Kish gasped and Nora, along with everyone else, tensed, ready for a threat.

Kish began to apologise immediately. "Oh my gosh, no, guys, not like that. I was just going to say, do you think they can breathe fire?"

Nora paused for a moment. It was plausible. Of course, there had always been the constant stereotype of dragons breathing fire, much of that legend derived from ancient lore and mythology. It would stand to reason that those that created these creatures would want to honour that traditional image of the animal. The logistics of that actually being possible, however, were far more complex. Due to the bird's influence, it seemed Mari's dragon would maybe contain bird-like wings. Thoughts racing, Nora flicked through the folder to the other pages. One labelled the *Maharai*. The picture atop the page had an egg covered in a scale-like pattern, metallic and glinting in the light cast in the photo. Then she flicked a couple more pages again to the next dragon type. There it was again. It made so much more sense now. Nora handed the file over to Reuben and pointed out the strands of DNA she had researched based on what could have been an obscure hunch. He looked at her quizzically.

She huffed. "Remember that weird biology-history incursion we had a couple of years ago? Think back to it, Reuben."

He looked back down at the diagram, his brow furrowed. Almost as quickly, they lifted and he turned to Nora in amazement.

"That's pterosaur DNA?" he breathed.

Nora nodded emphatically and they grinned at each other like children with a bar of chocolate.

"Where," Reuben began, "where did they find this?"

"I have no idea. I did see an article a little while ago that they found fossils off the coast of Queensland somewhere. The government must have poached it somehow."

"Well, technically they already own the land. So is it really poaching?" Gil quipped from the front.

"No one likes a smart ass, Gil," Mari called out.

Kish turned around in his seat but promptly returned to driving when they all began to yell obscenely at him to keep his eyes on the road.

He took a breath. "So, are our dragons part... dinosaur?"

"In a simplistic take on the matter, probably," Nora said calmly, "but what I'm confused about is the seemingly random collection of animals they've pieced together to create these dragons. Like, look at this, this is from a canine!"

"They experimented on a *puppy*?" Mari's face twisted in outrage. She held her egg away from her as if it stank of something terrible. "Is this the price I pay for being such an amazing thief? I don't know if I want it now."

Nora twisted in her seat to face Mari. "You don't care about the crocodile mistreatment but the minute a puppy is involved, you're willing to throw away this whole mission?"

Mari gave Nora a look that was almost condescending. Almost.

"A puppy's never tried to kill me, Nora."

Marilyn-Jo sank back into her seat, turning on her phone and tucking her egg in close. Nora hadn't believed for a second that Mari was serious about getting rid of the egg. Weird talking foetuses aside, she'd wager they had all made some kind of emotional attachment to their eggs. And as much as they were roped in now, she knew there would be absolutely no going back once they hatched.

*

It didn't take the group long to make it to the Reptile Park where Nora's uncle worked. Although, it took about an hour longer than it usually would, due to them having to take all the backroads to avoid detection. Though it was a pain, the nature around them as they drove was exceptionally beautiful. Kish slowed to a halt on the dirt road just beyond the fences of the park, the copious amount of trees between them providing adequate cover.

"Okay." Nora ushered them in closer. "I'll go in and find my uncle. I'll bring him out here if it's safe."

The others nodded and she moved to climb out of the van. Behind her, she heard Reuben make a sort of spluttering sound as if he was trying to say something.

She turned back. "Are you okay?"

"Uh, yeah, no, of course. Uh, just be careful," his mouth lifted in a small smile and she threw one back at him in return before getting out of the car, slipping on her sunnies and heading towards the park.

She folded up her usual glasses and tucked them carefully into her pocket. On the way over she'd tried desperately to tame her hair into a ponytail but without gel it was sticking up all over the place, curls shooting up out of her head without any rhyme or reason. She was fairly sure the average citizens here wouldn't recognise her unless there was a television blaring some picture of her and they scrutinised her with it side by side. The guards who let those people in, though… they had probably been briefed on all the 'dangerous criminals' in the area. Even though she doubted she would be spotted, a bit of extra precaution and distraction was always appreciated. As she continued towards the fence, she spared one last glance back at the van. She had had to leave Copper back with the others. Carrying a large white egg around a zoo wasn't exactly subtle. The unborn dragon had screamed at first, not that anyone else could hear it, but she had eventually coaxed the egg into a state of quiet whining. She could hear it now in her head. She wondered if she tried to talk to it through her thoughts, would it still hear her? Or did she have to talk out loud for it to hear her?

Copper? She thought of the word floating over in a tendril to the egg.

Nora! Its excited, child-like voice piped up out of the whining and Nora could swear she heard an excited squeal.

Once she had originally learnt of the dragon's telepathic abilities, she had immediately set to work to try and find out what words the foetus actually knew. It seemed not many, at first. Its own name and the word mother, which it repeated for a good hour. After that, Nora had been determined to teach it her name and things like goodbye and hello. Copper already had a rudimentary idea of language so it didn't take long for it to learn a few new words. She hadn't gone much further with that little project as of yet. But she would. Hopefully with the help of her uncle.

Nora ripped her eyes back to the task at hand. The others knew what they had to do. She circled around the perimeter of the park till she got to the far right-hand side. Somewhat hidden between the trees, she waited.

Boom. A resounding blast shuddered through the earth beneath her and she smiled softly. Well done, Kish. She had explained her plan to them not long ago. Kish would take the matches and limited fuel they had found left at Gillian's family cabin and douse as many cars as he could with them. The matches, well their job in the plan was obvious.

Nora could hear shouting from the front end of the park and above it all, Marilyn-Jo's shrill cry. Mari had jumped at the opportunity to cause that little bit of drama. She would cause a commotion at the front gate to get most of the guests and guards aware of the flaming cars and hopefully enough people would be alarmed enough to rush out the gates and assess the situation. Nora waited a few beats for the people in the park to run to the cars before she adjusted her sunglasses and sauntered towards the entrance quickly. In the short time the guards at the gateway abandoned their post, Nora slipped through and fast-walked as nonchalantly as she could manage over to the offices of the park's staff on the far side. She slipped past each of the enclosures before subtly knocking on the door of the office she hoped was still her uncle's. The door swung open and a man stepped out from it, hunched over. He had greying hair and pale, wrinkled skin, veins pulsing just visible beneath the surface of his almost sickly exterior. His small rectangular glasses were perched on his nose and he peered over them at Nora.

"Hello?" he rasped. "How can I help you?"

Nora smiled and folded away her sunglasses, quickly replacing them with her usual glasses so that she could see properly.

"Hi, Uncle Charlie. It's me, Nora."

Above those tiny glasses, his blue eyes, so much like Nora's mum's, widened and he immediately ushered his niece into the office.

Chapter 17

Jenkins

The dirt road shifted irritatingly beneath Jenkins' feet. He didn't think he would have had to come on this damned wild goose chase, there was a whole military squad here, for crying out loud. Why did they need *him*? The man he had met with earlier, Robert Gregorian, wasn't even here. He had merely assigned the task to some squad commander lady. Jenkins hadn't bothered to learn her name, or anyone else's names for that matter. Why should he? He didn't want to be there and it would be much easier to leave if no one knew he was there to begin with.

"Pick up the pace, Jenkins!" the sergeant's voice called from in front of him.

He was lagging behind but not so much that he couldn't hear her mutter, "Pathetic."

He scowled and dragged his feet harder through the dirt. Stuff whatever her name was. Maybe he should learn their names, if only to curse them under his breath. Jenkins wished he could have done something worthwhile, something *great* in his life. Yet here he was, edging on forty-one and acting like a sulking child. He'd got in these kinds of moods when he was younger too. His mother used to call him her "*bitter little possum*". Jenkins felt a pang of grief at the thought of his late mother but pushed it away. He was doing this for her, he supposed. Getting hired as a substitute teacher had been getting harder and harder. That was why he had taken the job at the airport, well not really an airport any more. He'd needed the money and the stupid cat his mother had left him was literally the spawn of the devil. It had a permanent diarrhoea condition and an anger issue that Jenkins had personally diagnosed. No one else thought cats could have anger issues. His mother hadn't even left him anything else. It all had gone to his half-sister who was barely out of university. She had tried calling him the other day. Maybe he should have picked up.

It was of no consequence now, he supposed. He was in the middle of freaking nowhere surrounded by a squad of Australia's stupid freaking military. He shook his head and decided to stop pouting if only to escape the cycle of thought he had trapped himself in. He picked up his feet and walked the hill to the cabin waiting, surpassing the sergeant as he did so. He had to admit, it was quite a picturesque cabin. He thought he might have liked to live somewhere like it if he had a different life. If he had figured out his passion instead of taking the first job he was offered. If he had any passion.

"Stand down, Jenkins."

Jenkins stopped abruptly, halting mere centimetres from the front steps. The sergeant marched past him up the steps. Before she went to the door she looked back, a single eyebrow raised. Jenkins scowled deeper. She smirked at him, as if amused by his pathetic expression of distaste. He huffed and followed up the steps after her. He stepped aside and tried not to flinch as she raised her leg and with one quick motion, kicked open the door.

"It could have been unlocked," Jenkins muttered.

She barely acknowledged his suggestion. "It wasn't."

Rolling her eyes, the sergeant waltzed into the cabin. Her dyed blonde hair was pulled into a meticulous bun, dark brown creeping in from the roots. Jenkins knew how he looked to her. Pathetic, weak. She wasn't far from the truth. Still, it stung just a bit. He crossed his arms and moved to the corner of the room; mouth twisted down severely. The rest of the army group filtered in, spreading out.

"Aren't you going to yell for them to come out with their hands on their heads or whatever it is that you do?" Jenkins asked sourly from the corner.

He sounded like a petulant child trying to prod one of the adults into just as bad a mood as he.

She rolled her eyes at him once again. It was a bad habit. At least that's what Jenkins had been told his entire life. It looked good on *her*, though, as much as it irritated him.

"They're clearly no longer here, *Jenkins*."

She enunciated his name strangely as if she were both showing her respect and yet insulting him in the same word. *Jen. Kins*. He kind of wanted to hear her say it again.

He grunted and leant against the wall. He'd seen plenty of the "cool" guys in the movies do it but he probably just looked like he was an old man who had been standing far too long.

"How do you even know they were here at all?" he asked gruffly.

The sergeant stalked towards him and Jenkins fought the urge to avert his eyes.

"We don't," she said softly, stalking ever closer, "but you better hope they were or you're straight back onto the street, old man."

Old man? *Old* man? He was only a couple of years out of his thirties and it's not like she was the youngest of the bunch, either. What, mid- to late-thirties, if Jenkins was any judge. She turned abruptly on her heel and over to the squad member waiting to report to her. The man was crouched at the fireplace, ashes pinched between his already dirty fingers.

"These are just barely days old, ma'am,"

"They were here," she muttered.

"Yes," he replied, "and I'd wager we'd be able to find some tracks leading out of here. Especially if they left in some kind of vehicle."

"Yes, I'd say that was the case, Morisson."

He nodded crisply and brushed his fingers of the ashes, shutting the fireplace door in one curt movement. Jenkins had to admit it was somewhat thrilling to be a part of something this big, however small that part was. He wouldn't admit that out loud though. He had spent too long despising everything and it didn't seem like an appropriate time to stop. He was finally at a point in life where he could blame his terrible mood on a mid-life crisis and his cat *was* technically dying. He had cause for displeasure now. It didn't take long for the rest of the squad present to rifle through the meagre things that had been left at the cabin. Then, the sergeant was clicking at him to come over, along with two other members of the party. She dismissed them with an order and began pulling Jenkins out of the cabin by the arm. He had expected her to have a strong grip, being in the military and all, but he was ashamed by the alarm bells of pain that rang through his forearm.

She pulled him out onto the driveway and let go of him suddenly, sending him careening into the side of the military state utility vehicle.

"Get in."

"Are we leaving?" he asked, righting himself.

"Soon."

He dusted off his jacket and threw one of his scowls at her.

She didn't notice.

"I don't need to get in until it's time to leave."

She levelled her eyes at him, completely unperturbed. "Did I ask?"

He scoffed and leant back against the vehicle.

"Don't lean on the ute."

Her voice was sharp, matter-of-fact. He crossed around to the other side of the ute and pulled open the door roughly, climbing into the passenger seat. The sergeant looked over as he did so but didn't seem to stop him. He left the door open, a dark cloud appearing and disappearing rapidly over his head. He didn't know what to think any more; he was in his forties and helping the government track down *teenagers* who had stolen dragon eggs, of all things. It was a tad ridiculous.

He watched as the sergeant was approached by the two squad members, she had given an assignment to earlier. They reported their findings to her and she nodded before dismissing them. She climbed into the driver's seat next to Jenkins and he finally pulled the car door shut beside him. "You found the tracks?" he asked.

The flick of her eyes to his was as good as a nod. The engine revved up and she reversed the ute, turning it around as to drive out of the remote cabin's long driveway.

"What's your name, anyway?" Jenkins made himself ask.

He figured if she knew his name, he may as well know hers. It would be unfair otherwise.

She blew out a breath. "Jane. Miller."

Jane. He made himself think the name. Jane Miller. He leant back in the seat, arms crossed, ready to go wherever Jane would be taking them. He had nothing to lose any more and yet for the first time in his bleak life he felt… content. He had never been ambitious and though he had wanted something *more* in his life, he was never overly in pursuit of greatness. He had supposed that had made him weak but perhaps, he supposed, it was his greatest strength.

Chapter 18

Marilyn-Jo

Marilyn-Jo fanned herself dramatically, savouring the deception. Tears streamed down her face as she sobbed onto the shoulder of the reluctant guard.

"There, there," his words were stilted.

"But Daddy's Mercedes!" she wailed.

She felt a hand tug at her arm.

"We'll be going now," the voice attached to the arm said.

Kish steered them away from the entrance and through, into the park.

"You had way too much fun with that," he accused with a grin.

Mari looked up at him, an identical smile splitting her face. "You're saying you didn't enjoy that little bit of arson?"

"Okay, now you're making me sound like a maniac. Come on, let's find Nora."

Once they were well out of the eyesight of the guard, Mari stepped out of Kish's embrace and abandoned the devastated rich kid act. She took a moment to look around her as they made their way towards the park's offices.

She'd been to the Reptile Park before, once, when she was little. Maybe eight or nine years ago? Reuben had wanted to look at the Galapagos tortoise *so* badly he had talked about it for weeks before their trip. He was fascinated with them and it had baffled Mari. Why had he cared about something so slow and boring? Their mother had explained to Mari the turtle's age but she could not honestly give two hoots that the creature was over one hundred years old. She, herself, planned to live that long, anyway. It couldn't be that hard to be old, right? Despite all this, Mari had rushed over with Reuben to the turtle's enclosure, excited nonetheless.

They had got there and the turtle was nowhere to be seen. A passing employee had explained that he was at the veterinarian at the time and the tortoise would be back in a couple of days. Mari had dismissed it and started to skip off to the next enclosure, already forgetting about it but then she had seen Reuben's face. It had crumpled when he realised he wouldn't get to see the one thing he had come to the reptile park for. She still didn't understand why but she absolutely could not bear seeing her older brother in that state. She knew he wouldn't want her to pat him or even touch him in any way as one might usually want when needing to be comforted so she wracked her brain for ways to get a smile on his face again.

Her mother had offered soothing words but Reuben had already retreated back into himself. As much as Marilyn-Jo had wanted to move on and go see the giant lizard and the snakes, oh the *snakes*, they sounded especially cool. And yet she couldn't just leave him there like that. Unless she had a super specific, very well-justified reason for leaving. Mari had made sure her mum was occupied with taking care of her brother before she slipped off, quietly at first and then suddenly sprinting towards the entrance with as much speed as her little legs could muster. She had finally made it to the gift shop. Mari tried to shrink herself down so she was as unnoticeable as possible. It wasn't hard, she was easily the shortest girl in her year at school and besides, little kids probably came and went through the gift shop all the time. The teenage cashier probably wouldn't even notice. Mari slunk through the shop until she finally came to the huge wall of stuffed animals. It was the most amazing thing she had seen in her entire life. It didn't take much to impress Mari. Even so, that wall of stuffed animals was positively *magnificent*.

Mari located the Galapagos turtle right down at the bottom, almost at the floor She crouched down and picked it up. It wasn't the best stuffed animal she'd ever seen. Slightly scratchy and nowhere near soft but it was the old turtle that Reuben loved and that was all that mattered. She looked back up at the wall. She could grab one for herself if she wanted. It wouldn't take too much effort, as long as it was on one of the lower shelves. But she didn't. She wasn't here for herself, anyway. Mari glanced quickly at the cashier, overly animated and serving some lovely-looking suburban family. A mother, a father and two pleasant children who looked like each other and their parents. It was unfair, no one looked at *them* weirdly. Little Mari had scowled before hugging the stuffed turtle tight and skulking out of the gift shop.

She had waited till the shop's door had slammed shut behind her before she sprinted away, lightning kissing at her heels. She had made it back to her mum and Reuben, still at the empty turtle enclosure. Her mum was frantically trying to get Reuben to walk with her, insisting that they needed to go find Mari. Mari had simply walked up and tugged on her mum's shirt.

"Oh!" her mum had gasped and bent down, pulling her into a lung-crushing embrace. "Marilyn-Jo Breneger, where have you been?"

Mari had shifted awkwardly out of her mum's embrace and lifted up the toy turtle she'd taken.

Her mother hadn't reacted the way Mari had thought she would. No smile stretched across her face, no congratulations, no hugs, nothing. She had simply sighed and rubbed her face tiredly, giving Mari an exhausted nod. Marilyn-Jo had gone and sat a little away from Reuben on the bench. His knees had been pulled up tight, shielding his face, his arms wrapped around them, he made no sound, no movement. Mari had simply placed the turtle between them and waited. And waited. And waited. What may have been worse than seeing Reuben so upset was seeing the bone-deep exhaustion of her own mother. It was streaked across her face in dull hues. More than that, there was the grief she knew her mum was feeling because she was trying her best for them and still, she felt she wasn't enough.

Suddenly, little Marilyn-Jo no longer hated that suburban family she had seen, her love for her own family was much greater than the feelings she'd briefly experienced when looking at them. They were probably terrible people, anyway.

Eventually, Reuben uncurled from himself and looked down at the turtle. Then he smiled. It was nearing dusk by the time they left the park and drove home. Years later, Mari realised that she had technically committed a felony that day but she also came to the realisation that her mum had probably gone in and paid for the turtle before they had left. Mari didn't know what she could have done to deserve a mother like her own.

*

She really had to stop coming to the Reptile Park as a borderline criminal but there wasn't anything she could do about that now. Kish led them over to the offices and Mari knocked when they eventually made it to the slim, wooden door. Nora creaked open the door and ushered them inside quickly.

"Where's Gillian and Reuben?" she asked, frowning.

Kish furrowed his brow. "They're back at the van. Wasn't that the plan?"

Nora groaned and smacked her forehead with her palm.

"Yes. Yes, it was. Uncle Charlie?" She called.

A stooped figure emerged behind the office cubicle, a crooked finger pushing his small glasses further up his nose. Nora's uncle had greying hair and an animated expression, almost manic. When he spotted Mari and Kish, his face lit up with a smile, his teeth crooked and yellow. Charlie rushed over to them and shook their hands excitedly. "You must be Nora's friends, it's a pleasure! A real pleasure!"

Mari shook his hand and smiled warmly. "I'm Marilyn-Jo, but you can call me Mari and this is Kish."

He grinned and nodded at them. "Well, hello. My name is Charlie but I'll respond to pretty much everything."

He still hadn't let go of Mari's hand and she tried to extract it, a sudden feeling of unease snaking through her.

"Well," Nora said, clapping her hands together, "shall we show you the eggs, Uncle?"

Nora led the way out of the offices, followed by Kish. Mari gestured for Charlie to go first, remembering the importance of politeness as a first impression. But Charlie merely smiled down at her and placed a hand on her shoulder.

"After you, my dear."

Mari grimaced but went ahead nonetheless and scurried to catch up to Kish. She was sure she was just overthinking Nora's uncle's weird looks. She trusted Nora and she was sure Nora trusted her own uncle, therefore, Mari trusted Nora's uncle. With Charlie escorting them, it didn't take much effort to leave the park and make their way back to the van, blessedly undisturbed. Besides the obvious commotion still petering out in the car park, that was. When they approached, Gillian must have guessed what Mari was thinking because he came over, lengthy strides and all, and wrapped an arm around her shoulders protectively.

"You okay?" he asked under his breath.

Mari smiled assuredly at him. "Yeah, I'm fine. Just getting some kind of weird vibes from Nora's uncle."

Gil frowned over his shoulder at the old man. "We'll have to keep an eye on him then, I guess."

Mari nodded and unwrapped his arm from her shoulder to haul open the boot of the van. She grabbed her egg, feigning calmness when all she could feel was a fierce maternal instinct, warrior-like in its rawness. She hoisted herself onto the lip of the boot, feet dangling off the back of the van. She was suddenly hit by a strange sense of déjà vu, not for a forgotten memory but of something that could have been. A road trip. Laughing around a campfire. Coming of age. If she had maybe made different choices. If she wasn't here and was still just a normal teenager, finishing up year ten. Yet, as much as that image carried an ache of longing with it, she knew she would not give up this little egg she had come to protect so dearly for *anything*.

Nora's uncle came over and the rest of her friends brought their eggs over for him to examine. Nora even fished the documents she'd stolen out for him to peruse. Mari sure hoped he was able to be trusted because they were putting themselves at extreme liability here. He came over to Marilyn-Jo and her egg first, reaching out a spindly hand towards the pastel pink of her egg.

Mari recoiled. "Hey, buddy, look with your *eyes*,"

She sensed the others' discomfort at her rudeness but she

held the old man's stare until he chuckled and hung his head in amusement.

"Of course. Apologies, Mari."

"It's Marilyn-Jo."

His smile faltered a little but he recovered quickly, pushing his glasses up the bridge of his nose and peering down at the egg. He clicked his fingers for Nora to bring him the file. He muttered what sounded like nonsense and then turned to look at the other eggs. Mari hugged her egg to her chest and watched warily. Finally, he stood up straight and addressed them all.

"Right. Well, I think the best course of action would be to take them back to the park where I can observe them until they hatch. They will need a stable and safe place to hatch, of course."

His tone was clear and precise and the others all nodded along with it. Mari, however, cleared her throat and said, "Nora? A word?"

Nora's eyes widened just slightly in surprise but she nodded, happy to oblige. Mari gave her egg carefully to Gil as she passed, before walking away from the group to talk to Nora.

Nora's brows were lowered, her glasses reflecting against the sun, her hair still slicked back into a ponytail, a few curls springing up.

"What's up?" she asked.

Mari fidgeted nervously. "Um, I just, your uncle. Something kind of feels off. Sorry."

Nora seemed to ponder this. She bit her lip and her eyes went downcast in thought.

"I had wondered that too, actually," she said after a little while.

"I don't mean to be rude or anything but—" Mari burst, before being interrupted by the other girl.

Nora shook her head. "No, no! It's totally fine. If you're really uncomfortable, we don't have to stay."

Mari smiled softly, grateful.

Nora sighed. "If I'm being completely honest, Mari, I haven't actually seen my uncle in years. My mum has all but disowned him and I have no idea why. Maybe it's this."

Mari didn't know what to say so all that came out was, "Oh."

"Anyway," Nora said, forcing a grin. Mari guessed she was forcing away thoughts of her parents just as Mari had done these past couple days.

They walked back to the group silently, yet not solemnly. Mari watched as Nora drew Charlie aside and said something softly to him. Disappointment shadowed his worn face and Mari almost felt guilty. Reuben peered up from where he was chatting with Kish and Gillian. Nora shook her head at him and he nodded imperceptibly, returning his eyes to the conversation. It didn't take long for Nora to give her uncle an awkward side hug goodbye and gather the rest of them up and back into the van. Mari felt guilty at robbing her friends of this hope of having a professional think it all out for them but she had learnt to trust her gut and she wasn't about to go against it when the stakes were this high. She climbed into the far backseat of the van and nestled her egg on her lap.

"I'll look after you just fine," she whispered.

Kish swung the van back out onto the backroads once again and Mari listened contentedly to the upbeat chatter of where they should head next. Definitely not back up to the Highlands. Maybe cross the border? What if there were patrols there?

Then Mari had felt it. She had rested her hands down on her egg when her thumb brushed over a dip in the surface. A crack. It was happening. The egg began to shiver slightly and another crack snaked along the circumference.

"Um, guys?" Mari ventured.

Their conversation continued on.

"Guys?" she asked, a tad more urgent.

Still, they didn't seem to hear her.

"Guys!" she yelled. Kish slammed on the brakes and she rocked forwards, panicking for the even more vulnerable egg in her hands, blaring alarm bells in her brain.

They all turned towards her, expectant. She lifted up the egg at them, displaying the cracks. "It's hatching!"

Her friends burst into a blur of talk and restricted movement.

"What do we do?" her brother asked over the panic.

Everyone seemed to settle as the reality of the question burrowed in. Mari sighed and closed her eyes. *Damn it all*, she thought. She would do what she had to. Even against her own wants.

"We have to go back."

They all stared at her incredulously.

"Are you sure, Em?"

Kish joined the sentiment. "Yeah, you couldn't stand that guy barely five minutes ago."

Mari groaned. "I know, I know! But I don't want my dragon to get some reptilian disease or something from being hatched in the back of some sketchy van—"

"Hey!" Kish objected.

"Plus," Mari continued, "you don't want the icky embryo fluid all over these seats, do you?"

"No," Kish conceded, "no, I do not."

That having been said, Kish swung the van around yet again and accelerated the derelict vehicle up to breakneck speeds to get back to the park. Mari fidgeted nervously, worry gnawing at her for her little egg, continually gathering new cracks. Finally, they made it back to the clearing of trees behind the reptile park from earlier. Charlie was sitting against the trunk of a tree, as if he had known they would return. Mari scowled with realisation. That conniving bastard. He had known the egg would hatch and she would have to come running back to him for help.

Nevertheless, Mari rushed out of the van and brought the deteriorating egg to the old man.

"This way," he said and quickly set off.

The others followed but eventually fell behind, unable to keep up the pace that Charlie and Marilyn-Jo had sped to. Finally, he ushered her into a dark room off to the side of the Reptile Park. Distantly, Mari wondered if it might have been a trap. Fortunately, Charlie merely lit a lamp in the corner of the room and pointed to a cot on the far side. A heat lamp was attached to it and he switched it on.

When Mari didn't move, he laced his words with urgency. "Put it in the cot!"

Mari jolted to attention and placed her egg in the cot. She couldn't bear to breathe a proper breath and yet she and Nora's uncle watched as it hatched and hatched.

Mari couldn't restrain her smile as a small beaked head poked its way out of the little, pink egg. It was followed by a long slender body. It had short legs that were yet to grow talons and its eyes had not yet opened. It was but a baby but it was beautiful. Mari could have held it between her two hands, if they were held about a foot apart.

Nora's uncle peered down at the dragon before turning to Mari. "Congratulations."

She smiled in thanks and then looking down at her dragon, she sat down next to the cot, heart full to bursting.

"I think I'll name you Kaida," she said softly, head leaning against the rails of the cot.

Kaida nestled into the heat of the lamp, already beginning to sleep as she turned her beaked head towards Mari.

Chapter 19

Kish

Kish rushed along with the others in a desperate attempt to follow Charlie and Marilyn-Jo. Nora's uncle and Mari eventually got too far ahead for them to keep up and the others lost them in the maze of the Reptile Park. Reuben bent down panting and Kish glanced back to see Nora tug him along.

"Come on, we're nearly there," she urged.

Reuben stood up and huffed. "I don't like running."

They resumed jogging and eventually made it to an office marked with Nora's uncle's name and Gillian burst open the door to the dimly lit room. Mari looked up and put a finger to her lips. Kish looked next to Mari's slumped frame at the cot sitting beside her. Inside the cot was a small, shrivelled-looking thing, somewhere between a bird and a snake with legs. Kish, not taking his eyes off the wrinkled, little baby dragon, slapped Gillian's arm gently.

"I can see the dragon, Kish," he replied calmly.

Kish came and crouched down next to Mari and smiled at her and then the dragon. It was kind of ugly, in a superficial way, but the miracle of life that it was made it kind of beautiful to Kish.

"Her name's Kaida," Mari told him and the others.

She stood up and slumped into Gillian who wrapped his arms around her.

"I'm so tired," she muttered.

Kish forced himself not to whip his head over at them and tried to maintain composure as a shot of some weird feeling spiralled through him. Mari and Gil were best friends, why wouldn't they hug each other? He presumed it probably wasn't *just* a hug, though. He'd seen the way he looked at her. Kish shook his head, he'd dealt with these thoughts. As in, he would no longer be allowing them.

Nora tapped his shoulder and he looked up at her. "Kish. Kish, you're cracking."

Cracking? He frowned at her, he thought he had maintained his facial expressions pretty well.

Nora gestured a bit more frantically at him. "Your egg, Kish. It's cracking!"

Oh! Kish's eyes widened and he looked down at the shining, red egg in his hands. Sure enough, cracks were splitting through the egg, getting wider each second. Kish pulled a face, panicked.

"Wha... what do I do with it?"

Nora's uncle broke his short silence. "Put it in the cot, boy,"

"What if it and Mari's don't get along, though?"

"We'll find out soon enough, just put it in the cot and everything will be all right."

Kish did as he was told and watched worriedly as a head and body poked its way out of the shell of the egg. It looked nothing like Mari's dragon. Kish's dragon was already covered in shining red scales with a square snout and deep brown eyes, so dark you could mistake them for black. The barest hints of upward scales jutted up along the ridge of the dragon's back and all the way along its tail, which ended in small, baby-sized spikes. The dragon stumbled out of the egg, the embryo fluid still sticking to its stubby, clawed feet. The little dragon locked eyes with Kish and suddenly it felt as if something had locked into place. Kish felt his own awe but there was something else there too, as if he could read the emotion beneath those bottomless eyes of the dragon.

"Totem."

Gillian coughed from behind him. "Totem?"

Kish dragged himself from the sight of his dragon to face Gil.

"Yeah, Totem. That's his name."

"May I ask why?"

Kish raised a brow. "You may."

Gillian rolled his eyes. Kish's own eyes snagged on Gil's arm still around Mari and he was suddenly glad he was irritating him.

"Okay, why Totem?" Gil asked.

"Well," Kish said, matter-of-factly, "one, it felt like it fit and two, it... sounds cool."

Gillian stared at Kish. As did the others.

He held up his hands. "Um, geez guys, I wasn't done. Totems, as seen in Disney's *Brother Bear*, are symbols of someone's strengths and—"

Gil laughed, amusement sparkling in his eyes as he stopped Kish's explanation. "We get it, Kish. It's a good name, okay? You don't have to keep justifying yourself."

Kish fought the urge to scowl and settled on a slight frown. Since when was he the one with the foul mood? He didn't know the answer to that, and he didn't really want to open the door to that question in his mind so he left Mari and Gillian. Instead, heading over to sit with Nora, cross-legged next to her uncle. She was gazing at the dragons, Mari's dragon, Kaida, dozing softly while Totem walked in circles around the cot, looking up at and smelling everything. Tiny puffs of smoke kept coming out of his nostrils, it was adorable. Kish saw Nora glance at her own egg, still smooth as porcelain. Kish felt spikes of curiosity and child-like innocence inside of him and frowned, perplexed. Maybe…?

Kish thought of his mum and dad at home and what he had been doing to his family lately and felt the familiar rush of hot anger course through him. Sure enough, Kish's half-formed theory was proven. Totem growled and jumped up and down as if in anger, plumes of tiny smoke pouring out of his nostrils. For some reason, Kish had been feeling the emotions of Totem and it seemed Totem could feel Kish's emotions too. Kish murmured this to Nora beside him and her eyes widened just slightly before furrowing her brow, the cogs clearly turning in her head.

"Hey, Mari," she called.

Marilyn-Jo's head snapped up and she crawled over to where they were sitting, leaving Gillian.

"What's up?"

"Have you been experiencing any of Kaida's emotions since she hatched?" Nora asked.

Mari frowned and looked over at the curled-up dragon.

"Well, she's been sleeping for most of this time but I did feel something kind of… lock into place?"

Nora looked over at Kish and he nodded. A panicked yelp burst Kish's attention and he rushed over to where it had come from. Gillian was holding his egg at arm's length and stood up abruptly. Cracks were running along the length of the egg. Everything was happening today, it seemed. Gil reached the cot in less than a stride and placed the egg in with the other dragons. Totem leant towards the blue egg and sniffed curiously.

"Totem, back off," Kish chided gently.

Totem merely sat back on his haunches and watched as Gillian's dragon climbed out of the shell of the egg. Gillian's dragon had the same build as Kish's, if slightly smaller, as well as shining, writhing dark blue scales. Its eyes were as dark as Totem's but with navy undertones and as it climbed the rest of the way out, it stumbled into Totem clumsily. Kish went to help them out but Charlie stepped forwards and held him back.

"They're fine," he said softly.

Kish watched as Gillian locked eyes with his dragon and he knew they were experiencing the same thing that had happened to Mari and Kish.

Gil smiled and stepped back as his dragon went to lie down, albeit not sleeping.

Kish clapped him on the back. "So, you going to tell us its name?"

Gil bit his lip and looked upward as if in thought.

He paused before saying, "Her name is Jay."

Chapter 20

Gillian

After all the excitement of the three newly-hatched dragons had died down, Nora's Uncle Charlie had bid them to get a few hours of sleep. He assured them that no one would disturb them in the little room he was keeping the five kids in. It was put out of use years ago, he had claimed.

Gillian woke now and sat up straight, pulling himself from his lean against the wall. He rolled his neck, wincing at the numb pain that sat there. He almost thought not sleeping would have been preferable. The room had darkened and there were no windows to let in light, bar the crack under the door. He moved away, careful not to disturb the peaceful slumber of those around him, lanky limbs awkward in the small space. Jay snapped her eyes open as Gil moved next to the cot. He had talked to Kish and Em about the sort of connections they had each made with their dragons. Gil smiled, even if they couldn't communicate directly with their dragons like Nora and Reuben could, they could at least still know the general gist of what they were feeling, making Gillian feel a lot more reassured about the protectiveness he felt towards the creature. Jay trotted sleepily over and slumped against the slats of the cot next to Gil. Even in the short time since she had hatched, Gillian could see the growth. A slight lengthening in her legs, able to stand with more confidence, little things. Gillian had seen the same happen to

Kish's dragon and even Em's appeared to be growing tiny feathers. Still, the changes were small and hadn't really built up to anything yet and the dragons were still relatively tiny. At least, compared to what Gillian expected a dragon would be like at its full size.

A day passed. And the day after that. Gillian, Mari and Kish hands down, refused to leave the room except for the direst of circumstances. That being, to relieve themselves or to use the primal showers Gil knew weren't meant for people but he also knew he needed desperately. Gillian knew the others felt the same thing as him. He just couldn't bear to tear himself away from Jay. This was such a pivotal point and he hadn't gone through the whole process of defying the government and going on the run just to lose that thin thread of connection with the creature. They had continued to grow quite rapidly over the few days, Jay already the size of a medium poodle. Em's dragon, Kaida, was almost completely covered in cream and pastel pink coloured feathers and a pale-yellow leather underbelly also developed colour.

Nora's uncle had reluctantly let the dragons out of the cot after the third day, they were simply getting too restless. Gillian himself was getting antsy to be on the move again. They had all resorted back to their phones, something Gil hadn't looked at since before the morning they had driven away and it was steadily running out of power. Charlie insisted he needed a little more time to study the dragons. He had kept his distance from the animals respectively over the time they had been there, which Gillian found slightly odd. They had all given him permission to find out as much as he could about the dragons, hadn't they?

In the late afternoon of that same third day, he had practically begged the three of them to leave the room. Nora and

Reuben had been making outings every day, their dragons hadn't hatched yet, after all.

"Please, you will all go insane if you stay in here much longer," Charlie had insisted. "The park is nearly closed and I've told the staff I have some guests. They won't disturb you. Take a walk, look at the animals."

Gil had glanced at Em and she had shrugged.

Kish had made a very unconvincing grunt. "I guess it couldn't hurt."

His face betrayed him, though. That was the thing about Kish; his emotions played across his face like a fine opera, open to anyone who bothered to look. Every giddy burst of happiness resulted in those giant, idiotic grins, but also every disappointment. Gillian couldn't imagine it. He had spent years building up a barrier between his mind and those around him. He had been told early on as a child what he was supposed to feel and if he had shown any deviation, it had resulted in tears and chiding. Gil had long since given up on crying. It had got him nowhere. The only weak link in his chain of emotional barriers was when it came to Em. Somehow, she had always pulled a blush out of him or some other key clue to his inner thoughts. Maybe she knew him too well, or maybe, he simply knew too little of himself.

Gil knew Kish didn't want to leave Totem behind; hell, Gillian knew the feeling. He hated the thought of leaving Jay but Nora's uncle had a point, they couldn't stay cooped up in that tiny room forever.

He stood up decisively. "Come on guys, it'll be fun. And our dragons will be fine for an hour."

Mari bit her lip and glanced at Kaida who was sitting next to her. Kaida promptly butted her small head into Em's leg as if urging her to go have fun.

The three of them had taken a while to leave the little room but once they had, it didn't take much for them to start enjoying themselves. Plus, if anything went wrong, they would surely feel the emotional change. Gillian's hands rested nonchalantly in the pockets of the new pants Charlie had found for him. He had found a few new sets of clothes for each of them. Gillian suddenly felt very grateful to the man, he had done so much for them when he was at risk himself, for harbouring them. Em was chatting excitedly to Kish up the front and Gil's heart twinged a little bit. Were they flirting? Although Mari expressed disgust at any kind of romance, he had seen her flirt effortlessly countless times. But with Kish? No, that would be absurd. Maybe Kish even had a girlfriend; they hadn't really had much time for that kind of idle talk. Even if they had, Gillian probably wouldn't have felt comfortable discussing those kinds of things. He caught up with them and they both turned to him.

"Gil!" Em smiled. "Wanna go see the snakes?"

"Sure," Gillian shrugged.

Mari grinned and started speed-walking ahead of them. This time, it seemed Kish couldn't be bothered to follow as quickly. Gillian coughed awkwardly.

"You been here before?" Kish asked.

Gil shook his head. "Nope, my mum and dad preferred more *dignified* outings. Their words, not mine."

Kish scoffed and looked at him with a smile. "I haven't been here before either. Not much time for it, I guess."

Gillian could tell that wasn't the whole story but he didn't want to push. Gillian inwardly grimaced, this conversation was so... *awkward*. It was all well and good that they were developing a friendship of sorts now, but it was so much easier back when Gillian could just wither with dislike. Now he had to be *civil* and *polite*. It was exhausting. Just the thought soured his mood a little. Maybe he could just ignore Kish and everything would be fine. Gillian huffed and tried to catch up with Em, at least with her some semblance of normalcy could be returned within Gil's mind. Kish hurried to keep up with him but Gil reached Em first and determinedly situated her between the two of them. Buffer initiated. Kish frowned; the opera of his emotions once again being put on stage. Em peered at the snakes through the glass, her head tilting slightly to the side. Gillian followed suit, as did Kish.

"I used to want to work here, you know? As a kid," Em said, her tone purely matter-of-fact.

There was no way that could have been possible now, although maybe Gillian was being cynical. Maybe their lives might go back to normal after all, eventually perhaps, if they were ever caught. The military's methods baffled Gillian and he had often wondered how they were not yet sitting in a cell but he supposed it was all the better for him and his friends.

"I wish we could have come here in the middle of the day, without disguises," Kish added.

"I wish we didn't have to wish for this stuff," Mari said.

"Keep wishing," Gil murmured.

Then he sat up straight. A shot of distress powered through him and he rose to his feet quickly. Something was wrong.

Chapter 21

Reuben

Reuben and Nora strolled through the Reptile Park, the second time they had done so that day. Reuben, though such a little achievement, was proud of the way he had been able to maintain a conversation and not sound like an utter imbecile over these past few days. They had tried to do only one or two exhibits each day so as to not run out of things to look at. Of course, Reuben never would run out because he wasn't usually looking at the animals anyway. He had noticed Nora come alive while studying the three newly hatched dragons and, weirdly enough, she seemed to be learning more than her so-called expert uncle. *He* had barely gone near the creatures.

Before their first outing, Reuben had slipped out and grabbed two backpacks from the gift shop. That way, they could keep their eggs with them without raising any suspicion. Nora's Uncle Charlie had insisted that the eggs would be completely fine if they just left them with him. Reuben was sure they would be, except for the skull-splitting headaches it would induce. At least Nora had understood his thinking. The hefty weight of the egg was settled against his back now as he leant on the railing of the enclosure they had visited today.

Once they had left the small room that evening, Reuben had been struck with an idea.

"Hey, Nora, you mind if I pick the animal today?" he had

said, eyes sparkling with the idea.

She smiled and shrugged. "Sure, I'm not fussed."

He had led her through the park, he knew the way well enough even though the last time he had traversed it had been nine years ago. He had studied the map online for weeks beforehand, the excitement making him obsessive.

She glanced over at him now and he looked up sheepishly.

Reuben gestured to the tortoise in front of him. "First time seeing him, actually."

"Really?" she asked.

Reuben nodded, suddenly kind of embarrassed. Nora had probably been here a dozen times with her mums to study the reptiles. She loved biology, of course she was probably so unimpressed with the tortoise by now. *Good going, Reuben.*

Nora cocked her head at the tortoise, the corners of her mouth on the cusp of a smile. "Same here."

Reuben fought to contain his surprise. *Yes!* He thought he did a well enough job of concealing it.

"When I came here, I really wanted to see it. My mum even bought me a backpack just like this one on our way in that had a little stitching of the tortoise on the front. But when we came to the enclosure, he wasn't even here."

"No way!" Reuben grinned. "The same thing happened to me! Except instead of the backpack, my sister stole a stuffed toy from the gift shop."

Nora laughed and Reuben grinned even further. He wanted to make her laugh again. He didn't, though, he merely turned back to the tortoise and shifted awkwardly on his feet. They waited there for a small while, chatting little, both mesmerised by the fixations of their childhood selves. Eventually, they decided to head back to the room and let the poor tortoise have some peace. It didn't take long to reach the room and they mercifully didn't bump into any of the park employees. Reuben didn't want to take any chances, despite Charlie's assurances that they would pay them no heed. Reuben creaked the door open and strolled inside, Nora behind him, only to look up and be stopped in his tracks by the scene before him.

Mari was almost locked in the middle of a step, leaning towards Nora's uncle, Gillian and Kish tensed behind her. Nora's uncle himself was holding Kaida by the neck as she was squirming. He was holding some kind of medical instrument and his glasses were perched on the edge of his nose.

"I haven't done anything wrong!" the man protested.

Mari stepped towards him threateningly but he held Kaida aloft.

"Don't come any closer!"

Reuben stepped further into the room. "What's going on here?"

Kish whirled to them, scowling. "This prick thought he could experiment on our dragons!"

Nora's brow furrowed as she looked to her uncle.

"Uncle Charlie?" she asked.

His gaze softened. "Please, Nora, you have to understand. I was only trying to better *my* understanding of them. They are really such a fine variety of specimens!"

Mari launched herself at him and he came at her with the medical instrument, releasing Kaida's neck to defend himself. The dragon tried to flap gracefully to the floor, but having not gained full control of her wings, fell in a heap. The medical instrument whizzed across Mari's cheek and Reuben blazed with hatred as he saw a thin slice of red open up, a tear of blood dripping down. Charlie righted himself but by that point Reuben had stormed over and shoved the man's frail body against the wall. Charlie's breaths were coming short now.

"Hey, hey now," he said placatingly, "I didn't mean any harm by any of you, I just—"

"You just what?" Gillian murmured menacingly, coming up behind Reuben.

Charlie gulped as Nora and Kish came to surround him.

"Please," he choked out.

Kish laughed. "Like that will do you any good, mate."

Nora's uncle's eyes were wide with fear and Reuben almost felt sorry for the man. Reuben himself wasn't much of a menacing sight but the four of them arrayed on Mari's behalf would certainly be a frightening view.

Reuben tightened his grip on the man's shoulders and lowered his voice. "If you *ever* hurt my sister or her dragon again, I will find you and you will wish you had stayed in your little den of cowardice and had never tried to trick me or my friends."

Reuben released the sorry excuse for a man and backed away.

"What the hell was that?" he heard Mari mutter to Gillian, her voice dull with awe.

That, he thought to himself, *is what I should have done years ago*. Reuben knew Mari deserved a better brother but he could at least try to be better now. Kish, Gil and Mari promptly gathered the dragons and followed Reuben and Nora out of the room.

"Oh, by the way," Kish leant back inside to address the fallen Charlie, "you probably shouldn't try to alert the authorities. You *are* an accomplice, after all."

*

Reuben, laden with uncertainty, gripped the steering wheel. Kish had passed over driving duties to Reuben so that he could take care of Totem in the back. He'd never driven a van like this before, only his mum's old Subaru. This vehicle was shaky and unreliable and shot Reuben through with fear each time he tried to brake. Why had he agreed to take *Kish's* van? Gillian's family probably could have afforded a whole new one. It was too late now, he supposed. They had been driving for almost half an hour when everything went to hell. Kish had yelled out and Reuben had slammed on the brake in shock.

"Totem! No, argh!"

Reuben had swung round to see Kish's dragon latched onto his shoulders, haunches raised and thick plumes of smoke coming out of his nostrils, claws digging into Kish.

Then Jay, claws clutching desperately onto Gillian's knees, had bent over and hurled directly onto the van's floor. Gillian had leant back in disgust. "Ugh, that smells like something died in a puddle of diesel."

Up in the back, Kaida was screeching and circling around Mari's head incessantly. Reuben switched the van's motor off and climbed out.

"Right, everyone out, now!" he called.

They did so obediently, albeit with a little trouble on account of the dragons. They filed out and stood before Reuben wearily.

"What's happening?" he asked them.

Kish rubbed the back of his neck. "Uh, I don't think they like the van very much."

Reuben tilted his head back and let out a long sigh which probably could have been interpreted as a string of swearing.

"Great," he muttered.

"We'll just walk," Mari shrugged.

The others mumbled their assent and Reuben agreed reluctantly. He didn't like the notion of hiking but really, what other option was there?

Chapter 22

Kish

They had begun the hike with vigour, eager to get away from what they had done. None of them had known what to do with the van since they could no longer use it. It wasn't like one of them could drive it while the others hiked, that would waste too much fuel and prove redundant. But they couldn't just leave it there. Gil had suggested they find a lake and shove it in there but Mari had vehemently voted against that notion. She claimed it was, and to quote, "littering on steroids". Then Kish had come up with a suggestion. He still had the lighter he had used to set fire to the cars last week and he proposed they do the same to the van. Distantly, Kish realised that his family had been down one vehicle the entire time he had been away. And he hadn't even let his sisters know where he had been going. There had only been one text from them this entire time, from Jill.

Jill – 6:17 p.m.
I saw the news. Don't message back, they can probably track your phone;). I told the others not to text you as well. Don't worry, we'll be fine.

He had abided by her request but by all things holy, he wanted to talk to his sisters. The aching of homesickness, the wish that he could just watch one more episode of *Criminal*

Minds with Jill, that he could have one more imaginary tea party with Sasha and Lydia. He hated that he left them but maybe once everything calmed down a little, he could go visit them. If things ever calmed down.

Mari had objected to burning the car at first, saying that that was just as bad for the environment but Reuben had countered with the fact that those were their only two options. Either that or leave the van there. Which none of them wanted to do. They wanted something monumental, a final farewell to the last remaining tie to their old lives. An old battered Hyundai, of all things. Kish had clicked the lighter, eliciting a small flame and a little whine of excitement. He had looked down at Jay and Totem who were dancing around and jumping at the flame. Kish wasn't bewildered for long. Jay had released a spurt of flame from her mouth and Totem had answered accordingly. Kish had only stared in awe, a dumb grin plastered across his face.

"This is *so* cool!" he had laughed.

The dragons had helped him light the van on fire and then they had stepped back into a line with the others. The five of them had lifted their hands to their foreheads in a salute. Five teenagers paying their respects to the noble steed that had carried them from the hands of imprisonment. They had meant to stand like that until the car burnt down but not one of them was patient enough for such a task. So, they had left the van and the memories it held, still burning, a dazzling shred of the past being left behind. Kish had to admit, he felt pretty cool walking away from, essentially, an explosion, silhouetted like a character in an action movie. Totem seemed to be feeling the same way, or maybe burning something with his own flame had given the dragon some sort of high.

Either way, the initial stretch of the hike went smoothly. It wasn't long before the sun had dipped fully below the horizon and they were plunged into darkness. They didn't say a word and yet they each knew that they needed to keep going. They were not nearly far enough away from Charlie as they would like and based on how they had treated him, it was highly probable he would turn them in.

Kish wondered what would be done to them if they were caught. He didn't really believe they would just throw him in jail, despite hoping that was the case. Would they hurt Totem? There were probably a lot of people like Charlie among them, claiming the dragons' pain would be in the name of research and the greater good. Utter bull, if you asked Kish.

If their pursuers caught up with them, Kish thought he would put up a good fight. Yes, they had military-level weapons and supplies but he had a dragon so...

Plus, he wouldn't let any of his friends get taken alone if he could help it. If he couldn't save them then he would go with them and they would figure a way out together. Hopefully, it wouldn't have to come to that.

Kish couldn't even imagine if it was his sisters in his friends' place, they were the only people he thought he might feel the same vigour towards their rescue. Everyone else would just get a regular rescue. The one you did out of the goodness of your heart and because you're not a total monster. He remembered a book Jill had read last year in which a girl had been held captor by some rich guy. The girl hadn't known whether this boy she loved would come to rescue her or not. Kish never wanted any of his loved ones to feel that way, he wanted them to know he would come for them.

After a few hours of hiking with only minuscule rest stops, the five of them were exhausted.

"Please," Mari huffed.

"I think we should stop here," Reuben conceded.

They waited until they rounded the hill they were on before falling gracelessly onto the grass.

"My arms hurt like hell," Nora groaned.

Kish turned his head half-heartedly. "Why?"

She gestured to the egg next to her. "I've been carrying this damn thing the entire time."

"You know," Mari murmured to them all, "if I don't have a six-pack by the end of this, I don't know what we're doing."

"I don't think fitness works like that," Reuben frowned.

Kish chuckled a little at them all. He often forgot he was the only one among them that had ever seriously done sport. He thought Mari had mentioned playing soccer a little but he didn't know whether she had stopped recently or a while ago.

"Did anyone happen to bring sleeping bags or anything?" Gillian asked the group, exhaustion dripping from his words.

The rest of them just let out a chorus of groans and lamentations.

Gil huffed. "So that's a no, then?"

They settled into silence.

"We could have taken the blankets Charlie gave us," Mari said.

"We were a bit preoccupied when we left," Reuben pointed out.

Kish rolled onto his side. "Look, we'll just sleep on the grass tonight and then tomorrow maybe we'll be able to find somewhere that sells supplies."

They all mumbled their assent and rolled over to whatever sleeping position was most comfortable. Totem trotted over to Kish and circled next to him, laying down in a curled-up ball.

Despite the uncomfortable terrain, Kish fell into the abyss of sleep with no problem at all.

*

Kish breathed in the deep scent of the cabin, the cosy scent of the smoke filling his nostrils. He was safe here in Gillian's family's cabin, the fire roaring in the grate. A bed filled with feathers cradled his half-asleep body and he hummed contentedly. No. They weren't at the cabin any more. Charlie. The dragons. Sleeping on the bare ground under the stars. But if he was right about that... why could Kish still smell smoke? Kish snapped awake, sitting upright immediately. He spotted it without much trouble. A blazing wall of flame moved through the trees just beyond where Kish and the others were sleeping.

Damn it, Kish thought to himself.

A little nudge of guilt was dripping away at the back of his mind and, sure enough, when he looked to where Totem had fallen asleep next to him, there was only grass.

"Totem!" he yelled.

Nora and Gillian startled awake, rubbing their eyes groggily as they looked with bewilderment at Kish. Then they looked beyond him, along his line of sight, and registered the fire just fifty yards away.

"Yours or mine?" Gil asked sleepily.

"Mine," Kish answered through gritted teeth.

Gillian sighed and pushed himself from the ground, Kish and Nora following suit. Without another word, Nora began to wake Mari and Reuben.

"Totem!" Kish shouted again.

Sure enough, a red figure began to emerge from the trees,

half leaping and half flying, still getting a hang of his wings. Totem flew the last stretch towards Kish and landed at his feet smugly. Somehow the little dragon was not so little, he had doubled in size overnight. He, now the size of a reasonable pony, had a hare caught in his jaws.

"Seriously?" Kish asked and gestured to the fire. "All that for a hare?"

Totem seemed to shrink down and he whimpered as if in regret.

"Yeah, you should be sorry. You didn't even get any for Kaida and Jay."

Totem hopped up and down, clearly trying to express something. Kish looked over to Gil and a freshly woken Mari who looked to their own dragons, trying to discern what the creatures felt.

"Wait, what am I supposed to be doing?" Mari asked.

Kish shrugged. "Do you think Kaida has eaten, does she feel hungry?"

"No?" Mari said.

Gillian shook his head too. Maybe Jay and Kaida had already eaten. Totem whined and Kish dragged his attention back to his dragon.

"Yes, you can eat the hare now."

Kish could feel the short burst of excitement from his dragon as he tore into the meat. Thank goodness the dragons knew how to hunt because Kish certainly couldn't keep feeding him scraps as he had done back at the Reptile Park.

"Guys," Marilyn-Jo hopped nervously from foot to foot. "We should probably move."

Kish gulped, the fire was just over twenty yards away now and he could feel the heat pulsing against them, eager to come and swallow them whole. They didn't need anyone to tell them what to do, the five of them started sprinting away, not caring which direction they were going so long as it was away from the fire.

"Kaida!"

Kish skidded to a halt and turned around to Mari running back the way they came, towards her dragon whose long body was levitating, held aloft by feathered wings.

What is it doing?

"Em! Get away from the fire!" Gil yelled at her.

Mari didn't seem to hear him or maybe she just ignored him but she kept getting closer to Kaida and the fire. Then the strangest thing happened. A massive wall of wind seemed to come from nowhere.

No, Kish corrected himself, *it's coming from Kaida.*

The feathered dragon was moving her wings up and down relentlessly, screeching at the fire, her body writhing in serpentine waves. The wind seemed to emanate from the dragon, driving back the fire until it was far enough away to give them time to run.

Chapter 23

Marilyn-Jo

They had run from the fire for a solid half an hour but it felt like a never-ending stretch of torture to Marilyn-Jo. She hadn't had time to register what Kaida had just done and honestly, she would need to sit down before she could even start. Try as she might to wait to process what she had seen, the thoughts and images still swirled haphazardly through Mari's head as she was running. She wanted to make sense of them but she couldn't do that while she was focusing on running by the time she had sat down, she probably would have worked through it already. Mari let out a grunt of frustration.

They eventually slowed down to a steady walking pace but it was still unbearable for Mari. Her legs were in absolute pain and she desperately just wanted a warm shower. She missed those suburban luxuries more than she thought she would. And deodorant. The others could use some of that if she was being totally honest. After an hour of the gruelling walking, Mari had insisted they take a break. Thankfully, her just as unfit friends agreed wholeheartedly.

"This isn't going to work," Nora pointed out.

"Not with that attitude, it won't," Kish retorted, stretching his muscled arms under his head as he stretched down onto the grass.

Reuben panted. "What won't work?"

"This," Nora gestured around them, "walking. Our pursuers have cars and the only one who exercised regularly before this whole thing was Kish. We don't stand a chance."

"She's right," Gillian added, "they'll catch up to us in no time."

Mari saw her brother ponder this. They all knew Nora spoke the truth but try as she might, Mari could not come up with a better alternative. Plus, they had thoroughly destroyed the van, there was no going back now.

"Imagine if the dragons were big enough for us to fly on," Mari mused out loud.

Even now, Kaida had grown substantially bigger in the week since she hatched. If she kept up the same growing speed, she would be the size of an elephant by the next week, but perhaps not quite so wide. Totem and Jay, however, were built like tanks. It wouldn't surprise Mari if they got to be the size of whales. Though, Mari was no zoologist so who could really tell?

"That would have been helpful," Reuben muttered.

"Hey," Kish protested, "they're still just babies, don't take this out on them."

Reuben glared and Kish backed down, cowed. Mari didn't know what crazy genes were given to her brother but she was in awe at his effect on people.

"Look," Reuben blew a breath out and slumped his shoulders a little, "let's just take a quick break and reconvene in an hour with some ideas?"

"Can we afford an hour?" Gil asked.

"We're going to have to be able to, Gillian."

They had all either split off or just sat a little while away, each of them claiming they needed a moment alone to think. Sitting down to just *think* sounded like a torturous exercise worse than running so Mari announced she was going for a stroll. Kaida followed her leisurely, her slim, dragon's body rolling lithely through the wind, lazy flaps of her wings keeping her airborne.

"Where should we go, Kaida?"

Mari's dragon responded by tilting her head slightly to the side.

"I don't know either. Let's see if we can find some water though, like a lake or something. I'm sure there's something around here."

Kaida seemed to perk up at that and sped through the air in front of Mari, straightening out like a bullet.

"Woah, okay, you can lead, then," Mari chuckled.

Her dragon seemed to understand because she started flying with new vigour, occasionally swooping down to the grass just to leap off again into the air. Mari followed Kaida through the forest, pushing away the killjoy thoughts that she probably shouldn't stray too far from the group. If Kaida could direct her here, she could direct them back. Plus, her dragon was presumably leading them to a water source, which contained a commodity that all humans, and probably dragons, needed to survive. The others would probably be grateful that she had left to find such a thing.

Before long, Marilyn-Jo was following her dragon through to a break in the never-ending ocean of trees. A flowing river parted the green expanse, at least three metres wide and who knew how deep. It was beautiful. The water rushed along in gushes of cool, clear splashes, rushing towards a destination unknown. Kaida was urging Mari towards the water but she shook her head. The water looked *really* cold, even though it was almost summer. Kaida huffed and nudged Mari's hands so that they were on her shoulder blades, fingers nestled in the soft feathers. Mari furrowed her brow bewildered. Then Kaida took off and Mari suddenly had to cling on tight to her dragon as she plunged them into the icy depths.

Mari's face hit the water with barely a splash and she closed her eyes as the cool currents slipped around them. Beneath her fingers, a thin, gelled layer slipped over Kaida's feathers. Mari opened her eyes beneath the water and recoiled against the rushing water. It took a minute but she adjusted and was suddenly able to marvel at the sun filtering in through the river's surface and the phenomenon that was her dragon.

They swam for a good twenty minutes before Mari sputtered to Kaida that she needed dry land. Kaida dutifully dropped Mari at the shore before slithering back into the water, floating on her back, talons sticking up in the air.

"We should probably take some water back to the others, right?" Mari speculated.

Although, clear as the water was, Mari didn't know if she was entirely comfortable with drinking straight from the stream, especially since Gil still had that wad of cash that they could use to buy filtered water at the next point of civilisation. With that in mind, Marilyn-Jo began to head back the way she thought they had come. Kaida leapt from the river and slid through the air, shedding her watery coat and ruffling her feathers once more. Together, they made their way back to the camp where Kish was attempting, unsuccessfully, to create a spark with some rocks he found. Totem tried to come and throw a spark onto the little tepee of twigs Kish had made but Kish nudged the dragon back with a hand.

"Step back, mate, I got this."

Mari approached them, amused. "You do realise you need

flint and steel to make a spark, don't you?"

Kish huffed and let go of the rocks. "Don't judge me, I'm pretty sure I saw Bear Grylls do this once."

"Right," Mari nodded, brows raised.

She folded to the ground next to Kish as Kaida came to lie down beside her, notably more graceful than Mari. Nora was dozing against a tree on the far side of the clearing and Reuben seemed to be studying the dragons' files yet again. Marilyn could easily just accept that the dragons were what they are and learn along the way what they could do, new information brought to her by the dragons themselves. She supposed her brother had never been like that. If he didn't understand something, he wouldn't stop until he knew the ins and outs of every possible fact about the thing.

"Where's Gil?" Mari asked Kish.

Kish shrugged, the nonchalance looking a bit too forced to Mari. "I don't know, I think he said he was going to see if there was any food in these bushes."

"Doubt it," Mari snorted.

Kish laughed as well but they both shrank a bit and tried to stifle their laughter when Reuben flicked a glance up.

"Right," Kish murmured, "Nora's sleeping."

Mari held a finger to her lips and widened her eyes in mock outrage. Their stifled laughter fell out again and before long, Mari's ribs hurt from them trying to keep the rising laughs in. A tap on her shoulder almost made Mari shout out but she managed to turn her head near silently.

"You thought I was a murderer, didn't you?" Gillian grinned down at her.

Mari scoffed and turned around. "No, of course not, that's stupid."

"Sure, whatever you say."

Mari rolled her eyes but was smiling nonetheless. Gillian's eyes flicked over to Reuben studying and Nora still dozing. Mari could almost guess what conclusion he was drawing from the situation; they may as well rest because none of them was going anywhere until Nora woke up.

"I'm going to go have a look at what Reuben's doing, see if I can help deduce anything," Gil said to them before promptly walking over and sitting himself down next to Mari's brother.

Chapter 24

Nora

Run.

Nora tossed in her sleep, trying to push away the nagging voice plaguing her dreams.

Run.

There it was again. Why did it keep trying to wake her? Couldn't it see that she was trying to sleep?

Run, Nora!

Nora jerked awake, banging her head against the tree trunk she had been leaning on, her glasses falling clear of her face. She hastily grabbed them and pushed them back up the bridge of her nose. That was Copper's voice. Her unborn dragon was trying to tell her something. No, not *something*. It was telling her to run. Nora jumped up, vaguely noticing the startled looks of those around her.

"We need to go," she said, putting as much urgency into her voice as she could muster, "now."

They all looked up at her with furrowed brows and confusion leaking from their gazes.

"Come on! I know this sounds crazy but Copper," she pointed to her egg, "was pretty adamant just then, telling me to run."

That was when the rumble of vehicular machinations reverberated through the forest scape and a myriad of muttered curses filtered through the group. Nora grabbed her egg and helped the others up from the ground as they too gathered their things. Then they were off, running through the trees haphazardly.

There is no way we can outrun them, Nora thought.

The words churned over and over in her mind as they ran and each time she thought about it, a stumble would come into her steps and she would falter. One of the others would always then grab her arm or her shoulder and restore her balance. She was bringing them all down, she was a liability. Nora thought back to her life back home, her mum's warm spirit and her mother's rare but precious smiles. And she remembered something her mum had been insistent about when she was growing up.

"It starts with a thought," she had always said, back before the grey had entered her blonde locks.

"It starts with a thought and then you let the thought take hold and it just spews more, similar thoughts."

Nora's young self had listened intently, perplexed at where her mum has been going with her words. Then her mum had leant back and reached out to tuck a curl behind her daughter's ear.

"Now what kind of thought you let take hold, that's up to you. You may not control what thought comes into your head but you can control whether it takes root."

Nora had nodded, thinking she had fully understood the concept.

Only now did she realise she had been so dreadfully wrong. For as long as she could remember, she had let the bad thoughts pile up, making her overthink everything. She knew it wouldn't be easy to dismantle that much right then and there but she could make a start.

We have a chance, she told herself, *we'll find a way out of this*.

The little nips of negativity were still there but she shoved back at them with a ferocity. She could deal with those once they weren't being chased by the military. Nora realised, slowing to a halt, that she could no longer hear the engines. They must be following them on foot now because the roads don't come in this deep. Nora started running again with the others, dark eyes scanning her surroundings. *There*.

She caught the attention of the others and pointed wordlessly to the sloping hill a little way off. They groaned but they all nodded, nonetheless. Nora guided the group up the hill, panting. The hill stretched over the ground below, covered in ferns and various flora.

"You guys go ahead, I'll catch up," Nora said between breaths.

"No," Mari said. "No way."

The others agreed with her adamantly. Nora took a deep breath.

"Look, I have an idea, I'll be fine."

They still looked at her, concern etched deeply into all of their features but, eventually, they accepted what she had said.

Nora smiled reassuringly at her friends. "Don't worry, I'll be fine."

They murmured various wishes of safety and luck before jogging off in the other direction.

"Wait!" she called, the final step of the plan clicking into place. "Could I borrow Jay or Totem please?"

Gillian nodded down to his blue dragon and she trod over to Nora. Then the others were off, jogging reluctantly away from them. If she was being completely honest with herself, the plan had not yet fully formed and she was fairly sure it was a pretty stupid idea. Yet, as stupid as she knew it was, she also knew it would buy the others much-needed time to get away. Nora readjusted her egg in her arms, she wasn't prepared to leave it in the care of others just yet. Not after what happened with Uncle Charlie. She led Jay and herself over to the place she had spotted from the ground. A reasonably sized boulder lay wedged just beyond the edge of the hill, ferns crawling every which way around it. Quickly, Nora explained what Jay needed to do, feeling very dumb while acting out extravagant charades in the hopes that the dragon would interpret what she was asking. Why couldn't she just talk to it the same way she did with Copper?

Soon enough, Nora heard the sound of approaching footsteps and she raised a finger to her lips, hoping the sapphire creature understood the gesture.

"Grimes, Norton, wait here with Jenkins and see if the sniffer dogs detect anything. The rest of you, sweep the square kilometre."

The strong female voice echoed through the leaves of the forest and Nora tensed. They had sniffer dogs. That did not look good for her plan. Although, once it was put into action, they would know that she was there anyway. Did that woman say Jenkins? Was Mr Jenkins seriously helping them track down his former students? She couldn't believe him, it turned out he was a spineless traitor after all.

Nora flinched as dogs' barks rang out through the air. Her time was up. She held up her palm to Jay, indicating that the dragon stay behind the boulder and swiftly removed herself from the cover of the enormous rock.

The woman she assumed was the owner of the voice before chuckled up at her.

"Hi! Nora, is it? I'm Jane Miller, I don't believe we've met before."

The woman had obviously dyed blonde hair pulled mercilessly back into a bun and held herself surely as if there was nothing she ever doubted. Nora wished.

"Hey?" Nora waved hesitantly down at her but adamantly avoided the gaze of her former substitute teacher.

"I think we can come to an agreement here, Miss Fairweather," Jane Miller began to walk slowly towards the bottom of the hill.

"That seems unlikely," Nora replied flatly.

Jane Miller smiled but Nora detected no warmth, only a woman on a mission. It wasn't even as if the woman had some personal vendetta against Nora and her friends. There was no emotion behind this chase for Jane Miller, she only wanted to do her job. Nora wondered if she would have become someone like this. Just another mindless drone who didn't question what she was told without bothering to worry about the people or things it affected. Nora hated to admit it but she knew it probably would have happened. She would think she was making a difference, but who knew if that would actually be a positive difference.

The odd thing, Nora noted, was that this Jane Miller woman didn't seem like a mindless drone. Nora sensed an intelligence there that was probably the reason she had been promoted to such a position. Nora kept her eyes trained on the woman, mind whirring as she tried to assess Miller's loyalties. Did she know what the military was doing? Somehow, Nora couldn't convince herself that this woman was devoid of empathy, couldn't convince herself that Jane Miller was really her enemy.

Nevertheless, Jane Miller had started up the hill at this point and Nora had completely ignored what she had been saying. It didn't matter, she was leaving soon anyway. Nora slipped back behind the boulder.

"Now," she whispered to Jay.

Nora pushed hard on the boulder, putting all her effort into getting it rolling. At the same time, Gillian's dragon prowled out from behind the rock and positioned herself at the tree on the outer circle of the area below the hill. A stream of fire flowed out of the dragon's mouth and caught onto the trees and leaves and bark, engulfing it in mere seconds. As the boulder rolled down the hill, heading for Jane Miller and the flames jumped from one tree to the next, Nora began to run. She could hear Jay's steady plods behind her, eventually easing as the creature lifted into flight. Even so, she could still hear the shout of frustration from Jane Miller and knew that she and her squad would be giving chase. Nora willed speed into her legs, hoping that sheer determination would carry her through. Hopefully, the fire would have surrounded most of their pursuers, leaving only Miller, who, Nora hoped, was slowed down by the boulder that came at her.

The ground rushed by underneath Nora and she fought to keep her fingers from slipping off of the egg in her hands. Her fingers, her knees, everywhere felt gross from being on the run but still she ran.

Nora didn't know if she was hallucinating but she was fairly sure that at that moment a crack ran down along Copper's egg underneath her palm. She had to be hallucinating, Copper could *not* be hatching now. That was not happening, Nora willed it to be so. Much to her dismay, she risked a glance down and there it was. The egg was falling apart right there between her hands. And despite it, still she ran.

Chapter 25

Gillian

Gillian and the others had left Nora back at the hill twenty-five minutes ago, if Gillian was any judge of time passing. They had peeled away slowly at first, not one of them eager to leave their friend behind. But Nora had insisted and so they had jogged away. Gillian was a little uneasy at having left Jay with her but he figured if there was anyone who would take the best care of his dragon it would be Nora. Much more trustworthy than her scumbag uncle, at least.

The four of them had jogged at first but had started running soon after, weaving between rocks and trees and vines. Now, they were bent over, panting and Reuben was getting antsy.

"I'm going back," he announced.

Gil straightened and ran a hand through his sweat matted curls.

"I'm coming with you, then."

Reuben shook his head and held out his egg. "No. You guys stay here."

Gillian tilted his head, bewildered. "I have more of a reason to go, Reuben."

"Gil, don't get involved," Em muttered somewhere in his peripheral.

Gil ignored her. "Nora can handle herself, Reuben, and she has Jay with her. A *fire-breathing* dragon, if you forgot."

Reuben just sighed and shoved his egg into Em's hands. With a small glance at them, he turned on his heel and began running the other way.

"Unbelievable," Gil muttered.

Gillian scoffed at Reuben's utter disregard for other people, it was astounding. How the guy had managed to make it this far in his life, Gillian didn't know.

Although, he conceded to himself, *it's not like he has that many friends.*

Or any that Gil knew of.

"We could follow him," Em suggested.

"Wouldn't we just call more attention to ourselves that way?" Kish asked.

Gillian forced his body to relax and slipped his hands into his pockets with a scowl. "Kish is right. Let's just wait here for them."

Kish and Em nodded and they all slumped down to the dirt-covered ground.

They only stayed there for a few seconds before the crunch of leaves underfoot rustled through to their ears.

"We should climb into the trees," Kish whispered.

"What's that going to do?" Gil replied sceptically.

"It's better than sitting down here. At least in the trees, the only way they'll spot us is if they look up."

Gillian bit back a retort and instead released a quick breath through his nose. Gil ran his hand through his hair yet again, there were way too many knots; he needed a haircut.

"Fine."

He and Kish rose and dusted themselves off as they scanned for trees with easy-to-reach branches. It wasn't much of an effort to climb the trees, what with Gil's long limbs and Kish, even, could be considered tall. Although Gillian was fairly sure he was the taller of the two.

Gil glanced down. "Em, you coming up?"

She nodded and shifted her feet beneath her. "Yeah, just, can you hold Reuben's egg while I climb up?"

Gillian reached out as she handed the milky white egg to him and waited as she, with great effort, hoisted herself up to the first branch. Once she had climbed up to where he and Kish were sitting, he handed the egg back to her. Kaida was right on her heels and slithered through the air to come to rest peacefully on the branches above them. Kish's glaringly red dragon had had less luck. Though he could fly, Totem was still bulky and practically destroyed the tree he tried to climb into.

"So," Kish said as he tried to settle into a nook between two branches, "what does your dragon do, Mari?"

She rolled her eyes. "What does my dragon do?"

Gillian himself contemplated Kish's question; it was a fair one. They knew for sure that Jay and Totem could breathe fire and Nora and Reuben's dragons clearly had some sort of telepathic abilities. But Kaida? The pastel-feathered, serpent-like dragon? An enigma of sorts, he supposed.

When Kish didn't elaborate on his query, Em sighed. "Well, you guys saw how she pushed the fire back with wind, right?"

Gil furrowed his brow. "So, she can manipulate wind?"

"And water, I think..."

Kish blanched. "Your dragon is the half Avatar?"

A squawk came from above them. Gil craned his neck to see Kaida swooping down. With an angry squawk, he knew was directed at them, she brought a taloned foot down to the ground, causing ripples of earth to cascade beneath them.

Kish raised an eyebrow. "Noted. Three-quarters the Avatar."

Kaida floated back up to her branch gracefully, wings barely having to move.

They sat for a moment, quiet. Then Kish opened his mouth as if to say something. He closed it abruptly before frowning and seeming to finally have the words.

"If we combined our dragons, we would have the full Avatar," he said decisively.

Gillian raised his eyebrows. "Are you saying you want to selectively breed our lab-born dragons to create the Avatar in dragon form?"

Kish nodded slowly. Gillian could see Em stifling a laugh in the corner of his eye.

Gillian took a deep breath. "We don't even know how, let alone whether, they reproduce."

"Eggs," Kish shrugged.

That was it, Gil couldn't take it any longer, he burst into laughter.

"Gil, stop," Em protested between her own peals of laughter, "someone will hear you!"

Then they were all bursting, doubled over between the branches of the forest, laughing till their ribs ached. Though Gil's grin stretched from ear to ear, it was bittersweet. Images of what could have been filled his head. Days without threats hanging over their heads, days without the dread of being caught, days of normalcy. Now his future probably held nothing but cages and grief.

"Oh no."

Gil looked up, the sighs from the end of their laughing fading into the air.

"What?" he asked Mari.

Worry was etched into her crystalline features as she held

Reuben's egg out for them to see. To Gillian's dismay, a tremendously fat crack had situated itself right onto the matte surface of the egg.

Kish blew out a breath "Shit.."

Then came the pounding of footsteps.

Chapter 26

Marilyn-Jo

Marilyn-Jo shook, body rimmed with nerves, something it never had before. The egg was shaking just as much and fresh bolts of panic shot through her. Reuben's egg was hatching. Reuben's egg was *hatching*. Did she need to put it down? Mari steeled herself. She was not some shaking, blustering girl. She was Marilyn-freaking-Jo and she saw only an adventure. Except, what if she did something wrong and let her brother down? No, she wouldn't. It was an egg hatching; how much did she really have to do?

She and the others tried their best to shield themselves from sight using the branches and leaves of the trees they had situated themselves in but if the owners of the approaching footsteps so much as just looked up, they were screwed. Though they didn't intentionally, all three of them still held their breaths as the oncoming figures came into full view. Then collectively blew said breaths out when the sight of those figures' identities brought on a flood of relief. She, Gillian and Kish climbed down from the trees to meet with their friends and Gillian reunited with Jay.

"Come on, we've got to keep moving," Reuben urged them on.

"Um, quick problem, dear brother," Mari said stickily, "your egg is hatching."

Reuben blinked quickly and demanded, "What?"

Behind her brother, Mari saw Nora's thin dark brows tighten.

"So is mine," she said, her teeth gnawing on her lower lip.

Reuben took a step back and his hands rubbed the back of his neck absent-mindedly. "We still have to keep going, these dragons are just going to have to deal with a rough birth."

They all nodded sagely back to him and set off with a reborn speed. As she ran, Mari heard Nora whisper an apology to her slowly dissipating egg.

The sparse grass flew by beneath her feet and she fought not to stumble as she ran and ran and ran. The dragons flew through the air above the five of them and though the pressure of the situation was paramount, Mari still managed to grin at the sheer reality of what was happening. They were being chased by the government for stealing dragons. She had a dragon who she had some kind of emotional connection with, it was the stuff of dreams and fairy tales.

"This way!" she heard her brother yell.

They veered off to the left, dragons following as well as the sounds of their pursuers. They were never going to shake these guys, not without some kind of miracle. They needed to scare them off somehow, put up a fight, it would work better than trying to outrun them. She voiced this to her friends but Reuben shook his head, brow furrowed, saying it was too dangerous. Instead, he led them down a steep incline and practically shoved the group into a gully behind some trees.

"What are you doing?" Gil hissed.

Reuben glared and shushed Gillian aggressively before signalling them to duck down and hide.

"This isn't going to work," Mari muttered, annoyance

seeping into her tone.

"Shut up," Reuben muttered right back at her.

Mari widened her eyes. "They're going to find us, Reuben. This is stupid!"

"They will if you don't quiet the hell down, Mari!"

The barks of the tracker dogs neared as did the footsteps and Mari fought the urge to scream in frustration as she finally abided by her brother's wishes and *quieted the hell down*. This was not how she wanted to go. How did he think a gully could conceal them? Mari pushed her back against the wall of dirt behind her, trying to make herself as small as possible and attempted to stop the incessant bouncing of her knee. She had to do something. It was better than being a sitting duck, waiting for them to slap the handcuffs on her wrists. She would, she *could*, show them a real challenge.

"Let's go, Kaida," she whispered to her dragon who obediently jumped up, sensing Marilyn's nervous energy. It seemed the dragon had inherited her restless spirit. Whispered protests were uttered immediately.

"Em—"

"Mari—"

"Marilyn-Jo Breneger, you—"

Mari ignored her friends trying to get her to turn back. She was about to save each and every one of them, whether they could see that or not.

She clawed herself to the lip of the gully, clutching at handfuls of dirt as Kaida helped to pull herself up with her talons. Once she cleared the edge of the glorified pit, Mari stood up straight, dusted herself off and located the military trackers. She made sure to go a little way beyond the gully before shouting out.

She cupped her hands around her mouth. "Hey, losers! I'm

over here!"

Yelling, pointing and scurrying followed as her khaki-clad pursuers rushed over to take her.

"Now, Kaida!"

She swung out her arm to indicate to Kaida in the air and the pink dragon sent out a plume of wind ballooning towards the officers, knocking them over like bowling pins. Mari laughed; she couldn't help it. Let them see her arrogance and know she had placed her confidence well. Yet the soldiers got back up like the little government pawns they were and came back at her. And again, Kaida sent a wall of wind to knock them back but they were unperturbed. Maybe if Kaida was older or more developed in her abilities, maybe she could have made something stronger but Mari didn't want to push her dragon. As Mari's own uneasiness grew, so did Kaida and they both shifted nervously as they thought of what to do differently. Mari had screwed them all. Damn it, her idiot brother was right; like always. Why did he always have to be right?

As Marilyn-Jo mentally hit herself for her blind-sighted ignorance, she didn't notice the two soldiers advancing from the group recover particularly fast from the last blast of air. Mari didn't notice as they levelled the taser at her. Though, their shout of "Surrender!" and the gun pointed at her snapped her back to reality. The reality in which Kaida was diving down, a sleek, serpentine bullet, heading towards them. She straightened out and slammed down onto the ground in front of Mari, releasing a roar of fury as she brought both front talons down hard onto the ground in front of her. In response, A terrible mass of earth was lifted from its nest and shot upward towards the sky in spikes, throwing back the three soldiers. Mari flinched as an unmistakable crunch echoed towards her. Shouts from the remaining soldiers to retreat fell on her ears and Mari stumbled forwards in shock. She felt her dragon's rage dissipate as they both made their way to their fallen pursuer.

"Mari?"

Nora's voice was kind and questioning. Why was she being kind? Marilyn couldn't think straight. There was only the crack again and again, playing through her mind like a broken record making her flinch and flinch and flinch. The body of the soldier was laying at an odd angle, his limbs twisted in an even worse position, his eyes almost glassing over in their attempts to stay open.

"Oh my gosh!" Nora rushed past her to the body and put an ear just above the soldier's mouth.

She shook her head slowly, face filled with anguish. The others came up to join them at some point. Mari couldn't remember. Her mind was in a haze. *No*, was all she thought between the resounding *cracks* in her mind. Was he dead? He couldn't be, he *couldn't*.

"No!" she screamed, falling to her knees and crawling to the fallen man. "No, no, no, no, no. He can still live. I didn't kill him, right? Right?" she screamed at them all.

Her friends just stood there as she stared dumbfounded at the man's face. What was his name? Did he have a family? Did she just make an orphan out of a child? How could she be so, so stupid? She should have listened to Reuben but she didn't and now here she was and she had killed a man and everything was a blur and she just wanted it all to go away. How could she have ever thought this was all some grand adventure? It wasn't, it never had been. They were on the run. They were criminals. *They were the bad guys* but Mari had been too naïve and drunk on her own freedom that she hadn't even noticed it and now here she was and she had almost killed a man. She had almost *killed* a man. She maybe had killed a man. She didn't deserve to still be here. She needed to turn herself in. This man deserved a proper ceremony. With flowers and... and she didn't know what else.

Silent tears began to fall down Mari's face and she curled into a ball, eyes trained on the man's pain-streaked face, quiet groans escaping his throat. Kaida tried to nudge her arms open but Mari wouldn't let her.

A strangled sound filtered out and Mari took a deep breath.

"What is... what was his name?" she whispered.

Was because looking at the way his body had twisted and the crack that kept replaying in Mari's mind, the man may very well exist only in the past tense.

Nora herself breathed in deeply and with tentative fingers, looked for an ID badge in the man's jacket.

"Jeremy Grimes," Nora replied softly.

Mari nodded; it was all she could do. Jeremy Grimes. Jeremy Grimes. She cemented the name into her mind until it became a part of her. She had to remember him, she had to. She had to. She had to.

"Mari," Reuben took a step towards her, pity drawn across his features.

She shook her head and pulled her knees closer to her chest. She had done this.

Chapter 27

Nora

Nora looked at the others helplessly. What were they going to do now? The idyllic haze that had thus far been protecting their childish minds from anguish had shattered, making their situation much too real for comfort. Kaida continued to nudge Mari persistently. The dragon was likely very confused by the whole situation.

Nora herself was still kneeling beside the man and a raggedy breath shattered the silence beside her. She looked up. Gillian, Kish and Reuben all had identical widened eyes, as she was sure hers were too. Nora placed her index and middle finger lightly on Jeremy Grimes' wrist. A pulse. A *pulse*! Why hadn't they thought to check the man's pulse before?

"He's alive!" Nora choked.

The others let out whoops of joy and jumped around, Marilyn-Jo merely looking up from where she was curled, a faint sense of shock shivered across her features.

Nora furrowed her brow and shoved her glasses up the bridge of her nose with a frown.

"Hold on," she said, holding up a hand for the boys to calm down. "Do any of our phones still have charge?"

Without a word, Mari uncurled herself and stood up, reaching into her jacket pocket and pulling out her cell phone, garbed in a sparkly pink case that seemed altogether inappropriate for their situation.

"What are you doing?" Mari whispered, voice shaking.

Nora fought to keep her concern from her features, she knew Mari would see it as pity. Yet, Nora hated to see the girl who had become sort of an unlikely friend be brought down this way. She was always so lively, had a comeback for everything. Nothing had seemed to bring Mari down for as long as Nora had known her.

"Calling triple zero," Nora replied, taking the phone gently.

Mari nodded and stepped back, seeming to keep her eyes anywhere but the man on the ground.

"Can one of you guys stay with him and ask him questions?" Nora asked.

The boys looked at her with blank expressions.

Gil cleared his throat. "What kind of questions?"

"Don't worry," Nora breathed out, "I'll do it, can you ring triple zero and get an ambulance here?"

Reuben started. "Won't we be caught?"

"You'd rather we leave this man to *die*?" Nora shot at him.

Reuben seemed to shrink back and shook his head. Nora nodded, satisfied, and handed Mari's phone over to Gillian who wasted no time in dialling an ambulance. While he tried his best to explain their situation and location, Nora crossed her legs and situated herself next to the fallen man.

"Hey, Jeremy Grimes? Can you hear me?"

Heavens above, she hoped he could hear her. A thin rasping gasp echoed out from the man's lips and she leant forwards to hear him.

"H… he—"

He coughed violently and Nora rushed to roll him onto his side as he continued to cough up blood onto the grass.

"Can you talk to me, Jeremy?" Nora asked him.

Yet again he could barely manage to get a few syllables out before coughing up more blood.

Nora turned to Gil. "Will the ambulance be here soon?"

Gil nodded ."Should be."

Nora took a deep breath and stood up, keeping one eye on Jeremy Grimes' deceptively still body.

"You're going to have to be the one to meet them here and tell them what happened," Nora said.

Gillian's face contorted. "Why me?"

"Because you're the one they talked to on the phone," Reuben said.

"What do I even tell them?" Gil spluttered.

The others were silent for a moment before Kish spoke up.

"Just tell them that you were going on a walk and came across him like this."

Gillian frowned but nodded, nonetheless.

*

Nora listened as the sirens of the ambulance echoed through both the trees and the phone in her hand. Before the ambulance had come, Nora had used Kish's phone to call Mari's, which Gil had stuck in his pocket. That way, the rest of them could hear what was going on without being seen. They had tried to be as covered by the foliage as possible but the fact of the matter was, their real asset was the distance and if anyone from the ambulance came close enough, they would be done for. Not to mention, they needed Jeremy Grimes taken away quickly because it was a given that whoever he was travelling with would be back soon for him. They could not be there when that happened.

So, there Nora was, huddled against the trunk of a tree in a forest she didn't know the name of, holding a phone out to a group of people she had barely spoken to before a couple of weeks ago while they eavesdropped on medical workers. *Exactly* what Nora had in mind when she thought of her future. She wondered what her life would be like now. Would they always be on the run? Maybe it had been a tad brash to decide to escape in the first place. What even would have happened if they had turned themselves in that morning? Jail? But the police didn't seem to be following them, disregarding their initial attempt. That was odd, when Nora thought about it because she didn't think they would be hard to track and yet... they had not yet been caught. She could owe that much to the dragons before her.

Speaking of, Nora thought.

Her egg was taking its precious time in hatching. The others' eggs had hatched almost immediately after the first crack and yet hers seemed to be breaking apart at an infinitesimal rate. Perhaps it had sensed the commotion around the accident and slowed down its progress. It was certainly plausible given what Nora already knew of the dragon's psychological capabilities.

Gillian's voice crackled through the phone's tinny speaker but Nora hated to admit, she wasn't listening. Her eyes were trained intently on the milky white egg, thin, veined cracks running down its surface. She felt a familiar presence enter her mind.

Now? Copper asked.

Nora nodded and almost immediately shards of egg scattered onto the grass around them, out of which her dragon crawled. It was about the size of a puppy who was a few weeks old and it had the fur of one too, almost beige in colour. Though, its body was different. It was quite similar to the physique of Totem and

Jay, in the fact that it had strong legs and a long tail stretching out behind it. Two horns poked up out of the fur on the dragon's head and it's ears rested either side, like that of a deer. Two small wings, the same colour as Copper's fur, unfurled from their back and stretched towards the sky as the dragon yawned.

Nora didn't dare speak in case it came through the phone call on Gillian's end so she just thought the word, hoping Copper would hear the message.

Hello, Copper.

Hello, Nora.

Nora smiled. The dragon, well 'dragon' in the loosest sense of the term, had an angelic voice and though it had only just hatched now, it seemed an older voice than before. Nora looked up to see that the others, bar Marilyn, were watching her and her dragon. Yet their eyes shifted as they looked down to see an identical process occurring on the face of Reuben's egg. The shards split outward and from the rubble stepped a dragon almost identical Copper. It had blindingly white fur and was minutely larger than Nora's dragon, but it still had the same horns and ears and bodily structure as Copper. Nora looked to her own small creature and smiled slightly as she watched it bound towards Reuben's happily.

The beeping intonation rang out as Gillian ended the call from Mari's phone. Barely a minute later he had stepped out into the clearing. Mari looked up, without a word and Gillian nodded. Jeremy Grimes was okay. Nora didn't want to think of the *for now*, but it sprang into her mind, nonetheless. At least he was in the care of professionals. It was out of their hands now.

"I see we have some new additions," Gillian said dryly, hands resting in pockets and leaning against a tree.

Despite the expected nonchalance of the position, every

muscle in Gillian's body seemed to be pulled tight, a spring ready to snap. Jay wandered over to him and nuzzled his legs, Gillian obliging her with a scratch.

"So, are they guys or girls? Are we able to tell now, cos we kind of had Char—"

A dragon's voice filled their heads, cutting Gillian off. It was deeper than Copper's and Nora realised it must be Reuben's dragon.

We are neither.

Reuben coughed lightly and gestured to his dragon. "Um, guys, meet Zephyr."

Gillian and Kish's eyes had gone wide, not accustomed to the beings speaking inside their heads. Mari just regarded the dragon blankly. Nora tried not to wince at her expression.

"Neither?" Kish asked.

Neither, Zephyr answered.

Gillian opened his mouth to ask another question but Copper sighed loudly, well, as loud as a sigh they could only hear within their own minds could be.

No questions, Copper said.

Nora startled, it seemed her dragon had been listening in and growing its knowledge of language without Nora knowing. She swore she could see the creature smiling as if it had pulled off a lovely surprise. She supposed it had.

"That's Copper, by the way, everyone," Nora explained.

"We should probably find somewhere to sleep tonight," Reuben said, rising from the ground.

The others murmured affirmation and nodded, all in agreement. Mari was still silent, Kaida laying peacefully beside her.

They went off once again and Nora knew she had to keep

going but exhaustion seeped through every bone and crevice in her body. She didn't know if she needed the whole endeavour to be over or just a good night's sleep but she did know that she would be getting neither anytime soon. Eventually, they came across a small cave-like structure and decided it would be the best option for their stay. It looked like it would rain, anyway. It didn't take long to get situated in the cave and Nora took no time in nodding off to sleep. Though the ground was hard and the air frigid, her body needed rest more than it wanted comfort.

Chapter 28

Kish

The wind swirled around Kish, blowing specks of sand and dirt into his eyes. He could barely see, save for three figures floating towards him in the darkness. Jill's eyes were glowing yellow, as were the twins', each one clutching tightly onto one of their older sister's hands.

"No, please," Kish begged.

They only came closer as the grit flew faster and faster around Kish, getting into his eyes, his nose, his mouth. There was no escape.

"You did this," *Jill's voice scattered through the air to Kish's ears,* "you abandoned us."

"No, you don't understand," *Kish's voice was clogged with dirt and sand and poisoned air. He clawed at it, trying to redeem himself to his sisters. They all glared at him one last time before turning and disappearing into the darkness, not one more word uttered. Kish grabbed after them desperately. He had lost his sisters. He wanted to scream but nothing would come up out of his throat except a pained gasp. He stumbled forwards through the flying sand and tripped over something, earning a face to the dirt. He pushed himself up and looked down at what he had tripped over. The sand and the wind was gone now. He was back between the trees, a shift of earth jutting upward over the body at his feet. Kish gagged as he stared down, not at Jeremy Grimes but at the lifeless form of Gillian Andrews. His eyes were glassy and his body limp and pale and yet still Gillian's corpse rose up onto its unstable feet and pointed a rotting finger at Kish.*

"Your fault," it rasped.

Kish screamed.

Panting, Kish pushed himself into a sitting position, running a hand over his face with a sigh. It was a dream, *just* a dream. Sure enough, when he looked up, Gillian's very alive body was propped against the cave wall, one knee hugged to his chest.

"You all right?" Gillian asked, that familiar rasp his voice took on when he was trying to be quiet brought Kish back down to earth.

"Yeah, just nightmares."

Gil's body tensed. "Me too."

Kish glanced over at the kindling and branches he had collected yesterday evening before he had settled down to sleep. He had seen the dark clouds above them and had figured it was best to gather the wood now before it became too damp to use later.

"Want to help me make a fire?" Kish asked.

Gil seemed to hesitate before giving Kish a simple nod.

He came over gently, making his way around the sleeping bodies of their friends with care, and began to arrange the kindling in a tepee-like structure.

Kish smiled, remembering a similar occasion at the cabin. "Good to see you've still got it."

Gillian rolled his eyes. "Were you actually going to make a fire or were you just hoping that I'd do it for you?"

Kish shrugged, unable to help the grin that was plastered across his face. He felt as if he should hate that he was so transparent. He watched as Gillian expertly used the sticks to create a spark and light the fire, the flame nibbling at the edges of the kindling tepee.

"We'll add the branches later," Gil said, still taking care not to raise his voice enough to wake the others.

He crawled over to where Kish was and they both sat back, pressing their backs against the cave wall.

"What was your nightmare about?" Gillian whispered.

Kish gulped before answering, slowly, "My family."

And you, Kish didn't say. He didn't want to think about what he had seen in his dream.

"Yours?" he asked.

Gillian's head tilted and he blew a breath out. "Same but I'm sure it was in a different context than yours."

"They—" Kish began, "they were angry with me. I had let them down, abandoned them."

"Mine were chasing after me, saying I was a disgrace to the family and should have lived up to the name."

Kish turned to face Gillian, trying not to be taken aback by the casual manner with which Gillian told him. Kish raised an eyebrow and Gil shrugged.

"So, really nothing new."

"What do your brothers even do, anyway?" Kish asked.

Gil sighed. "Honestly, I'm not completely sure. Something in the military, they've told me before what they do specifically but I can't remember."

Kish barked a laugh but covered his mouth when he realised the others were sleeping, eliciting a surprising chuckle from Gillian.

"The thing is," Gillian said, attempting to be serious again, "my dad served straight after school before coming back and becoming a lawyer. Griffin and Garrett plan to do the same. Garrett is in his last year, I think and he's already lined up a few opportunities with universities."

"He's the older one, right?" Kish asked.

"Yeah, twenty-four."

Kish nodded. It seemed they both had pressures within their families, albeit quite different ones.

"Hey," Kish said, nudging Gil's shoulder as casually as he could muster, "you want some breakfast?"

Kish regretted asking for breakfast. He had no idea how to hunt and his only knowledge of bush tucker was that one Bear Grylls video he watched like three years ago. He spotted a bird, perched on a branch just to the left of him, a rabbit skittering past the bushes. Could he really kill one of these animals? It was one thing to buy meat from a grocer but this? Bile rose up in Kish's throat as he thought of Jeremy Grimes. Of Gillian's pale corpse pointing a flaky finger at him. Nope, he couldn't do this. With a sigh, Kish went to turn back towards the cave when he spotted something.

A tangled mess of thorns and leaves and dark spots was billowing out between the trees. Kish grinned. Blackberries. He freaking loved blackberries. Kish hurried over to the bush and began looking for ripe berries. There weren't many because it wasn't for another month or so until they came in season. Each blackberry Kish did find, however, he cupped his shirt into a sort of pouch and placed them in there, taking care that they didn't roll around too much. Once he was done, he was a grinning mess, a smear of deep red blackberry juice staining his tongue. He hadn't planned to tell the others he had already snuck some, but he supposed they would probably be able to tell.

Kish sauntered back to the cave, his glorious find of blackberries pushing away the thoughts of his dream momentarily.

"Honey, I'm home," he called into the rock face when he arrived back.

Nora and Reuben were awake now and were chatting with Reuben around the fire. Mari was still curled against the far wall and Kish honestly couldn't tell whether she was asleep or awake. She was taking the incident a lot harder than any of them. Although, that was to be expected, he supposed.

She blames herself, he thought.

In Kish's mind, though, it was an accident. An accident that had got him dreaming about things he didn't want to dream about, but an accident, nonetheless. These dragons were too powerful for their own good. As if his thoughts had summoned him, Totem's red head popped up from behind Kish's friends inquisitively. The dragon jumped over the fire, earning shouts from the others, and bounded over to Kish. A thin coil of betrayal entered Kish's mind and he sighed, patting the dragon's scaly head.

"You were sleeping, mate. And it's just berries, see? I'll go hunting with you some other time."

Kish knew he, himself, wouldn't do any hunting but his dragon did have needs.

"Berries?" Nora's voice floated over to him.

Kish nodded and scooped the blackberries out of his shirt and distributed them amongst his friends. Silently he padded over to Mari and held out a few of the berries.

Just as quietly she reached out a hand and he dropped them into her palm, her slender fingers closing over the fruit.

"How has she been?" Kish asked as he sat down beside the

others around the fire, Totem close behind him.

"Hasn't spoken or moved," Reuben replied, voice flat.

Kish wondered how he must be feeling. If that had been Jill or even one of the twins, Kish would have been beside himself trying to help them. Soup, cartoons, just giving them space if they want. He didn't suppose Mari could have any of that considering their situation.

The conversation petered off and Kish peered at his friends, waiting for one of them to say something.

Nora took a breath in. "We have a proposition."

Chapter 29

Reuben

Kish eyed them suspiciously, lowering the berry he was about to pop into his mouth.

"What kind of proposition?" he asked them.

Nora huffed. "Don't look so apprehensive, Kish. Look, Gillian and I are going to go into town—"

"Wait, isn't that kind of dangerous?" Kish interrupted.

Reuben watched as Kish averted his gaze over to Gillian who was already looking at him intently. There was something in his neighbour's eyes that, Reuben thought, had not been there before. He wasn't sure whether it was what he thought it was but he wished the best for his childhood friend, nonetheless.

Gillian nodded almost imperceptibly to Kish. Kish, in turn, furrowed his brow and shot to his feet, anger seeping from him like a terrible wound.

"You can't do that, that's way too risky. That lady and her army are probably in that town, you know. You'll be recognised!"

"We'll be careful," Nora assured.

Reuben wasn't game to enter the conversation just yet. He had already discussed it with Nora and Gillian. They had decided it would be best for Reuben to stay and look after Mari. Nora had volunteered to go to the town and she had said Gil should come too because quote-unquote "his ridiculous lack of a haircut is a good disguise." Irrefutable argument right there. Reuben sighed as he returned his mind to the situation at hand.

"Why do you even need to go?" Kish spluttered.

Nora shoved her glasses up before pinching the bridge of her nose. "Kish. We need food."

"I just got food!"

"We can't survive on three blackberries a day, Kish!"

"You," Kish grunted, "you guys just can't go, all right?"

He was worked up, pacing.

"I'll go instead!"

Nora huffed, clearly over with it. "We went over thi—"

"Why do you even care?" Gillian shot at Kish, joining the argument. "If you can go, why can't we?"

Kish seemed to clench down on whatever he was thinking, lips thinning into a furious line as held Gillian's stare. Reuben shifted uncomfortably as the air in the cave zapped around that stare. He suddenly felt like an intruder, despite not having said anything. Kish shook his head and just turned on his heel and left the cave, waving for Totem to follow him out.

He is angry because he feels many emotions at once.

Zephyr's voice was contemplative within Reuben's mind, so much more dignified than when it was just an egg and could resort to only screaming.

I have apologised for that.

Reuben scoffed but he thought about what Zephyr had said. Too philosophical for that early in the morning but the dragon had a point.

"You probably shouldn't make a habit of looking into people's heads, though," Reuben whispered to the furry bundle curled next to him.

It seemed to harrumph and Reuben rolled his eyes.

"We should get going," Nora said quietly, clearly taxed from trying to get her point across.

Reuben thought back to Nora's quiet nature when he had first picked her up to come on this mission and she had barely spoken to them at all. Yet, now almost two weeks later, she had just upheld an argument with Kish.

Reuben nodded. "Good luck."

Reuben followed them out to bid them goodbye but as Gillian walked ahead, Nora grabbed onto Reuben's sleeve and pulled him back. She appeared to wrestle with her thoughts, eyes cast downwards.

"Hey," she started slowly, "before I go, I just wanted to ask…"

She trailed off, chewing on unsaid words. Reuben didn't say anything, terrified of saying something stupid that would scare her and then not being able to hear her question.

"Why did you ask me to help you?"

Her eyes were imploring, so dark they were almost black and Reuben swore that if he could, he would start walking into those eyes and he would just never come back. Why did he ask her here? Because she was the smartest person he knew and she could have done all of this without any of them helping her. Because he just wanted to be near her, all the time, so badly that it physically hurt not knowing whether she was going to be okay venturing into a town of certain danger. But he had a duty to uphold with his sister and he had to stay at the cave. So, he didn't say any of that. He couldn't. He wouldn't.

"You're very capable, Nora."

Nice one, Breneger, Reuben thought to himself, mentally slapping himself around the head.

Nora nodded, chewing softly on her bottom lip.

"Well, this is see you later, I guess."

Reuben smiled wanly. "See you."

As Gillian and Nora got further and further away, the bulge of cash in Gil's jacket pocket barely perceptible, Reuben almost expected his sister to shout something obnoxious from the cave and say "Bring us back something delicious" or "You guys better not die out there."

And yet she just stayed pressed against the rock wall, silent. Reuben wished he could help her, go talk to her. He remembered one time when Mari had been really sick back when she had first started kindergarten. She had been devastated at the thought of missing school but their mother had coaxed young Mari back into bed and, try as she might, could not get Reuben to leave his sister's side. He entertained her with jokes he looked up on the family computer, brought her lemonade with a wiggly straw, sat there as she slept. He was her brother; it was his duty to do so. Now he had to do that again but... different. She was in emotional turmoil and Reuben didn't think any number of jokes or lemonade could cure that. He shifted himself into the cave and over to sit beside her, clearing his throat.

"If you need to talk, I'm here. If not, that's okay."

Kaida's feathered head poked up at his words but not for long.

Reuben caught his own dragon's eye and shrugged as he saw the question in them. He could be here for his sister and that would have to be enough. Minutes after Gillian and Nora's footsteps had faded into the distance, the glowering figure of Kish re-entered the cave.

"They're gone, you can calm down now, Kish."

Kish huffed and sat down aggressively next to the fire. He shook his head dumbfounded.

"He... I, just—"

Kish couldn't seem to form the words but Reuben could catch what he was trying to say.

"I know," Reuben said quietly.

Kish sighed and rubbed a hand through his hair, seeming to shake the matter out of his mind before bringing his eyesight to meet Reuben's.

"So," he said, a hint of mischievousness creeping into his tone, Kish happily changing the subject, "what's the deal with you and Nora?"

"No."

Kish laughed. "Oh, come on dude. It's not as if everyone can't see it. Just tell me!"

Reuben lowered his eyes, glaring at a dead beetle to the left of his foot on the cave floor. Kish waited, surprisingly patient despite the manner with which he conversed.

Reuben pursed his lips in thought before answering, "Well, if everyone can see it, then you already know."

"Aren't you going to make a move?"

No. Maybe. Reuben didn't know. It had taken him forever to realise he even liked Nora. Which he didn't, he was being absurd. They were just good friends, that was all. Reuben highly doubted Nora liked him back and so he tried his best to shove the feelings down and away. Besides, he really didn't need any romantic feelings getting in the way of figuring out how to manoeuvre him and his friends out of the hellish situation he had landed them in. And the one after that. And the one after that. Reuben was the reason Mari wasn't saying anything. The reason Nora and Gillian had to go into the den of danger just to get them food.

Reuben realised he still hadn't answered Kish but then

remembered the electric stare he had been so put off by earlier that morning.

"Aren't *you* going to make a move?" Reuben asked Kish.

Kish scoffed. "I don't know what you're talking about."

Reuben rolled his eyes. "Okay, Kish, sure."

A pause filled the air around them, though it held no awkwardness.

Kish leant forwards. "You know what I think, Reuben?"

Reuben raised an eyebrow.

"I think we're mates now."

Reuben laughed and, gosh, it felt good. He missed laughing with friends. Even before this ridiculous venture, it had been a while. He just got too fixated on projects and interests that all his friends had just slipped away, not willing to put up with Reuben's occasional anti-social nature. And though he laughed, an unfamiliar warm ache spread through Reuben's chest. Kish considered him a friend, a mate.

"Yeah, we're mates," he grinned at the other boy.

A loud thud echoed through the forest and into the cave mouth through to them and they both stopped, heads turned towards the sound.

"What was that?" Kish asked quietly.

Reuben paused waiting to see if the sound repeated. It did not.

"Probably just a tree. I'll go check."

Kish stood up simultaneously with Reuben. "I'll come with you."

"No," Reuben shook his head, "one of us has to keep looking after Mari. I won't be long, it's probably just a tree."

Reuben knew Kish was deliberating, he could see it plainly on the boy's face. Kish glanced over at Marilyn-Jo's still form and seemed to come to a decision.

"Fine. But be quick."

Reuben nodded and with a quick wave headed out to investigate the source of the thump. He headed through the forest, feet squelching into the damp earth, the sky starting to cry lightly onto Reuben, as if in a bittersweet song. Zephyr padded along beside him, occasionally using their wings to attempt a new line of flight. They were still getting the hang of their body despite having doubled in size just overnight. It didn't take much longer to reach the fallen trunk of a tree. It was irregularly split, though still not quite natural. As if someone had tried to make it look like the tree had fallen of its own accord but had missed the mark minutely. Reuben frowned and looked over to his dragon in question. Zephyr sniffed the air and seemed to start to say something but could not finish.

Two sets of hands shot out of nowhere and Reuben was being roughly handled, a third figure coming up behind him and shoving a sack over his head. His hands and feet were bound and he tried to scream but couldn't muster the breath. Reuben felt himself being tossed haphazardly into the backseat of a vehicle and tried to maintain his breathing. What the hell?

Part 3

Holsworthy Base

Chapter 30

Jenkins

Jenkins followed Jane Miller through the twisting halls of a building he had never heard of. He supposed he didn't know much more than the prisoners they had just brought in, which was just kind of pathetic if Jenkins was being honest.

"What are we doing? Where are we going?" Jenkins managed to get out as he tried to keep up with Jane's quick, even pace.

"Shut up, Jenkins."

He spluttered, indignant. "You can't talk to me like that!"

"I just did."

Her voice had taken on an even quality since they had returned to wherever they were, rid of any inflexion. Jenkins scowled at Jane, knowing that she would know exactly which finger he was showing her back.

"Please refrain from such immature gestures while we are here, Jenkins."

She turned around abruptly and Jenkins skidded to a stop, just narrowly missing bumping into her.

"You have to be serious, all right, Jenkins?"

Her hazel eyes seemed to scream the question at him and the dim lighting of the corridor illuminated her taut blonde hair in an eerie way.

"I'm always serious," Jenkins grumbled.

Jane Miller blew a breath out through her nose and attempted to release the tension, only to clench her fists again.

"No, Jenkins," she said slowly, "you're always in a bad mood. There is a difference. Just... keep your head down, metaphorically not literally, and follow my lead."

Jenkins nodded, trying his best to look solemn and not just in a bad mood as Jane had put it. He had to admit, he was a little confused why she was so wary if they were on their own turf. There were no enemies here except two teenage boys. Jenkins was fairly sure they were harmless without their stolen dragons. Jenkins supposed he should blame himself for that and yet... how could you feel guilty for messing up something you were not invested in in the first place? If he really thought about it, if he had never let those dragon eggs be stolen, he would still be sitting in that cage of boredom like an absolute chump.

"What are we doing now?" Jenkins asked *seriously*.

Jane whirled around, eyes wide. "What did I just tell you?"

Jenkins mumbled an apology and kept following her, biting down on his questions. This place would be hell for a prisoner trying to escape. The military had left the walls unadorned, bare, all the same colour. There were no vases or chests of drawers along the walls either. Though, Jenkins supposed, if the prisoner in question had a hood over their head like the ones he and Jane had brought in, then it wouldn't really matter much whether the walls were adorned or not.

Jenkins sympathised with these teenagers. Sure, he had never been chased by the Australian military or been a disgraceful hooligan but, he too, in his way, had made a rash decision in his teen years that had impacted the course of the rest of his life. Of course, for him, that had merely been choosing a university degree, not becoming a fugitive but, still.

He thought he could picture what they were feeling fairly realistically. He had taken method acting classes last year, after all, he thought he could do a pretty good job of assessing what someone else's thought processes were. Jenkins recoiled within his own mind. Was he just bragging about method acting? To himself? He really had gone off the deep end. Jenkins wondered blankly what was going on with his half-sister, had she grabbed the cat in his absence? He hoped so. He didn't want to go home to some stupid feline anyway, especially a dead one.

Jenkins saw Jane Miller's eyes scan the hallway before flinging open a door and shoving Jenkins inside. Jane swung the door shut and came to face Jenkins, who was all of a sudden confronted by the sheer intimacy this supposed supply closet forced. Images sprung into his head and Jenkins tried to tamp them down but Jane had already guessed what he was thinking.

"Ugh, Jenkins! No. That's not why we're here."

Nevertheless, Jane Miller's cheeks were flushed with pink and her eyes were averted. She cleared her throat before returning her eyes to his.

"Look, my superior is here, so that means we're not able to deal with the prisoners as we planned."

Well, that explained her rigid composure earlier.

"Right," Jenkins replied.

She breathed in softly. "You have to be careful around him, he's…"

She trailed off, trying to find the words.

"Robert Gregorian?" Jenkins supplied.

Jane leant her head back to look at him, which wasn't much considering the cramped nature of the supply closet they were in.

"Why is he even here?" Jenkins asked her.

She shook her head and reached her hand up, as if to run

through her blonde locks but stopped when she realised it was encaged within a tight elastic band.

"I don't know, Jenkins, I don't know. He usually doesn't concern himself with such little matters as these. I don't even know why you met him."

She seemed flustered, which Jenkins had never before seen in the woman. He put his hands on her shoulders as a comfort, but he quickly realised his mistake when she glared at him and he quickly dropped them. Jane Miller took a deep breath in, as if that one breath gathered all her thoughts and arranged them into a completed puzzle.

"Okay, here's what we do."

*

Jenkins squared his shoulders. He was ready. He could do this. They turned a corner and were immediately met by the towering bulk of Robert Gregorian. Jenkins was mistaken, he could not do this. Jane squared her palm on his back and pushed him forwards, urging him to keep going. Her hand fell away but Jenkins kept putting one foot in front of another.

He raised his fingers to his forehead as Jane had instructed him. "General."

Robert Gregorian inclined his head towards Jenkins in greeting but focused on Jane Miller, who had done the same actions as Jenkins.

"Sergeant Miller, who are these?" he said, gesturing to the boys tied up against the wall.

Jenkins hoped they were sleeping, he didn't wish upon anyone having to be awake in the presence of Robert Gregorian, then you would actually have to experience the fear. Although, he supposed *Melissa* probably wouldn't mind being awake with him, considering she was his wife after all. It really was a shame about that but Jenkins had just come to the conclusion that he was going to die alone. No big deal.

"Prisoners, General."

General Gregorian heaved a breath and said slowly as if explaining to a particularly dumb child, "But who are these prisoners?"

"Reuben Breneger and Gillian Andrews, sir."

General Gregorian leant back, satisfied. He made his way deliberately over to the teenagers' slumped bodies and with one quick but rough movement, removed the hoods from their heads. Their eyes looked up; dazed expressions painted across their young faces in bold strokes. Dark circles rested under both boys' eyes and they looked thin, as if they hadn't been able to get enough food in a little while. Was that why the dark-haired one and the girl that had managed to get away had been leaving? To get food?

A surge of guilt swept through Jenkins. He hadn't cared before; he barely knew them but now he could see just how young they really were, how much of their lives could have been left to stretch out before them. Jenkins didn't want to do this any more. He didn't care if he lost his job. He looked to Jane, unable to hide his distress but she just mouthed one word, "Wait."

He could do that, he could wait. Maybe they could help them. But as Jenkins looked at Robert Gregorian, he knew in his soul that that was highly unlikely. As strong as his regret and guilt were, his fear of the military general was far greater.

Chapter 31

Gillian

Gillian fought not to let his fear show. Fought not to feel the fear. He took deep breaths in through his nose, out through his mouth. He had always thought that mindfulness, breathing exercises and stuff were pointless but now, as the bag over his head had scratched his face incessantly, he realised he needed it like a dying man needed water. A towering mountain of a man stood before them, peering down his nose with contempt. Tattoos snaked around his huge biceps, hands tucked behind his back military-style and Gillian couldn't quite discern the man's expression. He had heard the woman call him General, he was ranked high it seemed.

"What are your names?" he barked at them.

Wow, okay, straight to the point then, Gil thought sarcastically.

"She just told you," Gillian said with a mock matter-of-fact attitude, inclining his head towards the woman behind the general.

The man seethed and he crouched down to meet Gillian's eyes. Gillian was determined not to squirm, he merely levelled his gaze at the man; he would not be cowed. Not by this brute.

"You trying to be funny?"

Gillian raised his eyebrows.

"Funny doesn't run well here, boy."

Gillian had no doubt the man was telling the truth, his face was completely devoid of humour.

"Good thing I'm not funny, then," Gillian said promptly.

The slap came hard and fast, the bulky man's palm colliding with Gillian's cheek almost immediately. The pain flashed through Gil's cheek and throbbed.

He spat out the blood that had flowed into his mouth and cast his eyes to the floor. "Gillian Andrews... sir," he added.

The man stood back up and regarded Gillian with cold, black eyes.

The eyes of a beetle, Gil thought.

"Andrews? You related to anyone in the military, boy?"

Gillian almost scowled. "Yes, sir."

A moment passed as the general peered down at Gil.

"Not going to tell me? Fine. I'll get it out of you later." He moved over to Reuben. "And you? What's your name?"

"Reuben Breneger," Reuben replied flatly, though Gil could hear a vein of fear running deep within his voice.

The man seemed to chew on their names silently and Gillian averted his eyes to the two figures behind him. He thought he had seen some pity in Mr Jenkins' face but, once again, the man had done nothing. He was a coward, Mr Jenkins. An old, bitter coward. The woman next to him, though, looked alert. Gillian wasn't sure if they would have a friend or a foe in her but despite the latter being most probable, he couldn't help but hope.

"And you are?" he said, dragging his eyes back to the man who had slapped him.

He merely shot out a short, mirthless laugh. "You don't need to know who I am."

He flicked his hand, a clear signal; take them away. Four men emerged from the corners of the room to untie Reuben and

Gil's ankle restraints and shove them through the hallways. The blonde woman and Mr Jenkins led the eight of them through the building until, eventually, Gillian's handler pushed him roughly into a cell, Reuben into an identical one beside him.

"Where are we?" Reuben asked the blonde woman.

She just looked at him and walked away, taking the rest of the others with her. Gillian scoffed and Reuben looked over, puzzled.

"What?"

Gil shook his head, chuckling ruefully. "Nothing."

"What?" Reuben asked again.

"Drop it, Reuben, I'm not going to talk about this stuff with you."

"What stuff?" Reuben turned to him, incredulous.

Gil sighed and leant his head against the brick wall, black hair hanging down in loose curls.

"Just... I only came along on this thing for Em and now..."

And now he was locked up. What had started as a crush that was going nowhere had turned deadly. All those romantic feelings that Gil had held onto for years were suddenly just not there any more. He had known he held no chance and he had accepted friendship but all these years he had stubbornly maintained his feelings for his best friend because they were *comfortable*. And now, now he was a fugitive and nothing Gillian felt made sense any more. His head was just a mess of confusion and avoidance strategies.

"I know you don't like her like that any more," Reuben said softly.

Gil turned to him in alarm. "What?"

He didn't have any words. The boy before him baffled Gillian sometimes. He was so anxious and awkward in social settings and yet his perception skills for determining one's emotions was almost scary. Although, Gil's feelings for Em *were* the weakest point in the wall he kept around his emotions and were usually quite discernible. He smoothed his surprise at Reuben's bluntness and settled back against the cell wall, not even looking at Reuben when he coolly said, "Wow very perceptive, Reuben."

"Wow, way to use sarcasm to avoid talking about anything of importance," Reuben shot back.

Gil's lip curled, if Reuben wanted a fight, Gillian was only too happy to oblige,

"Oh, that's rich, coming from you," he replied.

"What's that supposed to mean?"

Gillian scoffed and rolled his eyes. "Reuben you never talk to anyone about anything."

Reuben opened his mouth to say something but Gil cut him off and kept talking.

"Because you always shove everyone away and then act hurt when they don't hang around to put up with all your crap. Is this enough 'talking about anything of importance' for you, Reuben? You know you're even doing it to Mari, your *sister*, and she keeps sticking by you!"

"I do not do that," Reuben protested.

Gil laughed humourlessly. "We used to be friends, Reuben, good friends. Do you remember that?"

"You ditched me for my sister."

Gil shook his head. "Whatever."

Reuben stood up and came to the bars between their two cells. "You know it's true."

Gil bit his cheek and sprang from the ground coming to meet Reuben at the bars. There was anger in Reuben's hazel eyes as

Gil was sure was in his own green ones.

"No, Reuben. I didn't ditch you for Em. She hung out with me when I got tired of waiting for you to come out of your shed. And you know what, I think you almost actually deserve all that's happening right now because at least it got you to actually leave that stupid bubble and do something with yourself!"

Reuben glared at Gillian, not moving. Gil's chest was heaving as he took huge breaths, trying to fill his lungs with air. Reuben turned away and Gil instantly shrank. The anger took a step back and an uneasy feeling snaked through his stomach. He shouldn't have said those things. Yes, he had been hurt by Reuben abandoning them when they were younger but that was a wound long since healed. Gil's arms came across his chest and he too turned away, choosing to hold onto the anger, an easier task than admitting his guilt.

The blonde woman from earlier rushed into the hallway outside their cells and gazed at the boys with disappointment.

"Seriously, can you guys keep it down? We have work to do, you know."

She gestured out of Gil's line of site and a burly man clad in military garb came and manhandled Reuben out of his cell.

"C block," the woman told the burly man.

Reuben didn't look back as he was taken away and Gillian tried not to flinch as the woman gave him a quick glare before she left promptly. As Gillian leant against the wall, closing his eyes and rubbing his forehead in frustration, a wave of Jay's emotions washed through him. She was distressed, he could tell that much. He just hoped she had got away with Nora and Copper when Gil had been taken.

Chapter 32

Marilyn-Jo

Marilyn-Jo groaned as Kaida's feathered head butted continuously into her side. She swatted at her dragon to go away but Kaida was relentless. Grumbling, Mari uncurled herself from against whatever she had been leaning on and sat up. A rush of dizziness overtook her and, with it, a wave of memories. A bone snapping; a body thudding to the ground. Pale skin, glassy eyes. Blood on *her* hands. Mari's breathing was suddenly too fast, too shallow and she needed to get away from herself.

"Hey, you're awake," Kish's voice floated over to Mari and she looked up.

Her eyes were wide and her breathing still came with difficulty but she was glad she wasn't alone. She scooted over to the fire Kish had prepared but didn't stretch out, instead remaining in a ball as if she could contain herself and prevent herself from hurting anyone else. Kish held out his hand, once again filled with blackberries and Mari obediently took some to nibble on. Her stomach had growled a little too much for her liking over the couple of days she had secluded herself.

"How are you feeling?" Kish asked gently.

Mari simply shrugged softly. That was the problem. There wasn't just one emotion she could pinpoint, not even sure if she was feeling anything at all. She was numb save for the plagues of guilt washing through her every minute. She glanced to the mouth of the cave where the sun was already dipping below the horizon as if soaking the last available minutes of the day into the sky in hues of pink and orange. Where were the others? Mari didn't think it would have been the best idea to split up. Kish must have seen the shift in her gaze because he spoke up again.

"Nora and Gil went to the nearest town because we needed food," Mari could sense the barely restrained resentment beneath Kish's clipped words, "and Reuben left to go check out a sound."

Mari's brows knitted together, unsaid questions about what happened wanting to escape her lips but she couldn't make herself speak.

"I don't know," Kish said, rubbing a hand over his face, "that was ages ago. I should have gone to go see if something had happened but I didn't want to leave you here alone."

Marilyn-Jo pursed her lips and considered it. The sentiment was nice but as she looked around, she realised she probably would have been fine. Kaida was with her and Mari was willing to bet the dragon wouldn't leave her side and if Kish was really worried, he could have told Totem to keep an eye on her.

Distantly, Mari thought of how pre-incident her would have reacted to what Kish said. She probably would have been mightily offended. Now, though… well, all she felt was a faint acknowledgement of Kish's reasoning. Mari glanced out towards the expanse of trees and wondered where her brother was. They needed to find him. His being away for so long could not be a good sign, especially considering the disappearing light.

Kish sighed. "All right, you want to come with me to check it out?"

*

Mari peered around herself cautiously. They had been wandering the woods around the cave for about fifteen minutes and still no sign of Reuben. They hadn't dared yell out his name in case whatever had caused his disappearance was still hanging around and they wanted to be alert. The same terrain stretched for kilometres out from where Mari was standing, just trees and grass and rocks and more trees. Somewhere out there was where she had almost killed Jeremy Grimes. The snap of bone and the thud of a body. His rasping voice. Mari doubled over, falling to her knees, faintly registering Kish rushing over to her. Unconsciously, Mari's hands went to her head as if trying to pull the horrid memories out. It kept replaying and replaying and replaying and—

"Mari!"

She looked up.

"Mari, can you hear me?"

Kish's persistent voice broke through and she nodded slowly, inhaling deeply. The images threatened to replay again but she stood up anyway. She took more deep breaths. And she didn't try to push away the memories as hard as she wanted to, she focused instead on staying on her feet. Keeping her arms at her sides. Breathing at a normal pace. She could do this; she *would* do this. Because, right now, she had to find her brother, people were counting on her.

Kish touched her shoulder gently. "You okay? Do you need anything?"

Mari shook her shoulder and tried her best to give Kish a convincing smile. He smiled back but it came across more like a grimace. The rushing of footsteps wafted through the trees to the two of them and Mari tensed. Kaida moved protectively in front of her. A shot of earth reaching towards the sky. Kaida's roar.

The snap of bone. Mari shook her head, physically trying to clear the thoughts from her mind. She tried to slow her breathing again and clutched her stomach as if afraid she may be sick. Mari tried to tell her dragon to stand down, but she didn't think any words seemed to come out of her mouth. It was going to happen again. Mari was cursed.

A figure burst through the leaves and branches, panting. Her brown skin was glinting with sweat and her fingers clutched her knees vigorously.

"Nora!" Kish ran over, worried.

"I'm fine, I'm fine," Nora waved for Kish to step back and only then did Mari notice that Gillian was no longer with her.

More so, both Jay and Zephyr had arrived with Nora.

Kish frowned and Mari could tell they were having identical thoughts. Where were Gil and Reuben?

"Is Reuben with you guys?" Nora asked fervently.

Mari shook her head and Nora spat out a curse, causing both Kish and Mari to recoil.

"Woah, what's going on, foul mouth?" Kish said, his joking demeanour doing nothing to lighten the mood.

"It's Gillian. He was taken," Nora said.

Jay seemed to twitch uncomfortably behind Nora as the words were spoken.

"What do you mean *taken*?" Kish asked slowly, despite the panic setting in.

"That blonde lady from before, Jane Miller or whatever, she and Mr Jenkins just jumped out of nowhere and grabbed him."

That's absurd, Mari thought.

How could he have been caught so off guard? Granted, they were all sleep-deprived and laced with hunger but surely two people couldn't have just *grabbed* him.

"Do you think Reuben was taken too?" Kish asked.

Nora pursed her lips, her face etched with worry, before nodding slightly. "That's probably the case."

Kish scratched the back of his neck absent-mindedly and muttered something indistinguishable.

"How'd you get away?" Kish asked.

Nora took a breath. "Copper and Jay were trying to fight off the rest of Miller's squad, so there weren't any people able to grab me. Then I ran."

They fell silent, the wind moving softly through the trees around them.

"What now?" Nora asked quietly.

There it was again. That question. It seemed to plague them wherever they went like an assassin. *What now. What now. What now.* Had they ever had a legitimate answer?

"Well, we're going to have to rescue them, somehow," Kish sighed.

Nora nodded and Mari knew she had likely already put the beginnings of a plan together and was just waiting for confirmation from Marilyn-Jo and Kish. Mari fought not to fidget under the stares of Nora and Kish as they looked her way expectantly. She wanted to rescue her brother and her best friend, she really did. But... how would she be of use? She would just slow them down when every second sound or shadow that jumped out at her would send the images and the crack of bone rushing back into her head. She would be a liability.

"I can't do this, guys," she said quietly, weakly.

Nora started towards her but Mari held up a hand.

"No, please, I'll only drag you down. Take Kaida, she can help."

Mari half turned before adding, "If there's anything I can

help with, I'll be back at the cave but I think… I just need to be alone for a little bit."

They nodded but Mari could easily read the pity written into the lines on their faces and she knew they would be back to argue the point with her eventually. She hated the pity, loathed it. She wasn't supposed to be weak, to be felled so easily. What was worse, she used to never stop moving. Fidgeting, running, doing some sort of activity whether to stimulate her mind or body. And now… she couldn't bear to move or think too hard lest it bring her to her knees. And it made her feel slow like she was stuck in wet earth, unable to shift her weight. With that, she walked away from her friends and prayed that they would be able to free her loved ones.

Chapter 33

Reuben

Reuben still seethed from his conversation with Gillian. With each echoing stomp of his footsteps as he was led away from the cell, the anger increased. How could Gillian say something like that? Ridiculous.

"Would ya calm down?" the guard escorting him said, annoyance dripping from his every word.

Reuben looked at him, confused.

"The stomping is a bit excessive. Like, just apologise to your mate and you'll be fine."

"I think that might be a bit hard since that could very well have been the last time I spoke to him."

"Oh yeah, right, prison and all that," the guard chuckled.

Reuben rolled his eyes. The guard eventually brought Reuben to what he saw was labelled 'C Block' and pushed him into the cell, surprisingly gentler than whoever had done it before.

"Right, here you are, mate. Let me know if you need anything."

With that, the strange guard just strolled away, whistling. Reuben looked around the room with distaste. There was barely anything within the small square cell, a thin mat on the ground with a blanket and a toilet in the corner. He wondered blankly whether this prison block had been brought up to code recently.

With a huff of breath, the adrenaline of his rage ran out of Reuben. He knew Gillian was right. Reuben barely ever left his shed, too caught up with whatever had snagged his interest. Reuben hated to admit such a thing but he knew he had subconsciously been looking at their situation through the same tinted glasses. Just another project. Just another fixation for him to puzzle out.

Yet it had proven time and time again that that was not the case. A man had almost died. Who knew if the hospital could even save him? Reuben had thrown away his friends' chances at the lives they had wanted. His classmates were probably undergoing the rest of their exams at this point, probably almost done with them. Reuben wondered what he would have done with his life if he had never picked up a dragon egg. If he had never gone to that abandoned airport. Maybe become an engineer, he had never really figured it out despite his mum and his teacher's constant worrying remarks.

Reuben, where have you gone?

Zephyr's voice was draped in the guise of calm calculation but streaks of panic were creeping their way into the dragon's inflexions.

Reuben sighed. "I don't know, I'm sorry."

Zephyr's distress seemed to grow infinitesimally and Reuben frowned in turn.

"Don't worry about me, all right? I'll be fine."

Zephyr seemed to give a *hurumph* sound, clearly not impressed with Reuben's seemingly blasé attitude. The dragon didn't say anything else and Reuben hoped they were helping his friends. Maybe Reuben would get out of this place. He didn't want his friends to endanger themselves, though. Mari probably shouldn't be doing anything involving prison breaks or heists or violence. The last time Reuben had seen his sister, she had been like a delicate piece of glass, on the precipice of shattering. *Delicate.* Reuben never thought he would *ever* use a word like that to describe his sister. She was headstrong, stubborn, bubbly. And if she broke, she joked about it. Not this time, though. Not this time.

"Oi, you!" A shout came from somewhere outside of Reuben's cell and his head snapped up, instantly alert.

The guard from earlier drifted into view, hands in his pockets and body somehow resting lazily on a lean.

"Oh, mate, you should have seen your face," the man laughed.

He rubbed at the stubble of his chin and chewed thoughtfully. "Anyway, I need ya to come with me, boss man wants a chat."

"Boss man?" Reuben asked slowly.

"Yeah," the guard said as he unlocked the cell door, "ya know, the top dog, apex predator, General Gregorian."

Reuben got up wearily and didn't move as the guard slapped a pair of hand cuffs over his wrists.

"Nothin' personal mate, just don't want ya escapin', ya get me?"

Reuben raised his eyebrows and nodded, indulging the man with feigned interest. The guard once again led him down hallways, paying no heed as to whether Reuben was listening to the endless stream of chatter spouting from his mouth.

"Have ya seen the new guy?"

Reuben suddenly jolted back to attention and peered at the man walking him down the corridor.

"New guy?"

"Oh mate," the guard chuckled, "you should see him, just

floundering around, like Sarge's little lapdog."

"Who?" Reuben asked again.

"I don't know, Jenkins or something. No idea what he's doing here at Holsworthy, he's got no qualifications or nothin'."

Holsworthy. Did this man just give away exactly where he was located? He needed to tell Zephyr. Zephyr could tell the others! Reuben hesitated. He didn't want them coming after him unless they had an airtight plan. He knew Kish would want to rush in but Nora would be more cautious, she could be the voice of reason… right? Reuben decided he would tell Zephyr later, there was no rush. Plus, maybe in the meantime he could try and find the cracks in the defence base's seemingly impenetrable security. The first break in the monotony of the hallways Reuben had seen thus far loomed ahead and Reuben gestured for the guard to stop. They came up to the window and Reuben peered out, unable to stop the look of ghastly terror from crossing his face.

Four rows of growing dragons were arranged across a courtyard, one to two soldiers clad in military uniform alongside each dragon. Both dragon and human stood at attention, eyes fixed on the commander at the front of the courtyard, methodically issuing commands in a booming, authoritative voice. As each order was shouted out, the dragons moved with their soldier counterparts into a new position, every so often arranging an attack. Reuben could see dragons resembling the scaled fire-breathing ones of Kish and Gillian and the snake-like forms of feathered dragons much like Marilyn-Jo's. There were none of the furred, horned dragons like Zephyr or Copper. However, Reuben could see different ones too. One dragon was covered in quills like a porcupine, wings like a bat's stretching above it's back. Then there was one that was built like an absolute tank, muscles stretching beneath taut leather, eyes glowing an unnatural red.

Reuben looked away. He had to get out of there. *How? How do I get past those things?* Was this what the government had really been breeding these dragons for? To fight in their wars, to take more lives, demolish more land? Protect people? Reuben supposed it could go either way. These dragons could change the world. Whether it was to save the innocent or to cause their demise was entirely up to whoever commanded their ranks. A shiver ran down Reuben's spine and he realised that it had been like this, nonetheless. Power still sat in the hands of those in charge, who had the decision of whether to cause great good or great evil. Instead of nuclear warfare, now they had dragons *too*.

"That's our new training regime," the guard explained. Reuben didn't think he had imagined the nerves trilling the man's usually so casual voice. "They're only lettin' the boys who have been here for years to train with the creatures. Ya know, the ones' that're really dedicated to all this. I try not to look at 'em for too long, mind you. Freaks me out."

As they moved farther away from the window, the guard seemed to relax back into his usual state, the fear of the dragon courtyard dissipating slightly. Although, the rest of the trip passed quickly and in silence. They came to a plain, silver-grey door and the guard escorting Reuben rapped promptly on the door thrice.

"Come in," General Gregorian's voice carried haughtily through the door.

The guard swung open the door and deposited Reuben in a cold metal chair, a clear match to the cold, metal table that lay between him and the army general.

"Thank you, Reid. Dismissed."

The guard, Reid, turned and left but slow enough that Reuben and Gregorian caught him muttering resignedly, "Why does no one call me by my surname like everyone else?"

Gregorian rolled his eyes. "Because you have a stupid surname. Now... *dismissed*."

Reid left for good, grumbling something that was, this time, incomprehensible. Once the sound of his footsteps had faded, the general moved his eyes slowly, deliberately, to face Reuben. Reuben did not fidget. He never did. He only met the man's eyes and made himself breathe evenly.

"Reuben Breneger, correct?"

Reuben nodded.

Gregorian inhaled deeply and steepled his fingers. He looked as if he were about to say something but instead stood, scraping back his chair, with his back to Reuben.

"Now tell me, Mr Breneger, who put you up to this?"

Reuben frowned across at the general's back.

"Up to what?" he asked.

General Gregorian swivelled around and smiled. It was a smile that radiated... *something*. It wasn't warm. No, it was nuclear. It was a nuclear smile that was about to blow Reuben into a million little pieces.

"This," Gregorian gestured around him, "stealing the eggs, compromising *my* operation. Who made you do it? Why *you*?"

Reuben supposed he should have been offended by the insinuation in that last word but he was merely amused. This man was furious, though concealing his anger well, that a teenager had been able to send a screw into the cogs of what he had thought was a well-oiled machine. Reuben thought about whether he should tell this man the truth. Would he be able to accept it? Mari would have messed with him a little. Nora would have twisted the question in some way, gaining the upper hand. Gillian would have offered up some sarcastic remark. But Reuben wasn't any of them. He was himself and the truth was the only tale he could tell.

"No one," Reuben replied flatly.

The general narrowed his eyes as Reuben sat there, waiting for the next question.

"Who are you?"

A loaded question. Who was he? Reuben Breneger. A teenager. A loner. A brother. Any of these could have been the answer. But Reuben voiced none of them. When he didn't answer, General Gregorian merely scoffed and slid back into the chair, leaning his elbows onto the cold, metal table.

"Why did you steal the eggs, Reuben?"

The man said it softly, like a father conversing with his son after the son had made some mistake. Reuben didn't fall for it. He hadn't needed a father before and he certainly wasn't going to be fooled by this excuse for a man trying to get Reuben to trust him.

"Why not?" Reuben said crisply.

"Why did you steal the eggs, Reuben?"

The same question. The same answer.

"Why not?"

Of course, at the time Reuben had thought he'd had a dozen reasons to do what he did. He told himself that in the days afterwards, trying in vain to ease his own anxiety and guilt. But what had slipped out now was the naked truth. *Why not?* He had lived, really *lived*, more in these past few weeks than he had in his entire life. Most people didn't get that. Ever. So yes, *why not?*

*

General Gregorian had spent what Reuben estimated to be roughly two hours questioning him. Reuben had told the truth. Well, as much of the truth as he wanted to admit, that was. After that, he had merely shoved Reuben into the corridor and trusted that one of his lackeys would escort Reuben back to the cell. Sure enough, the guard from before, Reid, was waiting just outside. Reuben wondered how much of the "chat" he had heard. Before long, Reuben was back in his cell with nothing to do but think. And pace. And think. And think. And think. And think. This was why he had always had a project; it occupied him, kept him away from his thoughts. Reuben scoffed at himself.

I'm pathetic, he thought, *afraid to be alone with my own mind*.

It's not like he didn't like to be alone. He loved that. But he was always doing *something*. Something that didn't leave room for him to think about every little mistake he had made or was yet to. The fight with Gillian filtered back into Reuben's flying vortex of thoughts. He supposed Gil had been right. They all were. He did get too invested, he pushed everyone away. Often, he didn't mind pushing them away. It was too hard trying to talk to people and figure out how to act around them and not overthink so much that he had to ask them what they said twice more because he had got twisted up in his own thoughts and hadn't heard. He didn't want to do that any more, push people away, that is. Reuben realised that these people, the ones he had dragged into this experiment, were his friends. The only friends he had truly had in years. He didn't want to lose that.

And he didn't want to lose Nora.

The minute Reuben had met her, he knew he was slipping down a steep slope and crazily, he wanted to fall. Headfirst, all in. Every time she laughed, the rock beneath him crumbled. Every time she met his eyes he felt as if the very air around him had disappeared. Every time *she*. Reuben was getting lost, slipping and slipping, he knew that. But if being near her did truly mean being lost then Reuben would abandon his compass. If her smile were the sun, then he would be Icarus. He didn't care that his wings would melt if only he could be close to her.

He needed to tell Nora this. All of this. Would she think him crazy? Would she think him pathetic for such pining? Would she…

Reuben tamped down the possibility of *what if*.

If she didn't reciprocate his feelings, he would be fine. He respected her too much to not be. But on even the slightest chance that she did, Reuben needed to get out of this blasted prison cell somehow. Somehow.

Chapter 34

Kish

Kish was thinking about nothing.

At least, he had been until he had fallen asleep and the nightmares had returned. He seemed to be cursed with plagues of images of his dead loved ones, pointing their decaying fingers at him in a horrible guilt trip. Kish was determined not to let the dreams follow him into the world of the conscious, he had too much to do. Rescue Gillian. Rescue Reuben. Keep an eye on Mari. Make sure Totem didn't start any more fires.

At the moment, Nora was pacing thoughtfully, a finger waving around in the air as she mouthed words to herself. Kish merely sat with his back against the tree, four dragons arrayed around him, all five of them watching Nora pace. Kish wondered if interrupting her thinking would be like waking up a sleepwalker; in other words, a bad idea. The eerie voice of Zephyr floated into the forefront of the teenagers' minds. The dragon had grown even quicker than Totem, Jay and Kaida had. All four dragons surrounding Kish were the size of a decent family car.

They are located at Holsworthy.

Kish shuddered at the sound of Zephyr's voice in his head.

"Holsworthy?" Nora asked, stopping mid-stride. "Where in Holsworthy?"

The white dragon didn't offer up any more details and Kish

wondered how the creature had obtained the information. Holsworthy was near where he and the others lived, maybe he could visit his sisters. Give himself some peace of mind. The others could visit their families too, they would all be discreet. It could work... if they actually managed to figure out where their friends were being kept.

"Is there a military base in Holsworthy at all?" Nora mused, a furrow appearing between her brows.

"That would make sense," Kish answered.

Nora gave him a look as if she had forgotten he was sitting there entirely.

"Or maybe..." she tapped her chin restlessly, "could they have taken them to a safe house? Are they high profile enough?"

"A prison?" Kish suggested.

"Aren't Gil's brothers in the military? Did he tell you anything about that?"

Kish shook his head and Nora grunted in frustration.

"We need a map!" she declared.

Kish himself had the thought that they could have just opened up maps on their phones like any normal freaking teenager but they weren't normal freaking teenagers any more and his stupid iPhone 6 had run out of power like a week ago.

"Where are we going to get a map?" Kish asked wearily.

"A town," Nora said as if Kish were a very small child that needed to have the obvious pointed out.

"Would there not be more of that Miller lady's squad in the nearest town waiting to get us too?"

Nora paused for just a moment

"We send the drag—"

"Absolutely not," Kish said, rubbing a hand over his forehead.

"You can't just shut down every idea I have, Kish. We'll get nowhere," Nora said pointedly.

"Okay fine," Kish conceded with a sigh, "say we get a map. Where would someone *here* have a map of Holsworthy?"

Nora frowned and the crease in her brows became even deeper as she resumed her pacing. She seemed to mutter to herself as she did so. Kish merely leant back and tried not to let the images from his nightmares re-enter his thoughts.

She sighed. "Maybe we just ask for directions to Holsworthy and then once we're there, we get a map."

"Or we could just ask where it is?" Kish suggested.

Nora threw her hands up. "My bad, Kish! I'm so sorry I didn't see what was clearly so obvious! Oh, wait. That's what I just said!"

Kish waited, lips thinned, eyes slightly widened. He coughed a little, awkwardly.

After a moment, he asked hoarsely, "You good, Nora?"

She sighed. "I don't know. I just don't know what to do any more, Kish."

Kish watched as Nora folded onto the ground, her face slashed with confusion and indecisiveness. Kish had never seen this side of Nora before, she had always seemed to have an idea of what was going on. Kish wondered if the next step had always come easy for her. He knew it had for him, most of his life. Take care of his sisters, finish school, get a paid apprenticeship. Easy and simple. Now he was just taking whatever was happening one step at a time. Maybe he needed to get Nora to think that way too, it certainly looked as if her thoughts were running in overdrive, telling her what *might* happen all the way up to twenty years in the future.

Kish stood up and moved over to her, shaking her shoulder

just softly to get her to look at him. Her curls had turned almost completely to frizz and dark circles rested beneath her eyes, smudged glasses teetering on the bridge of her nose. Kish wondered whether he looked this tired too. Probably.

"All right, here's the plan," he said. "We head to town—"

"What about Mari?"

"We'll stop by the cave and let her know. Who knows, she might even want to tag along. Sound good?"

"Yeah, okay, I guess."

A pause and Kish went to go and start back towards the cave when he heard Nora breathe in and in a quick rush of words, asked him, "Well, what about when we get to town? What do we do then?"

Kish spun on his heel and looked Nora dead in the eye, willing some of his calm into her.

"Let's worry about getting to the town, first," Kish said steadily.

Nora nodded but she chewed her lip absent-mindedly, surely running through all the possibilities of what could happen.

Chapter 35

Marilyn-Jo

Marilyn-Jo trudged through the brush sulkily. She wanted to help; she really, *really* did but... how much help could she really be if every twig snapping reminded her of the incident? Nora and Kish would rescue her brother and Gil just fine without her, they didn't need her. And though she had offered up Kaida's skills, Mari was grateful they had said no. She didn't think she could stomach being *completely* alone. Plus, there was little chance Kaida actually would have left her if she was really able to read Mari's feelings.

Mari made her way back to the cave as quietly and cautiously as she possibly could, words she had never cared to attribute to herself. With every step she took, a voice nudged her saying, *Go back. They need you. Go back.*

But then she would remember the way she had collapsed and she would continue on. A rustling echoed through the branches surrounding her and Mari whipped her head around, fearing repeated history. Nets shot seemingly out of the air and Mari tensed, eyes widening. Fear that was not hers coursed through Marilyn and she whipped her head around to where Kaida was collapsed on the ground, the dragon crisscrossed by nets and lead weights trapping her against the ground.

Mari tried to scream out but Kaida screamed instead and bucked her head as if urging Mari to run and get away. She didn't.

She just stood frozen, staring at the scene unfolding. She couldn't do anything. At all. Kaida bucked again and roared at her and just as the figures who had surely cast the nets began to move towards Kaida, Marilyn-Jo turned and she ran like the coward she had become.

*

Mari wished she would cry. Her brother was gone. Her dragon was gone. Her best friend was gone. And here she was in the middle of some random bushland, unable to find the last two people on this earth she might be safe with. Any normal person would cry but as much as she wished she would, Mari merely let the thoughts rush around her head as she gnawed on her lower lip in panic. The people who took Kaida were probably right on her tail. She had to move. Now. Mari glanced around her and stretched her neck, trying to listen for anyone nearby. She was glad she did as out from the thicket drifted two bickering voices.

"What do you mean where did *I* leave the cave? I didn't leave the cave anywhere!" The voice was agitated and male and... vaguely familiar? Though something was off, maybe a little higher than usual?

"Well, I can't find it!" a female voice replied.

Mari recognised that voice. A grin stretched her features, a grin of relief that her friends and had found each other. She rushed towards where she could hear their bickering.

"Nora! Kish!" Mari whisper-shouted as she neared them.

The two teenagers whipped their heads around and Mari could swear Nora literally sagged in relief as she enveloped Marilyn-Jo in a hug that could have ground bones into bread.

"Oh my gosh, Marilyn-Jo Breneger, where the hell were

you?" Nora breathed out, her voice devoid of any agitation.

"Woah, watch your language there," Mari managed a little chuckle.

Kish leant forwards in disbelief, his eyes wide. "Did you just… laugh?" he asked.

Mari shrugged. She could make an effort to be normal, at least, even if she still felt far from it. Kish grinned and it seemed to have a domino effect because a toothy smile broke into Nora's features as well. The four dragons ambled up behind Mari's friends and a pang of sadness zipped through her for Kaida. How had Reuben and Gillian managed to get taken but their dragons hadn't? If their dragons were free, why didn't they stop her brother and best friend from being taken? Mari shook herself of the feeling and forced a ready smile onto her face.

"All right," she said, "what's happening now?"

"Well," Nora said with a sigh as she pushed her glasses back up onto the bridge of her nose, "we were going to try and find a map."

"A map?" Mari asked.

Nora nodded, lips stretched thin and Mari could tell she had been worrying far too much.

"A map of what?" Mari prodded.

"Oh!" Nora seemed to come back to herself and Kish smacked her gently on the shoulder.

"Seriously, Nora? You had one job, *one* job," Kish tutted.

"Shut up, Kish. Anyway, Zephyr told us that they're in Holsworthy."

"Holsworthy?" Mari asked.

"Dude, you have to stop repeating the last word of whatever Nora just said," Kish pointed out.

"Sorry," Mari shook her head and tried to clear her thoughts.

She needed to be focused and not let the lingering memory of Jeremy Grimes stop her from doing the things that she needed to do. People needed her and if she walked away, that nagging voice would come back. And this time, Kaida wasn't there to keep her from the pressing loneliness. She did not want the voice to come back. She *would* stop her friends from getting hurt.

"How does Zephyr know that they're in Holsworthy?" Mari asked.

Both Kish and Nora merely shrugged and Mari guessed that was that; they were to just accept the dragon's word. That seemed about right.

"So, we're getting a map of Holsworthy and... what? Is there something in—"

Mari's eyes went wide in the middle of her sentence and she stretched her hand into pointing to the air excitedly, not pointing at anything but waving around in anticipation.

"I know where they might be!"

The others crowded in around her as if they held a terrible secret and none must hear them. Of course, they were surrounded by only a seemingly endless expanse of trees and dying grass and well, no one had ever known the grass to carry secrets.

"All right," Marilyn-Jo spread her hands as if a businesswoman presenting a *very* important idea, "when we were about eleven or twelve, Gil's dad took us to Holsworthy—"

"Sounds fun," Kish interrupted dryly.

"Shush, we don't have time for sarcasm, Kish—"

"Gillian would disagree, I think."

"Oh my gosh, what do you not understand about 'shush'?"

Mari stared at Kish and he backed down, forcing a somewhat awkward chuckle.

Mari continued. "Okay. As I was saying, you guys know

how Gillian was expected to follow in his dad and brothers' footsteps and join the military, right?"

Nora shook her head but Mari plunged on anyway.

"So, it was kind of a tradition in the Andrews household to take each son out to visit the military base in Holsworthy before high school. Gil asked if I could come and, eventually, Mr Andrews obliged."

"So, you think they're being kept at the base?" Nora supplied.

Mari nodded and the others grinned at her. They finally had something to go on. Marilyn-Jo had helped them find Gil and Reuben and probably where Kaida was being taken as well, she had helped. They wouldn't need her any more; she could go back to the cave and wallow in self-pity and guilt until they came back. But that nagging voice from earlier scratched at the back of her mind, telling her to keep going. Keep helping. At least, maybe, if she pushed through, it could distract her. And she couldn't hurt anyone by herself, right? She had made Kaida hurt Jeremy Grimes. Mari by herself was just a slight sixteen-year-old girl from Sydney. She couldn't hurt anyone... Hopefully.

*

Kish, Nora and Marilyn-Jo had started walking towards the town not long after, at least in the direction they thought the town was. Mari trusted Nora would know the way, she exuded the confidence of the kind of person that knew things like that. Before the bustle and business of the little suburb started, there was a general store leading into it, on the side of the road. They had decided that that was their target; they had managed to work out a whole plan on their way over.

After they had walked about halfway, Nora had stopped abruptly, causing Kish and Mari to glance at each other in mild confusion. Nora had whipped around to face them, forcibly bringing her muttering thought process to a halt.

"Copper," she had addressed her dragon out loud, "to what extent are your telepathic abilities?"

The dragon, too, had allowed them all to hear, *I am able to communicate like this. And I should be able to… how do I not say this crudely? Force people to do things?*

"Yikes," Kish muttered through his teeth.

Mari looked to the still growing lean, furred bodies of Zephyr and Copper. If possible, they were growing at an even quicker rate than the others had. Mari had half a mind to assume that that had been the point. As if they had made the progress of growth while inside the egg but hadn't the room to do it and so, had grown incredibly fast once outside the shell.

Copper sat down and tilted their head; *I do not know whether I am able to do that yet.*

"Do you want to try it out now?" Nora asked.

Yes. However, I don't believe it will have much effect on you, Nora, for you are too used to my communication.

"I'm sure Kish is happy to be your test subject,"

"Hey, no, wait a minute," Kish stammered.

Mari saw Nora give Kish a glare, trying to be subtle and failing. She knew that glare. The glare that said it couldn't be Nora and Mari was too *delicate* after the incident to help out. Well, no. Maybe she had accepted that fate an hour ago but she didn't want to wallow. Marilyn-Jo was *not* a delicate girl. She had never been and she never would be. Or at least, never again.

"I'll do it."

Nora flicked her gaze around with concern at Mari. "Are you

sure?"

"Yes, I'm sure," Mari rolled her eyes.

Nora, in turn, narrowed her own. "Don't you roll your eyes at me."

Mari rolled her eyes again, somehow reminding herself of Reuben. Her brother had made far too bad a habit of the action and had annoyed their mother to no end.

Mari faced the dragon, its horns having grown and curved slightly, looking as if to resemble a ram's when fully grown.

"Do it," she said.

Copper seemed to fidget a little, an awfully human action for such a creature.

I'm not sure how well it will work. I have never done this.

"Okay," Mari said, shrugging.

Maybe whatever the dragon did up there would make her forget about the incident. Or at least take her mind off the sound of cracking bones for just a moment. When Copper's voice re-entered Mari's conscience, it was different. Lilting, angelic, *persuasive*.

Walk to that tree, Marilyn-Jo.

Mari *almost* did as the dragon said. But it wasn't enough. It was like she was flitting between two planes of consciousness. One where her mind was blissfully empty and she merely did as told and the other where real life hammered in from all sides and her mind was an incomputable mess.

Walk to the tree.

A haze settled over her thinking. Everything was okay. She was okay. She just had to walk to the tree and then there would be peace. Absolute peace. Mari turned and lifted a foot as if about to do just that but at that moment, the haze lifted abruptly and Mari crashed back into her own thoughts and feelings.

"It didn't work," Nora said, the dejection slashed plainly across her face.

Mari and the dragon both seemed to be equally downcast about the result.

"Hey," Kish pointed out gently, "Copper is only like a week old, right? We can't expect too much of them yet."

He laughed, if a little mirthlessly. "I mean, Kaida had been alive for *at least* a week and a half when the um…"

Kish trailed off, looking unsure as to whether he was able to joke about the incident yet.

Mari steeled herself and willed it to be okay.

"I mean, he has a point," Mari said to Nora.

Kish's face fell with relief and he smiled slightly at Mari, she returned the small smile. They were in this together, all of them. They had to have been since the first moment they had left the Breneger household. Goodness knows what would have happened to Mari if she had gone by herself. Terrible things, surely.

Nora rubbed the crease between her forehead and pursed her lips in thought.

After a few seconds, she looked up and frowned not unkindly at Copper. "What if you combined your efforts with Zephyr? I'm assuming they have the same capabilities?"

Without warning, Zephyr and Copper's voices seemed to blend and surround Mari's mind.

Walk to the tree, they commanded.

Their voices had risen to a power while twisted together and this time, even as Mari tried to fight their instructive force, she still walked to the tree. When she reached the tree, their power seemed to fall away from her and Mari was returned to reality.

Wait.

The haze returned and Mari merely stood there, her mind content and rid of all worries. Her one desire was just to *wait*. Stand by this tree and wait.

"Stop it now, please," A soft voice ordered from somewhere in the other world.

The world where Mari had to worry about things and her mind was no longer her friend. She didn't know what the voice wanted to stop but it should learn to be like her, content and waiting.

"Copper, *stop it*."

The voice had grown more persistent and Mari wondered blankly why it was in such a fuss. Life required no such agitation.

"Copper!"

Just like that, the haze was ripped away and Mari stumbled from the sheer force of it. Nora rushed forwards and caught Mari's frail body with concern wrought in her every muscle.

"Mari, are you okay? Answer me, please."

Mari nodded and looked up at Nora in confusion as she straightened up. "Yeah, of course. Why?"

"You looked like one of those wax statues," Kish's voice was hollow, "lifeless."

Nora turned to Copper, anger writhing quietly beneath the surface of her maternal nature. "You will *never* do that to any of us ever again, you understand me? You put Mari in real danger there, you know that? Someone could have come along and we wouldn't have been able to get her to move. No, I'm not finished, Copper, don't you dare interrupt me. I am glad that you and Zephyr are able to pull it off but we do not want anyone in a state like that forever, so please, have mercy when you think you must be merciless. Otherwise, you will make us all liable for atrocities I don't even want to think about. And you do not want that."

Copper had seemed to wither under Nora's stare and laid on their stomach as if submitting and acknowledging Nora's command. Zephyr did the same.

"Thank you."

Nora turned away and her own eyes seemed to glaze over lightly, Mari guessed she was probably talking to her dragon privately now. Mari wished she could extend a message to her own dragon. She could feel the push of that Kaida's fear and Mari just wanted to ease her stress. All things going well, she could do that soon enough. All they had to do was rescue two teenage boys and a dragon from some military base in Sydney. Sounded easy enough despite the rope of unease coiling in Mari's stomach.

Chapter 36

Nora

Now that Nora had determined the telepathic capabilities of Copper and Zephyr, they could finally move ahead with her plan. She explained said plan quickly and precisely to the others and hoped they understood her hurried explanation. The dragons would need to stay hidden but have Zephyr and Copper within close enough range to be able to use their telepathic method of persuasion. Kish would be on the lookout, presumably keeping an eye on Totem and Jay in case they started any more fires, Nora and Reuben's dragons would be too focused on their own task to cause any trouble.

Be careful. Copper's voice floated towards her.

Nora merely nodded. They didn't need much from this little corner store, merely food and water and, well, anything else they came across that may prove pertinent to the rescue. Nora doubted the store had many relevant supplies anyway.

She, Kish and Mari were almost at the store now and Kish gestured for the dragons circling lightly in the sky above them to come down. He led them around to the back of the building where, if everything went as planned, the owner would not pay a visit while they completed their mission.

"You ready?" Nora asked Mari, willing her nerves to settle so she could ask the girl genuinely.

There seemed to be a war happening within Marilyn-Jo, she

was clearly reluctant about doing all this but there was that same, old grit inside her. The one that had been painted as charismatic and bubbly when they had first met but Nora knew now was pure, unfiltered determination.

After a quick intake of breath, Mari nodded vehemently. "Yes. Obviously."

"All right. Then," Nora herself heaved a breath and shook her hands as if trying to expel the nerves. "Let's do this."

As they crossed the corner, Mari whispered to Nora, "Should we have grabbed disguises or something because right now it seems that this is either very cocky or just very, very dumb."

"Or both," Nora muttered before pushing open the door in a burst of defiance.

The cashier looked up, a look of confusion crossing her face before she smiled brightly, though falsely, and readjusted her posture.

"Welcome! How can I help you both today?" she asked.

Mari immediately began a string of words, lilting her tone and giving eye contact at just the right moments as she made her way to the cashier. Nora had seen Mari flirt with practically everyone back at school so this simple human interaction shouldn't be too hard a task. She hadn't wanted to put Mari in a position that would require violence. Hopefully nothing today would require violence but... still. While Marilyn-Jo distracted the cashier, Nora began perusing the shelves. They didn't have a can opener so all these cans were out of the question. Besides, Nora didn't think *any* of them would enjoy Spam, even whatever they were feeding Reuben and Gillian as prisoners was probably better, in Nora's opinion. Chips were good but the sodium was too high and they would move through their water too fast as a result, Nora knew she needed to find something that would sustain them.

She knew this is what they should have done at the beginning of all of this mess but they had been in such a rush to leave Reuben's house that they hadn't bothered to pack anything. And now, Nora stank like the sewers down the road from her house, the thought caused her to shudder at the state of her hygiene. Were Reuben and Gillian actually getting to shower? Heavens, Nora missed showers. Even a clean river would be preferable to her current state. Following her own thought process, Nora grabbed a couple of spray deodorants off the shelf. She continued to walk around the shelves, the sound of Mari and the cashier's chatter acting as white noise.

Nora was glad the cashier was a girl around their age and not some middle-aged man because then, they probably would have had to use the dragon's telepathic abilities more than they already were. While she was still in the same aisle, Nora grabbed a couple lighters. It seemed like a good idea, though she wasn't entirely sure how many more fires she would need to start without the help of a dragon. She headed to the next aisle and grabbed a few more food items off the shelf before snatching a case of water bottles and heading up to the cashier girl and Mari. The girl didn't seem to notice her approaching at all and she wondered whether she could literally just leave unnoticed but she needed a bag and there weren't any for sale on the shelves. Nora cleared her throat and the girl looked up startled and then gave a somewhat passive-aggressive stare when she realised why Nora was up there.

"Hi, um, could I grab a bag, please?" Nora asked, eyes shifting to anywhere but the cashier's face, feet not staying still as much as she willed them to.

The cashier rolled her eyes and grabbed one from beneath the bench and handed it over to Nora. She seemed as if about to jump right back into her flirtations but then remembered the actual requirements of her occupation.

"You gonna pay for that?" she asked coldly.

Nora chuckled nervously. "Yes, of course, um, I'll just put these in the bag first."

Now, Nora thought frantically, *Now, Copper, now, now, now, now.*

Merely moments later as Nora dropped the final item into the little plastic bag she saw the cashier's eyes glaze over slightly and a thin smile rested on her features.

"Have a lovely day," she said sweetly.

Well, that was quick, thanks.

There was no reply from Copper and Nora assumed they were too busy handling the cashier girl.

"All right Mari, it's time to go."

They began to turn back but Nora quickly spun around and placed some money on the bench from her pocket. It wasn't much since she herself wasn't in possession of most of the large amount of money Gil had taken from his parent's cabin. But she had had a bit of cash on her and she felt bad just *stealing* it outright. Funny, that she got cold feet about the concept of stealing now.

She and Mari waltzed out the door and as they rounded the corner to the back of the building, Nora noticed the baseball bat swinging from Mari's fingers.

"Uh, Mari?"

She looked up innocently. "Yes?"

"Why do you have a baseball bat?"

Mari paused. "Well, I'm not going in unarmed and it's not like they sold guns or knives or anything."

It made sense but Nora wished Mari wouldn't just assume she would have to hurt someone when they went in to rescue the others. She didn't want to make her do anything like that. Hell, she didn't want to make herself hurt anyone more than she had to. But if she did have to, to rescue the others, she would. She had no doubt about that.

"I'll be fine, Nora, don't worry about me," now Mari was the one looking concerned and Nora indulged her in a smile that seemed to make her a little less tense.

They came around the back to see Kish leaning against the wall. He glanced up when he saw them approaching.

"Why d'you have a bat?" he asked, frowning

Mari huffed. "Oh my gosh."

Kish held up his hands and laughed. "All right, don't tell me, then."

Nora clapped her hands together and smiled as the two of them quickly raked their eyes back to her. Nora wasn't proud of what they were going to do next but they had all agreed it was the only way they could get to Holsworthy safely and in time.

"Time for phase two," she breathed.

*

"Go!" Nora yelled.

The air was rushing through her hair, making more knots than she was happy about. The tires screeched and the cashier girl's shouts were following them still.

"Can this stupid car go *any* faster?" Nora shouted at Kish.

He only responded with a yelled grunt and revved the accelerator harder. The car was beaten up and severely old but it sped along the potted road as if running from the forces of hell itself.

"This seems like a bad idea!" Kish yelled over the roar of

gravel beneath them.

Nora grimaced as Mari almost hurled in the back seat.

"The only bad idea," she yelled back, "was letting you drive!"

Kish swerved the car and they went down a side road quickly, the car tilting dangerously to the side.

She wasn't sure this was the best decision she had ever made but when it was put into perspective, all she had been making lately was bad decisions. Heavens, she even enjoyed some of them. Plus, that kid at the corner store would get a new car at some point... hopefully. How else were they supposed to get to Holsworthy? A plane? Out of the question. Walking? Absolutely freaking not. A car was the only way and since they had so ceremoniously lit Kish's van on fire and left it behind, the only available option left was for them to become thieves. Again.

Unfortunately, they had not been able to fit the dragons in the car. Totem and Jay were bigger than Kish's old van by now, roughly twice the size of this battered Commodore they were in, height and length. Zephyr and Copper were only about half that size, being a week younger than the others. Nora had taken too few moments recently when she had properly marvelled at the rate the dragons had grown. She had no idea what the government had been brewing the creatures for but evidently, they wanted them in action almost immediately.

The problem of the dragon's blaring conspicuousness had proved difficult to the planning of this getaway. They may as well shoot up a flare gun and yell for the military to come running if they let the dragons fly above them. Yet, they couldn't go in the car with them and walking would be just as bad, if not worse. Nora didn't want to push her dragon too much but she had requested of them if they were able to divert the eyes of anyone passing. She didn't think it wouldn't take too long as they took the back roads up to Holsworthy but it certainly wouldn't be quick.

They had driven at such a breakneck speed for as long as the little car could muster, which, it turned out, wasn't very long. Eventually, Kish managed to ease up on the accelerator and went at a more respectable pace. Nora could tell now that they were making some actual progress as he was getting antsy with each passing kilometre. But they were all antsy, they were tired and hungry and simply put, Nora just wanted her friends back. The sun seemed to have given up on the day and was sinking beneath the horizon. Nora glanced over and found that Kish's eyes, like hers, were beginning to droop.

"I think we should probably stop for the night," Nora proposed.

Kish nodded and the only response she got from Mari was a yawn. In turn, Kish pulled over to the side of the back road they had been on for the last half hour and continued to roll the Commodore a little way into the surrounding bush. She didn't know how he had managed to spot a gap in the foliage in the twilight but he had and she was grateful he did. The car came to a halt slowly and Kish flicked the engine off. Though he ran a tired hand through his hair, Kish climbed out of the car and leant against the hood, Mari and Nora following suit. They all watched as the four dragons came gliding in from the pink and orange streaked skies. It was as near to that from a fairy tale that Nora almost had to take a step back from it in shock. She had been too wrapped up in the scientific marvels of the whole thing and her own dire reality that she hadn't even realised the surrealism of the situation they were in. If only her younger self could see her now.

Zephyr and Copper came down last and Nora rushed over as soon as she realised their stumbled landing.

"Copper! Careful! Are you guys all right?" she asked, brows furrowed as she fussed over the collapsed dragons.

The dragons turned their eyes to Nora and all Nora could read was utter exhaustion. She had pushed them too far.

"Sleep," she told them, "sleep, sleep."

The dragons merely closed their eyes in response. Totem and Jay were still standing but they too looked pushed to the brink of exhaustion. Kish nodded and they folded themselves down onto the ground to sleep.

Nora met the eyes of Kish and Mari, still by the car. Without speaking, they all seemed to be in agreement; they were sleeping outside tonight.

Chapter 37

Kish

"How, exactly, does one break into a military base?" Kish asked promptly.

After two days of rest, they had all decided it was time to get back on the road again.

"With great difficulty," Mari piped up from the backseat.

Kish had been worried for her lately but he was glad she seemed to be on an upward climb now. Of course, he would never really know how she was going but at least she was talking and moving and even occasionally *laughing*. He had no idea what had changed but this appeared to be the Mari Kish had become used to over the past month. Kish didn't think the girl was usually silent when things happened until the incident with Jeremy Grimes had happened. He just hoped she wasn't repressing anything that would come out later.

Kish had often worked through emotional exercises with his younger sisters. He wanted to set an example that wasn't drowning yourself in liquor or abandoning your troubles when they got in the way. It had taken Kish a while, himself, to figure out how to regulate his feelings healthily and he still often got it very wrong, but he was open to trying new things. Anything to distract him from the rage that coursed through him every time he thought about his dad sprawled on the couch at five in the afternoon or glimpsing Derek drop his mother home after not

Kish hadn't seen her for days. Plus, Jill, Sasha and Lydia deserved better. He never wanted them to feel alone or scared or...

Kish's thoughts fell. He supposed he had done that, hadn't he? He had abandoned them, the exact thing he had vowed he would never do. Kish already kind of knew that but the thought had left him for a moment. He shook his head slightly and forced his mind to focus on what Nora was saying.

"Okay, but we really need to figure out a more airtight plan than Kish's."

"Hey," Kish said, "I don't see anything wrong with Totem and Jay just setting the place on fire."

Mari coughed. *"Arsonist."*

Kish swatted at her and she ducked, giving him a look that clearly said *you know I'm right*.

Nora sighed. "Guys, please. We need to figure something out."

Kish actually wasn't the one driving for once, Nora had offered to take up the wheel. Kish suspected it was merely some way for her to cope with not feeling in control. She had been murmuring things and then starting to propose ideas and then lapsing into silence the whole way. It was a slightly disturbing cycle, in Kish's eyes. Although, he himself was struggling to come up with a way to break into a military base and rescue Gillian and Reuben. Kish didn't like that almost the last time he had seen Gillian had been as a corpse in his dreams. He almost thought they needed someone on the inside, to account for their presence there. The problem was, Kish suspected they were all on the lookout for the three of them and... well, there was the potential of even *more* dragons in the base.

They really hadn't thought this out. But hey, they could

worry about thinking things through *later*. Nora groaned from the front seat and Kish returned to the present.

She tapped the wheel. "If Gil were here, he could probably tell us about the base—"

"But he's not," Mari interrupted, "so we need to figure this out by ourselves."

"Do you s'pose they have big meetings frequently? We could use that as a distraction," Kish suggested.

"A distraction," Nora said slowly, her eyes shifting into focus that Kish knew wasn't entirely on the road.

No, she had an idea. He could see it. It was probably an idea that would land them in a jail cell or dead, but really, wasn't that what all their ideas had been up until this point?

*

"Frick."

Kish gazed nervously at the base from afar. It was a sprawling mass of oddly sized buildings and shouted orders drifted on the late morning air over to Kish and his friends. The dragons were poised on the grass behind them, nowhere near at ease as they too watched the bulking shapes of what Kish presumed were other dragons, the little specks of their handlers moving alongside them within the courtyard. They had only been able to see this much due to stopping on the crest of a hill some way away. Anyone else looking from this far away may assume the figures were merely military vehicles but Kish knew better. There was no way a military vehicle could move like that, *no way*.

The base looked impenetrable. Not in that *Mission Impossible*, Tom Cruise can do it kind of impenetrable but *real life* impenetrable. Instead of feeling backed down by its sheer size, Kish felt emboldened. And maybe that was actually really stupid but he wanted his friends back and he had told himself he would rescue any loved one if they ever were to be taken or in danger. That was all there was to it, Kish wanted them back so he would get them back. Probably. And Nora herself had been adamant that she had, in fact, come up with a plan. Kish doubted any plan was possible when it came to Holsworthy barracks but he also knew not to underestimate Nora and was sick of trying to fight off the adrenaline coursing through him. He needed to harness it somehow and going on a reckless mission into a military facility seemed as good a way as any.

Although, that being said, Nora had given him only the barest form of a plan. Earlier that day, they had purchased – well, stolen – a map of the surrounding area. That turned out to be absolutely useless so they had turned to Google at the local library, which also turned out to be pretty redundant. It was almost as if the military were *trying* to stop people from easily breaking into their barracks. So, Nora had resorted to guesswork and plain logic. After that, they had come to this very hill and set themselves up with as expansive a view of the base as possible. Mari had found a notebook and a couple of pens in the back of the girl's car they had stolen, so they had taken turns jotting down the notes of the guard rounds they could see.

The guards at the front gate would stay from four till seven then switch and head over to man the main courtyard till ten. On the next rotation, they headed inside to the outer ring of buildings, staying within them till four o'clock again. Kish could only assume that they guarded the main hallways inside for another three hours until the night batch of guards came out.

It hadn't taken much explaining for all three of them to

figure out that they would need to slip in during that quick window of time when one group of guards left the front gate and before the next came. The next problem on their list was the cameras. If they merely took out the cameras, those inside the base would be alerted and he and his friends would be goners, immediately arrested.

"Reuben and Gil will most likely be kept near the centre of the base, to make it a longer way to go for anyone trying to get to them. AKA us," Nora said now, pacing the top of the hill.

Copper was trailing her heels, now sizeable enough that they could most likely pick up Kish or any of the others here and carry them off through oblivion.

"We're not going to have much time to get from the meeting area to the cell blocks—"

Nora was cut off as a sharp ringing sound pierced the air around them. Kish frowned and watched as Mari confusedly pulled out her sparkly, pink phone. She gulped and Kish knew she too was remembering the last time they had had to use that phone.

"Unknown number," Mari said quietly as if whoever the caller was could hear them through the ringing.

"Should I answer it?" She asked, voice hollow.

Kish and Mari turned to Nora, waiting for her to answer as she bit her lip indecisively.

"No," she said, nodding her head in her decision, "let it go to voicemail. If you answer they may be able to trace the call and figure out where we are. Of course, if they've already got your phone number, then they could probably track it anyway. But it's best to be safe in any case."

Mari nodded and set the phone down on the grass, pointedly ignoring its blaring colour. Several times over the last few days,

Kish noticed Mari flinching at sharp sounds or merely withdrawing within herself for varying amounts of time. He was worried but he could tell she was making an effort to not let it overtake her. The ringing finally petered out and just moments later the buzz of a text message appeared on Mari's screen.

"What does it say?" Kish asked.

"It's a voicemail," Mari said.

Silence settled among them during which Nora stepped towards Kish and Mari.

"Are you going to play it?" she asked.

Mari came back to focus. "Oh. Right. Yes, yes."

She swiped onto her phone and played the voicemail, setting it to speaker. A gravelly burst of static hit their ears and an intake of breath was heard through the phone's tinny speaker as if the caller was not sure how to approach what they wanted to say.

"What are you doing?" a muffled, male voice filtered through the voicemail.

"Shut up, Jenkins," a strong, female voice, closer to the speaker and louder.

The caller.

"You're going to get fired!" Mr Jenkins' voice was still muffled but more persistent.

All three of them rolled their eyes as they heard him speak. They quickly regathered their wits, though, as the woman began speaking again.

"Look, I know you kids have no reason to trust me, given that I've been the one in charge of tracking you down and bringing you to a cell but… you have to believe me when I say I thought we would just be disciplining you. You know, maybe you'd get a bit of jail time but now my superior has turned up and I don't know what's going to happen. I don't trust him and I want to help you guys. I get it if you don't trust me but I want to help."

"That was stupid."

"Literally just stop talki—"

The voicemail cut off and the three of them merely sat there in shocked silence. Not one of them wanted to trust the woman but they didn't voice one word. After moments of what seemed to be an eternity of pondering and trying to speak, Kish finally broke the silence.

"Nora, you actually met her, right? That woman?" he gestured half-heartedly to Mari's phone, hanging limp in her hand.

Nora nodded and seemed to come back to herself. She pushed her glasses back up the bridge of her nose as if forcing herself to think.

"Yes."

"Does this seem like a trap?"

Mari scoffed. "It sounds exactly like a trap. She's literally the one in charge of arresting us."

Neither Kish nor Nora answered her. Kish knew it sounded very much like a trap; he didn't doubt that at all. The only thing was, they needed to get inside the base and at the moment, all the information they had was this sketchy view from the top of the hill.

"What if we asked them for something?" Kish proposed slowly.

"A trap," Mari interjected immediately.

Kish held up his hands. "Woah, slow down. Hear me out, all right? We ask for a something, *as a test.*"

"Like what?" Nora asked.

"Like…" Kish shut his eyes to think before clapping and turning to the others with a grin, "what if we asked them to bring

Gil and Reuben out into the courtyard so we can see."

"If we did that, we may as well just ask them to bring Gil and Reuben to us," Nora pointed out with a frown.

Well, she had a point there. Although Kish knew they needed to test Jane Miller and Mr Jenkins in some way to determine their trustworthiness. Maybe they could never trust them. Maybe they just go ahead with their original thinking. Then, as Kish was about to voice another opinion, the wavering *ding* of a text message split the air around them. Kish and Nora frowned in the direction of Mari and she shrugged. Kish waited patiently as Mari opened her phone up and scanned the message.

"It's a map," she said slowly, as if not yet comprehending the image on her screen. Kish and Nora shuffled over on the grass to sit on either side of Mari, both craning their necks to peer over her shoulder. The screen was lit up with a glaringly white blueprint of the barracks below them. Kish scanned the sprawling expanse of boxes on Mari's phone screen, trying to take in as much as he could.

"Do you think this is a trap?" Mari asked, her sureness deflating the smallest amount.

"We'll have to compare the map and the base over there, of course," Nora said.

"There're barely any labels on here," Kish pointed out.

The others nodded and they broke away slowly from the knitted crowd around Marilyn-Jo's phone.

"Tomorrow," Nora said decisively, "we go in. For better or for worse."

Chapter 38

Marilyn-Jo

Marilyn-Jo breathed in, trying to even her breaths as they threatened to quicken and debilitate her. She swung her stolen baseball bat into the palm of her hand, trying to use the steady thump of wood against skin to soothe her rattling nerves. She closed her eyes for a mere moment and willed herself not to fall each time she saw someone in the same uniform Jeremy Grimes had been in that day. When she opened them again, she made herself follow Kish and Nora down the hill to the first point of the plan. They were hidden behind a little rise where they would stop until the change in guard. She still would have preferred asking Miller and Jenkins to bring the boys out to them but Kish and Mari were persistent about doing it themselves.

Mari set off with the others as soon as the first set of guards were far enough away. Ahead of the three of them, Totem and Jay were approaching the gate's cameras from their blind spots, leaning up on their haunches to not directly short fuse the cameras, but merely fog the lenses with their heated breath. As soon as the creatures dropped back down, Mari and the others rushed forwards and made it to the gate.

"How do we get over?" Kish asked, confused.

"Just wait," Mari told them, tapping her foot.

A moment later, the gate swung quietly open and they slipped inside, the dragons slinking behind them.

"Mari…" Nora said and Mari was reminded of a mother leading slowly to a chastising.

"What?" she said, feigning ignorance in the hopes of blowing off the question.

"You kept messaging them, didn't you?"

"I don't know what you mean."

"Marilyn-Jo."

Mari huffed. "Well, we're in, aren't we?"

Nora sighed and pushed her glasses back up her nose before pinching the bridge.

"Fine," she said, "but you do realise it's more likely they'll stab us in the back than genuinely help us?"

Mari didn't answer and merely waved her and Kish over to the back door of the first building on their left. It was a rectangular block, the first of three identical rows across and four down. She tried the doorknob and just as Jane Miller had explained yesterday, the door drifted open, unlocked. Mari darted in, gesturing for the others to follow her quickly and leaving the four dragons, dreadfully conspicuous, standing unsure outside the doorway. Mari chucked the military uniforms at Kish and Nora and they fumbled to catch them.

"Mari…" Nora warned yet again.

"Don't worry!" she assured. "We can blend in a lot easier with these."

Mari was careful to keep her voice low and tried to reassure the others as much as possible. She was sure Kish was fine with it, he was practically bursting with the need to get on with things. Nora looked unsure, though. Mari felt a little bad for upending this part of the plan but she was fairly sure there was no physical way for them to get it done without the help of Mr Jenkins and Jane Miller. Had Nora really thought that they would be able to wander around the base until they found the boys or someone caught them? The latter was far more likely without the help that Mari had acquired for them. Plus, they should be thankful. Mari had drained her phone battery for this.

Marilyn-Jo pulled the uniform up, over her clothes trying not to think of the snap of bones still so prominent in her mind since the incident. She wouldn't cause that kind of harm here; she *couldn't* cause that kind of harm here. Plus, anything she would do, she would do in self-defence and none of that would equate to the injury Jeremy Grimes had sustained, she wasn't physically capable of such things without Kaida's help. She wouldn't be able to hurt anyone, she willed it to be so.

"Jane is going to meet us here and take us to the others," Mari said, trying to spur as much confidence into her words as possible.

The others nodded, Kish bouncing lightly on the balls of his feet as Nora faintly chewed her bottom lip. A minute later, a short rap on the door echoed through the shipping container-like structure they were in.

Mari bounced forwards to lean over and peer through the peephole in the door.

"Is that her?" Mari mouthed to Nora.

Nora rolled her eyes and looked through the peephole, before sighing and yanking open the door.

Jane Miller narrowed her eyes and Mari fought not to shrink against her gaze. The woman was borderline terrifying and yet on Marilyn's right, Nora merely straightened her shoulders and looked down her nose at her.

"Fix your hair," Jane said crisply as she tossed a can of hairspray at Mari and hair bands at Nora.

Mari raised her brows and Jane merely gestured to her own,

slicked back hair; blonde strands pulled painstakingly tight into a bun at the base of her head.

"You didn't bring a hairbrush," Nora said flatly and Mari fidgeted uncomfortably.

Sure, this woman had been the figurehead of their anti-goal for weeks now and Nora was undoubtedly right for not completely trusting her but their tight-lipped glances were creating enough tension to pull a rope taut. And tension in the air meant tension in Mari. And tension in Mari meant awkwardly blurting out things and fidgeting constantly.

Jane huffed and held up the hairbrush dangling from her hands. "If you want to not get caught, I advise you to sharpen your skills of perception."

Nora snatched the hairbrush and began to attempt to pull her dark curls into a ponytail. After a while she just handed the hairbrush to Mari and pulled the hair into one of the hairbands. Mari turned away and began to brush her own, starkly different thin hair into a ponytail. She curled it into as tight a bun as she could manage before coating the whole thing in hairspray so thick it looked like fog.

"Um, do I need to be doing something?" Kish asked, uncertainty lacing his words.

"Hold on a minute," Jane Miller said.

Just as Nora was finally wrangling her hair into a bun and hair spraying, complaining about the lack of hair gel, the door opened once again. Jenkins walked, hunched, into the room, carrying a battery-charged razor. Mari began to giggle as Kish's eyes widened.

"No," Kish said slowly, hands going to his head.

Jenkins shoved the razor into Jane's hands and went back to lean against the wall, glowering at them all.

"Do we have to do this?" he asked Jane with a rather pathetic-looking scowl.

"Yes."

"Why?"

"Because we're good people, Jenkins," Jane replied with a huff, "at least, I am. And you're going to do it because I'm the only reason you're still here."

"Touché," he grumbled.

Jane returned her gaze to Kish and he let out a sort of whimper as she stalked towards him with the razor.

"Do I have to?" he asked quietly.

Mari was still giggling at his reaction but she forced herself to stop and pat him somewhat reassuringly on the shoulder.

"Don't worry, Kish, I'm sure you'll look great mostly bald."

Nora snorted.

"I'll look like an egg!" Kish whined.

"Do you want to rescue your friends?" Jane asked.

There was no hesitation when Kish replied affirmatively. Jane didn't even respond; she merely clicked the button on the front of the razor and let the buzz fill the air. She shoved Kish none too gently onto his knees so that she could reach his head, he was at least half a foot taller than her, if not more. Just like that, she sheared the razor across Kish's scalp. Chunks of his matted hair fell to the ground repeatedly as Jane continued to shave his head clean of hair. Once she was done she smacked his head lightly to get him to stand up. Kish rubbed a hand over the stubble of his head and looked at the others in some kind of awe.

"I'm one of *those* kids, now," he muttered.

"What?" the others replied simultaneously.

Kish waved his hand at them in disregard. Mari took a deep breath; it was finally time. They were about to rescue Gillian and

Reuben and Kaida. Nora would go after Reuben, Mari after Kaida, obviously, so Kish had been left with getting Gil. Mari sensed he didn't mind that much. Jane Miller and Mr Jenkins had explained that offering small bits of assistance were all they could do; they didn't want to do too much lest they lose their jobs. Mari didn't want to push it too much since Jane had already seemed incredibly reluctant for Marilyn-Jo to rescue her dragon. Something about the integrity of one's occupation and duty to country but also trying to uphold one's own moral values at the same time... it had all been a blank of white noise to Mari as she had tried to listen and failed miserably as she got distracted.

In any case, she had something to do now.

Jane pursed her lips in thought before she turned to them and asked formally, "Would you like the guns now?"

"Excuse me?" Nora asked at the same time as Kish coughed and spluttered, "What?"

Of course, Jane Miller had already warned Mari about this but she was still so unprepared for when Jane just went to a cabinet on the side of the room and pulled out a pistol in one hand and a rifle in the other.

Mari had been opposed to violence for as long as she could remember. Yes, she loved cool swords and blades but guns, to her, were disgusting. They were ugly and they were used to do ugly things. She did not want to carry a gun. Otherwise, who knew who she might hurt? What if she accidentally fired it and killed Nora? Or Kish? Or Reuben? Or Gillian? Or one of the dragons?

She couldn't take that chance. Jane Miller caught her look and addressed them all again.

"It's not actually loaded. I'm not stupid."

Kish and Nora took the guns with a gulp, looking at them

warily as they hung from the tips of their fingers. Jane groaned in frustration and adjusted their grips on the pistols, before gesturing for them to tuck it into the holster hanging from their belt. She started to hand one over to Mari but she shook her head. If Mari took that gun, she could easily kill someone, something she was particularly averse to doing.

"Like I said," Jane said softly, "it's just a blank."

Mari could practically see the sighs of relief flowing from Nora and Kish; she, too, relaxed a little.

"So are we just defenceless?" Kish asked pointedly.

Jane shifted her eyes to look at him. "I don't really want you kids going around shooting my peers. If you get into any real danger you can always knock someone over the head with the butt of your guns."

"We need to go now," Jenkins said, pushing himself from the wall.

Mari guessed now was the time. They had the map. They had the uniforms. They had the guns. Now all they needed was a dragon and two teenagers.

Chapter 39

Nora

Nora took a deep breath and willed herself not to look back yet again at the disappearing figures of Kish and Mari. She prayed desperately for them to be all right. For their plan to work, the three of them would rely on stealth to get Reuben, Gil and Kaida out. Once Kaida, particularly, was freed, that was when they would need to increase their speed. Jay was with Kish at the moment, the two of them posing as one of the handler and dragon pairs they had seen roaming the base from the top of the hill. Nora had been reluctant to acknowledge the fact that she didn't see any dragons in the base that looked like Copper or Zephyr. So, she had taken Totem with her instead to lessen suspicion. A giant, furry beige dragon with curled horns and dark eyes would surprisingly be quite out of the ordinary.

According to the map Mari had described, Reuben should be in one of these rectangular, block-like buildings spanning the centre of the base. They were arranged in rows, somewhat haphazardly as if people had built sections of the block buildings at different times and hadn't bothered to try and make them align perfectly.

Nora squared her shoulders and summoned the scraps of her confidence as she walked into the first building she saw. The door swung loudly shut behind her and Nora glimpsed Totem's blaring red scales in her peripheral. He had to stay put for this to work, Nora was sure Kish had told him that. Guards in similar garb to what Nora was wearing were stationed at different points in the hall. There were about four in total but Nora just walked in clipped steps to the one nearest, his black hair buzzed short and brown eyes staring straight ahead.

"Excuse me," she announced, pushing clarity into her words.

The guard turned his eyes to her, unimpressed.

"I'm looking for a prisoner," she continued, "under the instruction of the general."

The guard harrumphed but turned his entire head this time to look her condescendingly in the eye.

"Well, they're not going to be in here, are they, *sweetie*?" he said haughtily.

Nora bit back her rage and forced a small smile onto her face.

"Of course," she replied with just as much faux sweetness. "I was just wondering whether you knew the specifics?"

"Well, which prisoner?" he snorted. "We only got two."

Nora was about to explain herself further when she noticed one of the other guards striding over. He had a lazy smile on his face that was somehow reassuring. He had a more genuinely sweet demeanour than the turd she had been talking to.

"Sorry about Andrews, here. He's a bit of… well, I won't be crude with you. Anyway," the guard stuck out his hand and Nora shook it, confused but going along nonetheless, "I'm Norton. You new here?"

Nora snatched onto the lie. "Yes. Yeah, I am new."

"So, who are you looking for?" Norton asked.

"Breneger, I think he said," Nora said, trying to think of the kind of language whoever the general was would use.

"That's the kid in A Block, right?" Andrews said, frowning at Norton.

They began discussing it and Nora merely slipped back out. Norton had pretty much confirmed Andrews' A Block theory. As she exited the building, Nora noticed the large, metal-plated D on the side of the crate-like building she had just left. If she kept following these buildings, presuming they were in alphabetical order, she could hopefully end up in A Block and therefore, find Reuben. Totem obediently came up to her and followed alongside, playing the part of a dutiful dragon companion perfectly. Nora tried to picture the map on Mari's phone in her head, where all the identical buildings were situated. She turned and spun around, merely trying to ooze enough confidence that no one would come up to her and question her presence. After what seemed to be an eternity of searching, Nora managed to come across the building with the A on its side. She breathed in deep. Reuben had to be in there, he *had* to be. Else, the whole plan would be delayed and they would run out of time. Nora quickly gestured to Totem to stay outside the door and went into the shed-like structure. She stalked along the hallway, trying to ignore the sets of eyes from the guards trailing her as she passed locked rooms and closed doors. Her eyes flicked to each window as she passed, hoping to see a figure with unruly light brown hair and piercing hazel eyes. Panic began to set in as Nora realised she was nearing the end of the whole block. This was *not* happening; this was *not* the plan. A flash of déjà vu hit Nora as she remembered the same panic from way back at the start of all this. When they had strayed from the plan and grabbed dragon eggs from Richmond Airport.

Just as Nora was about to turn back and descend even deeper into her panic, she glanced at the last room's window and then did a double take. It wasn't Reuben but she was sure she recognised that uncut mop of black curls. Some semblance of her sanity returning, Nora went up to the door and rapped hard onto the metal door. The boy's head snapped up and confused, green eyes met hers. It was Gillian. Oh, she could just laugh. Gil didn't say anything, he merely raised an eyebrow at Nora and with a sinking feeling, she realised her mistake. Jane Miller hadn't given them the keys. For all her talk of wanting to help them, she had neglected to give them the keys to actually liberate their friends. That cold jerk. If only Gil and Nora's roles had been reversed and he could have picked the locks. Nora chewed her lip in thought for a mere moment before deciding quickly what to do. She took a quick step towards the nearest guard.

"Excuse me. I was sent by the general but he didn't give me the keys to transport this prisoner," Nora said flatly.

The guard gave her a confused look. "The general?"

She nodded.

"I didn't know Gregorian was here."

Damn it.

"Well, he is," Nora said arrogantly, willing the guard to believe her.

Instead, he called out to one of the other guards and queried whether this General Gregorian was at the base or not. The other guard laughed and Nora's heart sank.

"Yeah! I saw him before I made my round here, totally took me by surprise!"

Nora pushed down the relieved grin threatening to take over her face. The original guard chuckled at the other before handing her the key and continuing the conversation with the guy across the hallway. Nora, looking as professional as she could, unlocked the door and roughly grabbed Gillian by the elbow.

"Go with it," she whispered through her teeth.

Gillian merely resumed his bored expression, tinged with

strong hues of distaste for those around him as Nora led him down the hallway. She locked the cell's door behind her before marching them down and out of A Block. She didn't know where Kish was for her to have got to Gillian first but she needed to grab Reuben now and she doubted it would look normal if she marched Gil over to Reuben's cell and then escorted them both out.

The sunlight burst forth and hit Nora's dark eyes as she stepped them out into the air. It only took a moment until a tall, brown-skinned boy with a freshly shaved head rushed past them with a shining blue dragon on his heels. Nora went to call out to Kish but Jay had already doubled back and pounced on Gil. Gillian laughed as he struggled to get out from beneath the dragon's head.

"Take Gillian, I'm grabbing Reuben. Meet us at the gate," Nora told Kish promptly as he came back to them.

"What?" he asked, voice cracking the tiniest bit.

But Nora was already going, leaving the two dragons and Gillian in the care of Kish. She looked back and they were already standing somewhat awkwardly with an uncomfortable amount of distance between them. They'd be fine.

As Nora walked, the buzzing energy from her brain being translated into step after step, she wracked her brain for the other block Norton and Johnson had mentioned in their discussion. It wasn't D or A, she knew that. Running out of time, Nora just flung open the door to the building closest to her. Did it say C? It didn't matter. She had to hurry, the guard from A Block had probably already realised she had left without giving him his key back. She charged past the guards lining this building, stealing glances through the windows on each side of the hallway. No, no, no, no, no. There.

Oh, thank the heavens, Nora breathed out and as she went to unlock Reuben's cell, the soldier nearest to her called out.

"Hey, what are you doing?" she glared at Nora.

"General's orders!" Nora yelled as she promptly unlocked the door and burst through.

Reuben jumped to his feet, his eyes suddenly coming to clarity as they locked with Nora's. Nora shook her head and made herself focus. She raised a finger to her lips and grabbed Reuben's elbow before leading him out of the cell and locking it behind her. She was honestly surprised that the one key worked for all these blocks, she wouldn't think the military would be so lax with security. She could tell Reuben was itching to tell her something but she just kept walking. They needed to get out of here, now. Down the hallway, she led him until finally they got out of the block and she relaxed her grip on his arm just the slightest. That was all it took for him to spin around and grab her by the shoulders. Nora tried to regain her grip on his elbow, in case someone saw them.

"Reuben, we have to go," she persisted.

"No, wait, just—"

Nora frowned up at him. His brows were furrowed and he kept trying to form the right words. What was he doing?

Reuben breathed in. "Nora, remember when you asked why I asked you to come on this mission?"

"Yes?" Nora replied, unsure where he was going with this.

Of course, she remembered. He had said she was *very capable*. She supposed it was what she should have expected, Reuben was a practical guy. He didn't think about... well the things she thought.

"I lied," he said quickly.

Nora looked at Reuben again, confused.

"I mean, you are capable, obviously," Reuben corrected, leading into a ramble, "but that wasn't the only reason. You're amazing, Nora. You are smart, like *so* smart, and I know you don't think you are but you're good at literally everything you try and you're kind and you're beautiful, but like not in a shallow way, if you know what I—" Reuben groaned and ran a hand through his hair. "I'm messing this all up. My point is, I like you, Nora. A lot. Like a lot, a lot and—"

Nora didn't let him finish what he was saying. She merely wrapped her arms around his neck and kissed him. Reuben's hands came up to cup her cheeks and after a few moments, she pulled back, biting her lip nervously.

"We should probably go now," she said softly.

Reuben stepped back, a blush creeping up over his neck as he coughed lightly. "Right, yes, of course. Let's go."

Chapter 40

Gillian

Gillian shuffled his feet, pointedly avoiding Kish's gaze as he scratched Jay's head affectionately.

"Thanks… uh… for rescuing me," he said, words stilted.

"Yeah, no problem, anytime."

There was a deep pause in which Gillian figured they should have started leaving and yet they merely stood there, the only sound their slightly quickened breathing.

"I probably could have figured something out," he said to break the silence. "I didn't need your help getting out of here."

Kish snapped his eyes up and Gil met his coffee-brown gaze with a challenge. Kish raised an eyebrow. Gil shrugged and stepped forwards infinitesimally.

"I don't *need* you, you know," Gillian pointed out.

Kish turned towards him now, a cocky grin stretching across his features as he leant forwards slightly, hands resting casually in his pockets.

"Maybe not," Kish said slowly, "but you *want* me, don't you?"

Gil went to say something but nothing could make it past the flustered blush reddening his skin. He quickly scoffed and rolled his eyes, dismissing the notion as he turned away. Gillian gestured to Jay and they began walking off, ignoring Kish's quiet chuckle as he jogged slightly to catch up with them.

"The gate's that way," Kish pointed his thumb over his shoulder in the opposite direction they were going.

"Why'd you follow me then?" Gil harrumphed.

Kish merely shrugged and followed Gil yet again as he turned on his heel and went in the direction Kish had pointed. Why did he have to be just so… so *infuriating*? He just had to act like he knew everything. Gillian fumed but it was no use. He wasn't really angry at Kish and yet he didn't know what else to be. In any case, getting out of this military base would hopefully occupy them enough to take Gil's mind off it. They just had to get to the gate and get out of this place as quickly as humanly possible. Kish and Gil were almost at the gate, about to make the last turn when Gillian stopped dead in his tracks.

"You have got to be kidding me," he muttered.

"What?" Kish asked, coming to a halt beside him.

Standing right past the corner were two men, both with jet-black hair shaved to the scalps. One with identical green eyes to Gil and one with brown. Garrett and Griffin, his older brothers. Gil tried to shrink back away but they had already seen him and odds were, walking towards him. Sure enough, mere seconds later Garrett crossed the corner and Gil felt that familiar wash of rage at his eldest brother's smirk.

"Hey, little brother," Garrett drawled, brown eyes glinting with cruelty.

"Hey," Gil replied, clipped.

Gillian noticed Griffin hanging back, arms crossed, face betraying nothing of his thoughts, the so-called forgotten middle child once again. Griffin had been like that for as long as Gil could remember, content to sit back and not get involved. And yet he was still brought up as an arguing tool by his parents when Gillian was classed as the disappointment.

"What are you up to?" Garrett asked, feigning nonchalance when really Gil knew he was one word away from snapping.

Gil used to be afraid of his eldest brother; the unpredictable, short-fused golden child. But his brother had been away from home too long now and Gillian had got far to used to not having to deal with him.

"Oh, you know, the usual," Gil replied causally.

"Should we be running?" Kish whispered.

"Who's this?" Garrett grinned unkindly.

Kish went to answer but Gil pushed him gently to the side. "What do you want Garrett?"

Garrett frowned, a breath coming out raggedly from his nostrils as he clenched his fists. "I was talking to your friend, Gillian."

"Garrett, let's go," Griffin's voice floated over, just as Gil remembered it. Not strong enough.

Garrett stretched his smile wide as he turned back to their middle brother. "Now, wait just a second, Griffin. Don't you want to have a chat with our baby brother? Don't yo—"

Garrett cried out as a string of flame flew onto his clothes and Gil grinned at Jay, her nostrils flaring in shared anger at Gil's brother.

"What the hell?" Garrett shrieked.

"Go," Griffin told them.

Kish and Gillian didn't need any more encouragement. They rushed past Gil's brothers, their dragons trailing them, just fast enough so Gil could still turn back, look his middle brother in the eye and say, "Grow a spine, Griff."

Gillian felt kind of bad for his brothers, despite how badly they had treated him when he was younger. His parents had coddled and praised Garrett his entire life, deeming nothing a mistake and if there ever was one, well, the right people were bribed to change such a thing. Garrett had grown up believing he could do no wrong, that he was apple of everyone's eye. Griffin had fallen back behind the curtain, learning to be silent in the wake of Garrett's spotlight. Griff and Gil had grown closer when Garrett had started his time in the military, away from their brother's overbearing, manipulative presence. Their brother wasn't there to lord over them and thus, they had actually grown to know one another for perhaps the first time in their lives. Then four years later, Griffin too had left to join the military and it had all gone away. That was two years ago now.

Gillian had all but forgotten his family in his effort to put them in his past and yet here they were again. Although, Gil's brothers became the furthest thing from his mind when he and Kish finally made it to the meeting point. Nora and Reuben were backed up against the gate, a ring of military surrounding them, that itself backed by a wall of varying dragons. There were so, so many dragons. Kish skidded to a stop alongside Gil and spotted the scene, rubbing his forehead.

"Oh, stuff this," Kish grunted.

Chapter 41

Reuben

The wall of khaki-clad soldiers were closing in around Reuben and Nora as they backed further and further up against the gate. Zephyr kept trying to talk to Reuben to see whether they and Copper would need to come and help but Reuben mentally pushed them away as strongly as he could. This was a doomed situation; he wouldn't rope the dragons into it.

"Halt and come with us," a gravelly voice commanded over a megaphone from somewhere within that crowd.

Reuben scanned it and gulped. The real worry, he thought, was the barrier of dragons staring menacingly down at them from behind the line of military personnel. Reuben could only assume that each of those dragons was bonded to a member of the military just as Reuben and his friends had done. A clatter of feet and Reuben's eyes were drawn away from the imminent threat at hand to see Kish and Gil stop just beyond the ring surrounding Reuben and Nora, Jay and Totem standing behind them looking like absolute tanks. Which would have been reassuring if it wasn't for all the other dragons that looked just as, if not more, deadly. Reuben glanced over at Nora and they met eyes briefly, they weren't coming out of this without some kind of miracle.

Reuben wondered blankly where his sister had gone. Had she even come on this mission? The last time Reuben had seen her, the incident had taken a real toll on her. The incident…

If Reuben remembered correctly, that had all happened because Kaida had believed Marilyn-Jo was threatened and had leapt to her aid. That's when the thoughts began falling on each other, a domino trail of ideas. If these dragons were bonded to the soldiers in a similar way, it stood to reason that they would act *similarly*, right? If Reuben and the others just managed to *threaten* enough of the soldiers around them, enough dragons would leap to their aid, sowing chaos and eventually turning on one another once the cramped space inevitably caused them to bump heads.

"Nora," Reuben said softly, not turning his head to avoid suspicion.

He felt her eyes flick over.

"Remember how Kaida reacted the day of the incident?"

Nora's brow furrowed imperceptibly.

"When she caused the incident, why did she do that?" Reuben pressed.

A breath escaped Nora's lips. "She thought Mari was in danger."

Bingo. Reuben knew the cogs and wheels were already away in Nora's head and she had predicted exactly what he was thinking. They didn't have any weapons at their disposal except the blank gun at Nora's hip which was all but useless from this far away. If Reuben could get the plan to Kish and Gil, they could get their dragons to shoot off a line of fire to achieve what they wanted.

Zephyr, you heard the plan, right? Reuben pushed the thought outwards, hoping that that would reach the dragon.

Yes, the answer was immediate.

Reuben forced himself to breathe as the voice continued to blare over the megaphone, telling him and Nora to come forwards and surrender themselves.

Kind of creepy, but I'm glad. Can you get it to the others? he asked.

Zephyr didn't reply but Reuben got the sense of an affirmative and hoped his dragon was already doing what was needed. Sure enough, barely minutes later he saw Kish and Gil step back and their dragons spring into action. Their brightly coloured scales shifted in the dipping sunlight as their haunches shifted and their powerful bodies moved into a deadly stance. Then came the fire, rippling strands of pure heat just pouring from their jaws and at the once impenetrable wall blocking Reuben and Nora. The soldiers all dropped to the ground, trying to roll the flames out. By that time, their dragons had set their sights on Jay and Totem. Reuben would have been afraid for the dragons but as he watched it became clear that they knew what they were doing. As another of the same dragon went to release its own fire on Jay, she rushed in front of one of those quilled dragons, leaping into the air just as the flames left the other dragon's jaws. Seeing this attack, the quilled dragon roared in rage and shot its quills in the general direction of the scaled dragon. Reuben saw these land both in the attacker and some surrounding soldiers and dragons.

Reuben was astounded at the chaos erupting around him, though he had come up with the plan, he had almost thought it not possible for such mayhem to ensue.

"Let's go!" he shouted over the din to Nora.

She shook her head as she pushed up her glasses, eyes scanning the sky above them.

"No!" she yelled back. "We have to wait for Mari!"

Mari was here? Did that mean she was feeling better? A better question, why wasn't she back here yet? Was she hurt?

Had she been imprisoned? Reuben jittered slightly on his feet, warring between going to look for her and waiting for her to meet up with them. Just as Reuben was deciding to push through the throng of chaos, a whooping figure appeared in the sky. Mari's ebony curtain bangs were flying around her face and she was grinning, one hand pumping the air while the other was clutching onto the back of Kaida's neck tightly. Kaida swooped down from the air and as much as Mari's smile was genuine, Reuben noticed the gulp and the falter in his sister's expression when she saw what was happening below her. Nevertheless, she and Kaida landed at the feet of Nora and Reuben with the stupidest grin Reuben had ever seen.

"Hey guys," Mari panted.

"Hi," Nora said quickly, "how did you get her out?"

Mari smiled and merely tapped the side of her nose.

"Okay, we better get out of here, you guys call your dragons in," Mari told them.

"I am not sitting on Zephyr, no way," Reuben said adamantly.

"Doesn't matter," Mari shrugged, "they can carry you."

Reuben went to argue further but Kaida had once again plunged her and Mari into the clouds and with a gulp, Reuben realised the guns being lined up in their direction. They had to move fast.

"Zephyr!" Reuben yelled at the same time as he heard Nora yell her own dragon's name.

Sure enough, the hulking, furred figures of the dragons appeared over the lip of the base's wall, pale wings flapping relentlessly. Zephyr dove over the wall and plucked Reuben off of the ground with their… Reuben didn't know what they were. Paws? Feet? Claws? Somewhere between all three. In any case, they carried him high above the concrete ground, making Reuben's head spin. Dizzily, he regarded the other dragons doing the same to his friends. Reuben raised a fist to his mouth to avoid spewing his meagre rations, the other hand clutching desperately onto Zephyr's leg. And then he passed out.

Chapter 42

Marilyn-Jo

Marilyn-Jo's eyes kept fluttering closed even as she told herself she must stay awake. She glanced down at the ground, the sudden shock of the height jarring her awake. They had flown for hours now, the darkness of the night settling around them. Mari had tried to capture her own interest with the stars appearing every minute but try as she might, her body just kept wanting to sleep. She couldn't sleep though, not while she was still sitting atop Kaida's back, lest she fall and plummet to her untimely death. She patted Kaida's neck, sure that the dragon was feeling just as exhausted as she was and Kaida in turn began to glide down to the ground. Mari trusted that the others would be coming down too. As soon as Mari was met with the solid ground again, she slept.

*

The sun was well and truly up by the time Mari cracked her eyelids open. The sky was insanely blue, not a blemish corrupting it at all. She rose from the grass and stretched her limbs, swearing she could hear a creaking in one of her joints. The others were mostly all awake already, bar her older brother. He was still either sleeping or passed out from the night before.

She went over to sit where Nora, Gil and Kish were chatting

quietly in a circle, their dragons lounging lazily behind them. A chorus of, "Morning," and, "Hey Mari," greeted her as she sat down with them.

"You guys got any breakfast?" Mari asked.

She was met with scoffs and forcefully uneasy laughs.

"Not yet," Nora told her, "we're going to need to establish where we are once Reuben wakes up. Hopefully, if we're near civilisation we can go grab some food."

"Do you guys still have all that money we took from my parent's safe?" Gillian asked them.

Mari shifted uncomfortably and made herself meet her best friend's eye. "I only have a bit left in my pockets, sorry."

"Same here," Nora added.

"I didn't get any in the first place," Kish said when their eyes turned to him.

The sound of rustling grass reached the group's ears and Mari turned to see her brother yawning as he rose from the grass. Somehow, as soon as he had woken up, Reuben had infused himself with some kind of energy that persisted despite the obvious muscle pain Mari assumed he would be in from exerting himself. Reuben strode purposefully, and perhaps a little creepily, over to them.

"I was thinking—" Reuben declared.

Gil interrupted dryly. "You were literally just passed out."

"Yes. Anyway," Reuben continued, ignoring Gil's shocked muttering, "they've tracked us pretty easily before, right?"

"Well, that's to be expected," Nora replied.

Reuben looked affronted. "What do you mean?"

Mari laughed. "Reuben, we're just teenagers. They're the Australian military for goodness' sake."

Reuben furrowed his brow and pointed at all of them. Mari

shifted; she knew what this was. This was Reuben's lecture moment; he had learnt it from their mother. Except his lectures were always *a lot* more obnoxious than her mum's.

"No," he told them, "no. We may be teenagers but we are never *just* teenagers. I'll be damned if I ever let us be *just* anything. That's lame. Pathetic. May I remind you all that we managed to break into *two* of their facilities and escape with minimal consequences."

"Minimal consequences?" Gil squeaked.

"Well, we were in jail but that was only for a few days or a week at most, I didn't really keep track of the time," Reuben said matter-of-factly.

Marilyn-Jo didn't know if she was merely making things up but she could sense the tension between Gil and her brother. Though Gillian had frequently denied it, Mari had always thought he harboured some kind of resentment towards Reuben and now it was, well, glaringly obvious. She knew he didn't hate Reuben, or even dislike him, per se, but Gil was always very good at holding grudges, even unintentionally. Even if Gil thought he had forgiven and forgotten what someone had done, Mari often noticed it wasn't quite the case for Gillian's subconscious.

"Something happened in the prison between you two," Mari affronted the two of them.

Kish's eyes widened and he looked away, a confused look flashing across his features.

"What do you mean?" Reuben asked her.

Gah, he was like a broken record. Nora hummed thoughtfully and turned to Mari.

"I noticed that too," Nora said. "Gillian is glowering at your brother more than normal."

"You guys need to sort that out," Mari told them and

promptly stood up, taking Nora with her. "Kish, look after them for us," she called over her shoulder as they walked away.

Nora and Mari walked a little ways away, waiting a few moments for their dragons to come up to them.

"How do you feel about flying, again?" Nora asked.

Mari grimaced but she nodded nonetheless and with that, the two girls shook their dragons to consciousness and once again took to the sky.

Chapter 43

Nora

Nora paced uncertainly back with the others after flying for what felt like forever. She had flown over the city until she had spotted her house, scrawled a quick note and shoved it under her front door and then got the hell out of there. It had been a stupid move, to fly in plain sight over Sydney and *hope* that all the barracks in the city wouldn't spot her or shoot her down. To be honest, she wouldn't be surprised if they had seen her which meant there was a whole new, much worse option; they had seen her and *chosen* not to do anything. Which could mean but one thing; they were preparing for something. Nora did not like the sound of that.

Mari made it back to the others shortly after Nora had returned to their tense silence. She now lay sprawled on the grass, arm shielding her eyes from the sun as she watched Nora pace.

"Nora, could you not?" Mari called out.

Nora stopped abruptly in her tracks and turned her head. "Not what?"

"The whole pacing thing."

Nora sighed and conceded, she too sprawling herself down on the grass with a sigh. She didn't know if her mums had seen the message she had conspicuously shoved beneath their doorstep, if they had reported it, though she doubted that option, but she really, desperately hoped they were coming. She hadn't wanted to send them a text message or ring them lest the phone call get tracked and her conversation was heard, their location discovered. And yet she'd done something even more stupid and probably far more telling.

Nora pushed the thought out of her head and tried to be more like the girl sitting next to her, though she doubted Mari's mind had ever been calm, let alone what it had been like since the incident.

The rough squeal of rubber on grass snapped Nora out of her reverie. The car seemed to inch its way over the hill to where Nora and her friends were sitting and she watched as the others perked their heads up to see what was happening. Each dragon around Nora began to rise onto their haunches, growls emanating throughout the trees in warning.

"What's happening?" Gil called out.

"Guys stand down! Tell them to just hold on!" Nora fought to remain calm as her friends tried futilely to control their animals.

She jogged quickly over to the car and rapped on the window, sure that this Mercedes was the one her mums had bought a little while ago. The window rolled down slowly and Nora prepared herself for the inevitable lecture that was about to occur. Instead, the tinted window disappeared to find her mother's face streaked in tears, dark eyes glistening, thin hands clutching the steering wheel tightly. She clambered out of the car door, arms engulfing Nora in a crushing hug.

"Hey," Nora said slowly, "Mum, you all right?"

"No! Of course, I'm not all right! You just disappeared for months and no phone call and then you were on the news and—"

Her mother broke off in a sob and Nora's mum came to wrap her own arms around the two of them, that same long grey cardigan almost drooping in the mud.

"Shhh, Debbie, it's okay, she's here now," Nora's mum assured, stepping back.

Nora took a moment to take in her parents. They had aged while she had been away, probably due to the stress of it all. Or maybe Nora just hadn't seen their faces in a while. She saw her mum take a wide look around her, jaw going slack as she took in the towering beasts around her, her fingers going straight to her grey-tinged blonde locks and toying with them somewhat anxiously.

She cleared her throat. "Well, they must have grown quickly."

At that point, the others had started to gather around them and Nora noticed Reuben trying, a little unsuccessfully, to push himself forwards. Finally, his hunched frame stumbled towards her parents, hand outstretched. Before Reuben could get a word out, Nora's mother had started storming towards him, her finger outstretched with unbridled maternal rage.

"You! You, young man, are the boy that ruined our daughter's life! She could have died out here! Do you have the slightest idea how worried we have been? And we talked to *your* mother too, you know…"

Reuben seemed to shrink under the demanding rant of Nora's mother as Emily and Nora had to drag her away from Reuben before she finally relented.

"Well, I should probably make some introductions, shouldn't I?" Nora proposed, forcing some cheerfulness into her voice.

She was positively ecstatic to see her mums again but this moment was getting riddled with far too many tense silences for her liking.

"This is Reuben, who you just berated, Mum," her mother mumbled a quick apology though did not look very sorry. "This is Kish, Marilyn-Jo and Gillian."

"Oh! Gillian! We remember you!" Nora's mum exclaimed, grey cardigan flying as she threw her hands up in recognition. "You and Nora were in chess club together, right?"

Gillian laughed. "Yeah, I almost forgot about that again."

If Nora remembered correctly, Gillian had won exactly once and that was only because the club coordinator had told Nora to be a quote-unquote "good sport" and let him win. And that was ten years ago. Nora's mother clapped and looked them all in the eye.

"So, what's you kids' next move?" she asked.

They all blanched. They had hardly had time to think of what to do that afternoon let alone a next big move.

"We could try and figure out a way to clear your names, twist the truth somehow so that you're in the right and the military is in the wrong," her mum mused, finger tapping softly on her chin, "and who better to twist the truth?"

"The media," Gil offered.

"Exactly."

Reuben furrowed his brow. "What are we going to tell the media, though? We need something big enough to catch their attention."

"A scandal," Mari said with flair.

"I know!" said Nora and they all looked to her, expectant. It was a far-fetched idea, sure. But that was all the last month had been; a string of far-fetched ideas that they had *just* managed to pull off. She continued her explanation, laying out the steps clearly. "We'll lure them to a big event of sorts but we won't tell them it's televised. They'll get there, we'll be wearing mics and one of us needs one of the higher-ups to confess to all the cruelty towards animals laws they undoubtedly have broken in creating dragons. Plus, if that fails, the whole country will see them manhandling teenagers and I'm sure people will protest that."

"A ball!" Marilyn-Jo cried.

Nora and the others looked at her oddly. A ball? What did she mean, *a ball*?

"Like you know, in *Bridgerton* and Jane Austen novels and that era in general. With dancing and dresses and fancy music. Imagine them tackling us against that setting!"

"She has a point," Nora's mum turned to look at them all, as did her mother.

Her mother softened her face, ironic that this be the thing to do it after ten years. "Okay, kids, let Emily and I sort everything out with the venue and decorations and everything, all right? Now, who should we mail the invitations out to?"

"Jane Miller," Nora said.

"No," Gil and Reuben's voices were in unison.

Nora turned to them puzzled but she supposed it was good they were sort of getting along now.

"There's this Robert Gregorian fellow. He's in charge of it all, head of the operation kind of gig. He's the one who came up with it."

"Okay, send them to Robert Gregorian and Jane Miller and I'm sure they'll bring a whole host of the military," Nora supplied.

Her parents nodded and with a lingering hug, they got back into their car.

"We'll be back, kids." Her mum smiled.

Before they left, Nora's mum called out and waved her hand out the window, beckoning Nora to come over. She gathered up her cardigan across herself before casually dumping three bags of food and water into Nora's arms. Nora thanked her mums endlessly and fought not to let tears fall as they drove away through the trees. She hadn't realised *quite* how much she had missed her own mums. She had seen them every day for eighteen years since she was born or there abouts. But now, they had a ball to plan.

Chapter 44

Marilyn-Jo

The next week passed in intermittent visits from Nora's mums and endless pacing for Mari. She had to keep herself occupied, keep herself moving or else images of Jeremy Grimes would push past and torment her. Within four days, Nora's mums announced they were ready. Of course, that was the point when Mari realised that none of them had suitable clothes for a *ball* nor had most of them had a shower in more than a week. And they all stunk. Real bad. Lo and behold, Debbie and Emily had indeed taken care of everything and somehow managed to find tuxes for the guys and tracked down the dresses Nora and Mari were going to wear to their respective formals that year. Marilyn-Jo had completely forgotten about her year ten formal, understandably she supposed. But she had really been looking forward to that, to having fun and partying and chilling with friends. Although could she really call any of them *friends* after what she had been through with these four people? There hadn't really been many friends before this, either, she supposed.

Marilyn-Jo was now sitting in Nora's house, at the kitchen bench while trying to dry her hair after the best shower she had had in her entire sixteen years of living. The smell of pancakes wafting from the stovetop threatened to topple Mari's now frail body off the bench stool and disintegrate her into a pile of drool. Emily was mixing the batter, looking completely relaxed as she chatted with her daughter. They had all decided it would be best to leave their dragons where they had been situated. Mari was confident that Kaida would be able to take care of herself as would the other dragons. Plus, the emotional bond would tell her if anything was wrong and Nora and Reuben could easily communicate with Copper and Zephyr. So, it would be *fine*. At least, that's what Mari told herself.

"Hey, guess what I found out," Nora said.

"What?" Mari replied.

"Want to know what a group of dragons is called?"

Mari shrugged. "Sure. Seems like something we should know."

Nora grinned. "A thunder of dragons."

Mari laughed, as did the other girl.

"So, we stole thunder?" Mari asked, chuckling.

Nora merely nodded, an identical smile splitting her features.

After a few minutes of their giggling, Debbie rose into the room with a clap, the others filing into the kitchen behind her. At the sight of pancakes on the bench and the nod of approval from Nora's mums, Gillian practically attacked the plate in his eagerness. The others were quick to grab a plate too, though certainly not at the same speed with which Gil had. Debbie cleared her throat, bringing the teenagers' attention to her. Mari's fork stopped midway to her mouth before she quickly gulped the bit of pancake down lest it had fallen on the perfectly polished tile floor.

"We've sent the invitations out to your families and year groups and some of our own friends, as well as those people you requested. We've also organised a caterer and all the other things needed for a ball," Debbie told them.

Marilyn-Jo saw Reuben shift from behind Nora's mother uncomfortably.

"Why do we have to have a *ball*?" he asked. "Can't we just have a discreet meeting instead?"

They all shook their heads at him and he groaned.

"Then can't we have something else? Why a ball? That's so weird and old-fashioned," Reuben persisted.

"*You're* so weird and old-fashioned," Mari shot back.

Emily came in between them. "Okay kids, calm down. Reuben, if not a ball, what do you suggest?"

Reuben fidgeted on the balls of his feet and shrugged. "I don't know. A dinner? Literally anything else?"

Mari scoffed.

Emily frowned, though there was no animosity in the gesture. "I'm sorry, Reuben, but it's a bit late for a different plan."

Reuben grumbled and Mari, though she would never admit it, could see the unnecessary extravagance they were putting into this. But they needed a spectacle and Mari needed some fun.

"How are we paying for this?" asked Gillian, ever practical.

Nora's mums waved their hands and dismissed the notion. Marilyn-Jo was struck by how cavalier their attitude towards their own finances was. She had seen the same thing within Gil's family growing up. The only difference was, she had seen none of this sort of generosity, or any generosity for that matter, when at the Andrews household. Apart from Gillian. Gillian had always seemed eager to dispose of the money funnelled through to him. He hated it. He had often ranted to Mari how he wanted to be rid of the money, rid of the name, rid of that person his parents wanted him to be. It was more than just the shame of his family's attitudes, though. Marilyn-Jo knew from the years surrounded by Gillian that he did not like relying on anyone else. For anything. If he could do something on his own, provide for himself on his own, then he would do it. And when he couldn't, he grew incredibly sour.

By that afternoon they had persuaded Reuben to agree, albeit reluctantly and by the next morning, they were setting up.

"We need to have the cameras set up first," Nora was saying, "that way if they get it in their head to ambush early, we'll still have footage."

The hall stretched as if to the ends of the earth, situated in some building Marilyn-Jo had never heard of. There was a small circular stage in the far left corner where some band was setting up their instruments and practising for the night ahead. Marilyn-Jo could feel the anticipation tingling through her body and though she knew she would probably get thrown in a cell by the next morning, she didn't care. They would go out with a bang so loud people would come running. And when they did, those prats in the military would be sorry they ever messed with them. Of course, Mari realised that they had been the ones to mess with the military in the first place, but that was entirely beside the point.

They did not end up arriving early to ambush them. In fact, they were *late*. By an hour and a half. By then the hall was almost full and the dragons had been called back to stand at the entrances and stroll menacingly along the marble floors. Many of the teenagers Mari had formerly gone to school with were gazing at the towering creatures with awe, dozens of phones whipped out to upload videos of them to social media.

Good, Mari thought, *let them film*.

The dragons weren't the only thing that turned heads, though. Marilyn-Jo knew she was dazzling, even more so than normal. The dress was strapless with a flowing skirt and a deep blue that sparkled under the light of the chandeliers. Modest but flattering. *Very* flattering, if she said so herself. She strutted through the hall as if the lives around her depended on the very sight of her. That was the confidence that had got her through all those years at school. Through the loneliness and the whispers. They could whisper all they wanted about her and her family and their *differentness*, she would still be straight-backed with her head held high looking as brilliant as ever. And that confidence would get her through this now and allow her to do what she had to without thinking of Jeremy Grimes.

What if he comes tonight? Mari's thoughts spiralled.

Unless he was dead. Unless he was dead. She had pushed away that possibility but she knew that was an option. Even though they had called an ambulance and done all they could. He could still be dead. She could have still killed a man.

The chattering around the hall fell to an abrupt silence and Mari turned her head, her hair falling perfectly into place around her shoulders in the loose curls that Nora's mum had done for her. There in the doorway stood a towering wall of a man, head shaved to a light buzz and aviator sunglasses shielding his eyes despite the formal attire. That had to be Robert Gregorian. Beside Gregorian stood Jane Miller and behind her, looking extremely uncomfortable, was Mr Jenkins. The bastards had claimed to help them but Marilyn-Jo suspected now it was merely an act to ease their weak consciences. *Yes, let's help these children out but no, not when they actually need it. Here's a haircut, don't die kids!*

Mari scoffed and started to make her way inconspicuously towards the others. She found Kish first, then Nora, then Gil and finally, Reuben. Reuben held his hand out to Gregorian as if going in for a handshake. The military general extended his own hand only for Reuben to sweep it towards the room as if that was what he was going to do the entire time.

"Welcome," Reuben said, greeting their enemy with a wicked smile.

Gregorian scowled and practically barged inside. Mari scoffed, so much for manners. A whole host of military folk filed in after the front three and to Mari's surprise, in came Gillian's brothers. Garrett was strutting inside, smirking at the crowd as if they all owed him their lives just because he had deigned to bless them with his presence. Mari wondered if that was what her confidence looked like. Of course, people like Garrett were precisely the reason she had needed to build that persona. Mari glanced over at her friend to see how he was handling the sight. The only sign of his discomfort was a slight downturn at the corner of his lip. That's when Garrett spotted the three of them standing there and turned on his heel with the most arrogant smirk Mari had ever seen on someone. Like the obedient little lapdog Gil's other brother was, Griffin followed along.

"Gillian, brother, fancy seeing you here," Garrett said, slime dripping with every enunciation.

Gillian rolled his eyes but it was Mari who shot back, "What do you want, Garrett?"

Garrett spun his brown eyes over to her and chuckled.

"Hey kid, long time no see."

Kish pushed forwards and looked Gil's oldest brother in the eye. "She said, what do you want?"

Garrett didn't bother to step back, he only grinned lazily at them all before looking challengingly in Gillian's direction.

"Still getting others to fight your battles for you, little brother?" he asked.

Gillian huffed and pushed past his brothers, leaving Kish and

Mari to hurry after him, albeit shooting back death glares as they went. Griffin had remained silent as always and Mari wondered just how he could stomach spending so much time around a guy like Garrett.

Chapter 45

Reuben

Reuben smiled wide as he watched the military filter in through the grandiose doorway of the hall. Finally, *finally*, something was going right for them. That damned Robert Gregorian would think he had won, the brute. He would think he had outsmarted them, would think that Reuben and the others had merely invited them as a chance to discuss peace, naïve teenagers with no real knowledge of these kinds of affairs. But they would be the ones doing the outsmarting and oh, how that felt good.

Once they had passed by, Reuben turned to Nora with an excited grin and she smiled back. He was momentarily taken aback by how beautiful she looked then. Of course, he thought she always looked beautiful, but the dress she had chosen, presumably for what would have been their year twelve formal made her look absolutely stunning. Her curls were done up in a loose bun at the top of her head with diamond clips sparkling through the dark. Her dress was satin and fell to cover her feet in a deep red slip.

"Reuben," she said, "you're staring."

Reuben blushed immensely and quickly looked away quickly. Nora laid her hand gently on his arm and chuckled somewhat awkwardly. "It's okay," she smiled.

"I'm going to go break up that little party over there," she told him, gesturing to where Marilyn-Jo was trying to drag

Gillian and Kish away from the snacks table. Any other night, Reuben would be over there with them, attempting to get as far away from the socialising as possible but not this night. There was too much anticipation coiling up beneath his skin, too much to be done, too much to go wrong. Nothing was going to go wrong though, Reuben told himself even though that was technically statistically impossible. The fact was, though, they were *trying* to get arrested. As long as Gregorian and his lackeys had the same objective as they had had for the last month, it would all go according to plan. Even if the cameras Reuben and his friends had set up didn't work for some reason, there were about two hundred teenagers here with some form of social media at the ready, already filming dragons. There was no way that not one of them wouldn't upload a video of the arrest. Sure, there would be different arguments about it. *The kids are criminals* or *this goes against their rights*. Everyone would have something to say and Reuben was counting on that. After about twenty-five minutes of the military being there, dancing, mingling, Reuben heard their general bark over to him. Reuben was grabbing a lemonade, not allowing himself alcohol that night. He had to be alert for this to work.

"Boy! You! Breneger, over there!" the general shouted across the hall.

Reuben rolled his eyes at the crassness but turned around and walked politely over.

"Why, hello, General. How are you this evening?" he asked as any good host would.

"Cut the crap, Breneger."

Reuben took a sip of his drink and raised a hand in mock outrage to his chest. "Whatever do you mean?"

Reuben saw Mr Jenkins shift uncomfortably behind the

general. He was a weak man, Jenkins. He always had been.

"Why did you call us here?" Gregorian grunted.

Reuben opened his mouth to tell another polite and obvious lie but the general cut him off by raising his hand.

"It was a rhetorical question, son."

"Not your son."

"Whatever."

A rhetorical question? Reuben didn't let the panic register on his face. Did this man actually already know what Reuben and the others were up to? If so, they were in way, way too deep.

"You called us here," Robert Gregorian continued, "because you want to frame us. For inhumanely handling you or animal cruelty or some bull like that. Get everyone to defend your rights or whatever the hell you want so that when we do arrest you, we have to let you go because technically *we're* not the law."

Okay, so they did know what was going on. Reuben also couldn't help but notice the military general's flippant attitude towards human rights. Rude. Reuben could find a way out of this, though, surely. Right? *Right?*

Reuben. Zephyr's voice was urgent, probably concerned about the panic in Rueben's mind.

Reuben shoved the dragon's conscience out of his thoughts. Zephyr didn't need to worry. Didn't need to worry the others. Reuben could take care of this.

"I don't know what you're talking about," Reuben lied.

Gregorian sighed. "Here's the thing, kid. There is a bomb in this hall."

The immense weight of panic must have shown on Reuben's face because Gregorian chuckled.

"What?" he asked. "Did you think you could give us the address and just expect us not to come here earlier to scout it out and plant anything of our own?"

Reuben was naïve. Reuben had no real knowledge of these kinds of affairs. How could he have been so near-sighted?

"I thought you were supposed to be the good guys," Reuben said softly.

Gregorian laughed just as softly. "Oh, we are. We are the good guys."

"What do you want from me?" Reuben asked, pained.

"I want you to take the cameras down and I want you to tell everyone to go home. Then we can take you away discreetly and it's a win-win situation for everyone."

Not for Reuben. Not for his friends. But at least they would be alive.

"And if I don't?"

It was a stupid question. He knew what would happen if he didn't but he asked anyway, if only to buy a few more moments.

Gregorian leant in close. His breath smelt like off whisky and mould.

"Then we leave and we blow this place to shreds."

"You're a psychopath."

Gregorian shrugged. "Maybe. But I win either way so it doesn't really matter."

"Won't you go to jail for this? You *should* go to jail for this," Reuben shot at the man.

Gregorian smiled softly and looked Reuben in the eye with what some may mistake as pity.

"Why would anyone think it was us? We'll take some civilians out with us. Claim that we tried our best but those teenagers, they were far too messed up in the head. They weren't thinking right. They'd rather go down in flames than to go to jail. Tragic, *real tragic.*"

Reuben shook his head and marvelled at just how sick this man was. How could Reuben have ever been the bad guy when people like Gregorian existed? Their crimes didn't even come close. Nevertheless, Reuben's choice was easy and he turned to start taking the cameras down. That was when he heard the bang.

Chapter 46

Kish

Kish didn't see the explosion.
　But he felt it.

Epilogue

The heat of the bomb going off radiated through the hallway.

"What the hell was that?" Gregorian was roaring.

Jane's brows were knitted together and Jenkins was trying to get his ears to stop ringing. The bomb seemed to have gone off in some side room, a small explosion by any means, nothing of the sort the general had been describing to the kid. That same kid was turned towards the doorway from which the explosion had blown from in shock, his face painted in hues of anguish. The flames had shot out through the thin frame of the doorway of the side room, collapsing the wood and blasting out a force of wind knocking bodies into the air and slamming into the marble floors. Jenkins had watched in detached horror as that black-haired kid with the rich parents had cried out, his voice cracking with pain and ran to one of the fallen, the body's chest only barely rising and falling with breath.

Now Jenkins watched, silent, as the Breneger kid turned to the general.

"I was doing what you said!" he yelled, coming up to Gregorian and shoving him. "I was meeting your demands! Why'd you set the bomb off? *Why?*"

Gregorian shoved Reuben away and scowled at him. "Get off me, son."

"I'm not your son!" Reuben roared.

He shook his head before turning on his heel and running towards where the bodies had fallen. Jenkins watched yet again as Gregorian barked the order to disable the cameras. It was done almost immediately for him. And then Jenkins just stood there as Robert Gregorian and the others converged on the teenagers, still lying over their fallen friend, trying to get the boy to wake up, his breaths coming shallow in a quick rise and fall of his chest. They yelled and screamed and kicked as their hands were shoved behind their backs and they were dragged away from their friend's motionless form.

"You can't do this to us!" one of them screamed.

Gregorian must have given up caring because there were about three dozen people here with their phones out, if not more. He would deal with it. Yet, Jenkins still just couldn't comprehend why the bomb had been set off then. The kid was complying, why'd he set it off?

"Let go of him!" the black-haired one, Andrews, yelled at the man who was chucking the unconscious boy over his shoulder. "Let go of him!"

Andrews was blatantly ignored, pushing his shouts louder.

Jenkins looked over at Jane Miller, her face carefully composed even as her lip twitched with unnamed emotion. Jenkins could tell she was fighting against the instinct to go help the children. But Jenkins also knew that, though she was a much better person than him in a million and one ways, they were also one and the same in one particular way. They *wanted* to help. Yet, wanting to help and actually helping are two very, very different things. A difference that is a canyon between life and death. Good and evil. Moral and immoral. People liked to think they were one or the other but that was rarely the case. Most people were somewhere in the middle, merely trying their best. Their best that sometimes, just sometimes, wasn't quite good enough.

"Why'd Gregorian set the bomb off?" Jenkins whispered to Jane without turning his head.

She practically choked out the words. "He didn't."

"Then who did?"

Jane's eyes lifted towards the sky and it was almost the same as if she had put her head into her hands and let out a long sigh.

"I don't know," she told him softly.

"What do you mean?" Jenkins glanced over at her, brows knitted in confusion.

She struggled to retain composure. "Gregorian was bluffing," Jane got out, "we didn't have a bomb."

He couldn't have been, though. Right? He couldn't have been because then who would have set the bomb off? Who would have put the bomb in the hall? Who would want them all dead? The kids, the dragons, the general? Somehow, even in the finality of the arrest taking place before Jenkins' eyes, this whole affair was far from over.